8-10

		DATE DUE	
AUG 26 2010		MAY 13 2012	
SEP 1 2010		DEC 20 2010	
OCT 31 2010			
NOV 26 2010			
DEC 03 2010			

The Urbana Free Library

To renew materials call
217-367-4057

The
Ammonite
Violin
&
Others

The
Ammonite
Violin
&
Others

CAITLÍN R. KIERNAN

Subterranean Press • 2010

7/10
25°°

First Edition

ISBN
978-1-59606-305-1

Subterranean Press
PO Box 190106
Burton, MI 48519

www.subterraneanpress.com
www.caitlinkiernan.com

Table of Contents

To the memory of Diane Arbus,
in lieu of the eloquence of silence.

Making Her Own Light: An Introduction

by Jeff VanderMeer

Some writers cannot help themselves. Some writers, by the sheer complexity and reach of their imaginations, will always be somewhat unclassifiable. For this reason, it's their view of the world we value, not the category in which a publisher places them. These are the writers who create what they find to be perfectly normal, only to be told it is strange. Such writers I value the most, for they are *sui generis*. Caitlín R. Kiernan is one of these writers, and in *The Ammonite Violin & Others* she goes to very strange places, indeed.

In effect, she has created a collection that positions supernatural elements of myth and folktale in a place far more primal than even their original context. In a radical move that no doubt came to her as naturally as a dolphin takes to swimming, Kiernan has managed, through texture and point of view, to show us the *reality* of these archetypes. Angela Carter, in a collection like *The Bloody Chamber*, reclaimed iconic stories for feminism, but still used her lush prose in a stylized way that mimicked the flatness of tales, which are generally two-dimensional compared to short stories. Kiernan has accomplished something much more subversive—hers is a kind of dirty, modern lyricism. Like many of the Decadents, her prose is, yes, lush, but it's also muscular, allows for psychological three-dimensional portraits of her characters, and has the flexibility to be blunt, even shocking. Mermaids, selkies, vampires, and fairies all make appearances in this collection.

However, the method of description and storytelling creates a sheer physicality and alien quality to the context for these creatures that both humanizes them—in the sense of making them real, if not always understandable—and makes it impossible to see them as just people in disguise or as caricatures we can dismiss because they exist solely for our passing frisson of unease or terror (which is so often the case when writers describe "monsters").

Part of this authenticity—part of the reason I find them disturbing—comes from the simple fact that the people in these stories don't really survive their encounter with the supernatural. Whether in, among others, "Madonna Littoralis" or the two "Metamorphosis" stories, this inability to survive can be literal or figurative, or both—and it occurs because the supernatural isn't so much something terrifying in Kiernan's view—it can be, but that's not the true point. The supernatural to Kiernan is also something beautiful and unknowable in intent, and often wedded to the natural world. In a sense, trying to know something unknowable will always destroy the seeker.

In almost all of these stories, too, the characters seem to encounter the supernatural as part of a need for connection, even if the thing they connect with is Other and will be the death of them. And, once the connection is made, the implications of that *passing over,* are never what they might have seemed to be before the crossing. For example, the powerful, controlled yet intensely interior narrative "The Cryomancer's Daughter (Murder Ballad No. 3)" burns with its description of an obsessed, unequal relationship: "...she reaches out and brushes frozen fingertips across the space between my shoulder blades. I gasp, and at least it is *me* gasping, an honest gasp at the pain and cold flowing out of her and into me." That there is often a graphic sexual component to these stories shouldn't come as a surprise—it supports this idea of trying to connect, even if the connection can turn from erotic to grotesque, the two elements commingling until it's not always clear which is which.

Kiernan also discards the typical plots that you see in fantasy or supernatural fiction. There are few twists here, little action in the conventional sense. Such artifice would form a barrier to getting at truths about the relationships in these stories, some of which form intricate snapshots of dysfunction and the attempt to communicate (underscoring that even in normal human relationships, we are all encased in our separate skulls and, ultimately, unknowable).

This focus contributes to the sense that we're reading something *new* here, even though these stories fit comfortably within Kiernan's overall oeuvre—something that is unrelenting in peeling away layers of falsehood in an attempt to get somewhere real. It's not just the characters but *readers* who receive what seem like true glimpses of what it might be like to encounter the inexplicable, with all blinders off, stripped of any niceties. I won't lie—Kiernan's approach can be brutal at times, the true fodder for nightmares, but it's also brave and true.

"A Child's Guide to the Hollow Hills" exemplifies these qualities, with its depiction of a faerie girl mistreated by the Queen of Decay. She's trapped by the Queen when she chases a lizard—"verdant, iridian, gazing out at me with crimson eyes"—through the forest and becomes a slave, and then even less than that.

The descriptions in this story, which serve to underscore the themes, are devastatingly brilliant. The Queen is "fashioned of some viscous, shapeless substance that is not quite flesh, but always there is the dim impression of leathery wings, as of some immense bat, and wherever the Queen brushes against the girl, there is the sensation of touching or being touched by matted fur and the blasted bark of dying, lightning-struck trees." The girl sits on a "black bed far below the forest floor," while the "Queen of Decay moves across her like the eclipse of the sun," surrounded by "mirrors hung on bits of root and bone and the fishhook mandibles of beetles."

Here, then, is the true terrible *unknowableness* of that which is often sanitized or only brought forward for our amusement, revealed as terrible because we cannot truly fathom it. Even more important, perhaps, is the sense that this is all part of the natural cycle from the faerie Queen's point of view, as much as the pattern of the seasons, and that the natural world around us is a deeply alien place, even though we try so hard to control it. Thus, it's appropriate that the story ends with the lizard that led the girl to her fate. The lizard is the real main character in "A Child's Guide to the Hollow Hills," the secret sharer: that which we forever chase without realizing the depths of what we chase. It's a stunner of a story, and it's one that only Kiernan could have written.

Throughout *The Ammonite Violin & Others*, these moments proliferate, mixed with moments of pure horror—"It's loose in the room with us," "I cannot look away"—that always serve to support something beyond just unsettling us. These stories are, ultimately, driven by deeply human, deeply humane, deeply secret moments.

In the second story in *The Ammonite Violin & Others* the beleaguered narrator tells the reader, "There are things that are born into darkness and live their entire lives in darkness, in deep places, and they've learned to make whatever light they need. It sprouts from them, lanterns of flesh to dot the abyss like bare bulbs strung on electrical cords, and I wish I could make my own light at the bottom of the walls of the earth."

Caitlín R. Kiernan creates her own light in this remarkable collection, and shines it on dark places. In doing so, she gives us gritty, lyrical, horrible, beautiful truths.

Madonna Littoralis

L ike the hooves of Neptune's horses or only the waves breaking themselves upon the shore, my thoughts have broken apart again, shattered white foam spray on sharp granite boulders, and I'm staring at the tub or I'm staring at you stretched out naked upon my bed or I'm staring into that other darkness huddled beneath the rocks. That darkness filled up with the semen reek of seaweed and stranded things, with the sound of dripping water and lapping water and someone whispering half to herself, and I do not know if I'm meant to listen or to turn away. I *always* turn away, in time, when push comes to shove, but for now I listen, and the bathroom light off the old tub glints too brightly incandescent from cast iron enameled white and rusted claw feet on ceramic tiles the color of a broken promise. I listen, and you pause, smile that smile that will never stop frightening me, and then continue again.

"Jenny Haniver," you say. And I ask *Who? What was that?* and so you whisper the name again—"Jenny Haniver."

The cold Massachusetts night, night below the lighthouse and the sand and the rocks, in that hollow the sea has worried deep into the edge of the world, and I am crouched at the entrance, because I haven't yet found the courage to crawl inside. That would be *felo-de-se*, just like the white bathtub, and you roll over onto your back and smile for me.

"Oh, it's a pathetic, shriveled thing," you say. "An ape above, a mackerel below. You know the sort. Even P. T. Barnum had his Fiji mermaid."

I squint into the stinking sea-cave darkness, seeing nothing at all and thinking that I really should have brought a kerosene lantern or a flashlight. Knowing that I never have and likely never will. It's not permitted; there will be light, of a sort, farther along.

"The Fiji mermaid," you say again, repeating yourself because I must be hard of hearing. "Exhibited throughout North America and the Continent in 1840, '41, and '42, to the wonder and astonishment of thousands of naturalists and other scientific and scholarly persons, whose previous doubts as to the existence of such an astonishing creation were entirely removed."

"Now you sound like a carnival barker," I say, and there's that smile again.

"Step right up," you say. "Just two bits, my lady, and I'll show you everything there is to see." And you spread your legs wide, and for a long, disquieting moment I can seem to find no difference between the sea cave and your exposed sex. I cannot, for that moment, place myself in time or space, and it might be night on Cape Anne or only another night in my room. My dislocation passes, slowly, and the lamp light casts your restless shadow on the walls.

"Something I haven't seen before?" I ask, and your laughter is an undertow dragging me down and down and down, silver bubbles leaking from my lips and racing towards the drowning sky. You draw your knees together once again, hiding the passage below the lighthouse, hiding my dreams, and roll over so your back's to me.

"You don't ask much, do you?" and I don't want to answer, but I answer, anyway. I always answer. Then I want to know if it was really from Fiji, the Fiji mermaid.

"Who knows. Barnum leased the thing from a man named Moses Kimball for twelve dollars and fifty cents a week."

I look over my shoulder, because there's unexpected music from the hallway; I turn towards the open bedroom door and stare out the entrance of the cave at the waning moon laying molten silver across the Atlantic. I know that the two of you—you and her—are coconspirators, secret accomplices, comrades in my undoing. Wicked, wicked things, my loves, my licentious saints of tide and beached whales and dry, salt-stained kisses.

"Stop stalling," you say. "Come to bed. I'm so cold," and I turn back and stare at your shoulders and keep my seat. The moon is one night past full now, a pocked and shining coin tacked up somewhere beyond the windowpane.

And sang in a voice so hoarse,
"My comrades and my messmates,
Oh, do not weep for me,
For I'm married to a mermaid,
At the bottom of the deep blue sea."

I have been down here so many times that I've long ago lost count. Awake and dreaming, I've traced the winding path between the low dunes and through the rocks, past the winking, white-washed tower of the Annisquam lighthouse. When the tide is out, I can always reach the cave, and she is almost always there, the lady and her court, the maiden empress of urchins and stingrays. If I were a sane woman, I'd go home to Boston and forget what I've seen and done. But if I were merely sane, I would never have found this place.

I wonder how many have died here, how many have lost their way or lingered too long, hypnotized by the siren songs, by her hurricane voice and the booming voice of the ocean echoing off the high granite walls, and then found themselves trapped when the moon dragged the waves back in again. I've seen their bones, crusty and sharp with tiny barnacles, green with algae. I've seen skulls that have become cradles for anemones and scuttling crabs. Before it's done, I'll take my place among them. I know this because she's told me so again and again. There was a time when that knowledge frightened me. There was a time when I still valued my life more than the sight of her.

I wonder what it will take to get the tub clean.

"I'm growing bored," you say and sigh and roll over onto your back again. "Are you going to sit there all night or are you going to fuck me?"

He said that as he went down,
Great fishes he did see;
They seemed to think as he did wink,
That he was rather free.

"Soon the stitches will have to come out," you say and laugh, and I'm not imagining that you're laughing at me.

"People believed in it, the Fiji mermaid?" I ask.

"People believe what pleases them most. People see what they want to believe. Show them a baby orangutan sewn to a fish's tail, a little *papier-mâché*, and they'll see what they *want* to see."

I close my eyes, shutting out the cold light through the window, and what was that name you used? Jenny Haniver, Jenny Hanvers, Antwerp Anvers, *jeune de Antwerp...*

She came at once unto him,
And gave him her white hand,
Saying, "I have waited long, my dear,
To welcome you to land.
Go to your ship and tell them,
You'll leave them all for me..."

I don't remember standing and walking to the bed. I can't recall standing over you or taking off my dress and my stockings and my boots. Your eyes are black and bottomless, and your teeth are razor shards of alabaster set in purple gums.

...For you're married to a mermaid,
At the bottom of the deep blue sea.

"Yes, that's my girl," you murmur, and your breath is no different from the air imprisoned beneath the lighthouse, sea-damp exhalations from the crystalline lips of the cave. "My father was a taxidermist," you whisper playfully in my ear. "My mother was a shark got caught on his line. They made me from love and needles, from fish heads and silken thread."

"Maybe they should have thrown you back," I say, and my fingertips brush quickly across your glistening thighs, then loiter a moment on your pale belly. I touch the smooth place where your navel should be.

"Maybe they did," you reply.

I am very near the heart of the cave now, moving past twin columns carved and shaped by the constant attentions of the sea, the perfect lancet archway fashioned by nameless architects, its keystone marked by the idiot countenance of some dim, abyssal god. And here is the pool, glowing phosphorescent with the false light of jellyfish and tiny squids, the yellow-green glow of a hundred thousand coelenterate tendrils washed up here and clinging to the rocks. She's floating facedown in the shallow water just a little ways out from the pool's nearest edge, her long hair spread wide for a strangling halo, the fins along her spine sagging limp and tattered, and a more careless or indifferent eye might easily mistake her for a dead thing.

I look away from the tub. There are spatters and bloody smears on the floor at my feet, already drying to a crust. There's more blood waiting in the sink, clinging to the scalpels and Metzenbaum scissors I dropped there when she finally stopped breathing, the retractors and stainless steel hooks and hemostatic forceps. Blood in the tub and on the floor, in the sink and on my hands. All the cleaning to be done, though I'm so tired that I only want to close my eyes and pray she'll have given my dreams back to me. Certainly, she has no use for them now, for the sea is ever dreaming, that ever slumbering, sunless kingdom of nightmares which lies so many thousands of leagues down, balanced always on the bright edge of waking.

"Did you actually write that?" you ask me, and I nod yes. You shake your head and frown; your lower lip looks swollen. "Well, it's wretched," you tell me. "No wonder no one will publish your silly book. Is that really the best that you can do?"

Later, I'll admit there's much more blood than I'd expected. Later, I'll say something like, "You'd have thought that I'd used a hacksaw and an axe." I reach for a clean towel to wipe some of it away.

And you impatiently guide my left hand to the cleft between your legs, the skin shaved smooth, and the ocean inside you is beginning to leak out. It moistens my rough fingertips with a few sticky drops of brine, and you're still talking, describing again for me exactly how it should be done.

"You would tightly bind my legs before making the first incision," you whisper, as if someone else might overhear. "You would press the blade *here* and draw it slowly down."

I'm in the cave beneath the lighthouse, and outside, the ocean roars and rages as I wade into the glowing pool. The water is cold enough to steal my breath, and I pause, gasping as it washes about my legs and quickly soaks through my woolen trousers. At that moment, I can almost believe it is a conscious thing, that chill, and that it means to drive me shivering back out onto the rocks. The jealous souls of all those who have come before me to keep her safe and keep her distant and keep her to themselves.

"If I cried out, you would ignore me and keep cutting. It wouldn't be anything but cowardice, anyway."

I grit my teeth against the gnawing guardian cold and the pain that comes before merciful numbness and take another step towards her. The bottom of the pool is slick and uneven, and I almost lose my footing, splashing about like a clumsy child, and now the water has risen as high as my waist. If I drown, if I slip again and hypothermia takes me before the water rushes up my nostrils and down my throat and fills my lungs, then I can take my proper place with all the others whom she's called out from warm beds and the listing decks of sailing ships.

"If I should scream, you'd cut that much deeper," you whisper urgently, commanding me, and then you thrust your hips against me. And I hold my breath, wanting and dreading what comes next, the part you keep hidden decently inside, the secrets you say you show no one but me.

My father was a taxidermist. My mother was a shark got caught on his line.

I try hard not to look into the tub. There's nothing there I ever want to see again, nothing I haven't seen before. It's only dead flesh, cut away and discarded and unloved.

In the pool, she slaps once at the surface with her broad tail, and the freezing spray peppers my face. She drifts a moment longer, then turns her head and looks at me. Her eyes are something more than empty. Her eyes are the moment before the universe winked on. Her eyes are void and absence and the first twelve seconds after death.

"Don't you *dare* fucking pussy out on me," you hiss, digging your sharp nails into my back. And when you enter me, I bite my lip to keep from screaming, bite down hard enough that I taste blood. I've never yet seen that hidden part of you; you've told me that you'll kill me if I ever look, and I believe you. It slides deep inside, folding me open, a bristling, stinging fist or fingers sprouting barracuda teeth or a gouging scrimshaw tongue. And now you shut your eyes, your neck bent sharply back so that I can see the old scars on your throat, three ragged pink slits on either side.

They made me from love and needles...

And I'm alone again, curled up in a sandy place near the mouth of the sea cave, though I have never been able to recall how it was that I escaped the pool—if I was found wanting, lacking, and *driven* away, or if I was only too afraid to reach out and take her hand. The moon is bright and bitter above the thundering breakers, no warmth at all from her light as I lie among the weathered stones like Andromeda waiting for the slithering, snake-jawed agent of Poseidon to finally be done with her. I'll find my way back home before dawn, past the old lighthouse and the marshy banks of the Annisquam River.

You wrap your legs around me. You encircle me.

"Sew them closed," you murmur, and a single drop of sweat rolls off my chin and lands on your right breast. "Sew them closed forever," and in that room with its lion-footed tub, I make another careless vow and reach for the leather satchel near the door.

Orpheus at Mount Pangaeum

I open my eyes, thinking that it must be morning by now, hoping there *might* be morning in the empty spaces after my dreams, but there's no less darkness than before, and the air stinks of mildew and old dust, bare concrete and ice. No less darkness than before, but no less light, either. Two naked incandescent bulbs which hang like fairie pears fashioned from glass and tungsten filaments, strung from the high ceiling on yellow electrical cords. And so there is light, and so there are shadows. Some of the shadows move, reminding me I'm not alone. I shut my eyes again, remembering that it can never be morning down here, remembering that and all the stairs leading from the door in the building's subbasement. We must have walked for an hour, going down. I said to you, "We've been walking for a coon's age," and you didn't laugh. You didn't even stop and look back at me, scowling over your shoulder. You only shrugged and took another step *down*. So, I am remembering the long descent, the cement stairwell and the musty air and the sound of our footsteps, the glow from your flashlight growing dimmer and dimmer as though the darkness above and around and below us had weight like water piled above the deep places of the world, and all that weight was crushing the light back in on itself. I'm remembering your anger when I said we should go back.

"There's always a siren," she says, "singing you to shipwreck." And I know that's only a song I've heard somewhere. I know she's only listening to my memories, so she's watching as we went down the stairs through the night that will never have a morning, and she has heard me try to call you back. She laughs, and her claws click softly against the concrete.

"Kiss me," you said, but I knew that wasn't what you meant. You say kiss me, but you mean another thing entirely, and you show me your white teeth filed down to cannibal points. I always think about how much that must have hurt, and it's no wonder there's almost always dried blood caked at the corners of your mouth. Most of it must be your own. You said, "Kiss me." Language only something that's there to mean what you need it to mean at any given moment, and I put my arms around you tight and let you lap at one of the scabby, always-bruised places at the nape of my neck. But lapping at damage done is never enough, and I know that, and if it had ever mattered I wouldn't have followed you through the city and down to the basement and the subbasement and down those stairs into the sea. A dentist sharpened your teeth for you, eight incisors and four canines. I used to know his name. He charged you $250 for each tooth and used a drill. "Kiss me," you said, and I held you as tightly as I dared, because I'm always afraid of drowning, of that water so deep that my feet will never find the bottom, and your sharpened teeth broke through my skin again.

"Why so green and lonely?" she asks me, and I open my eyes again. She's sitting on the floor near enough that I can see the beads of sweat standing out on her forehead and cheeks and bare chest like beads of milk on her ebony skin. I can see the tiny bones and bits of filth plaited into her hair, and I can see her pupils, a glimmering color that is almost, but not quite, gold. Her pupils like the horizontal bars of a sheep's eyes, or a squid's, or...but then she blinks and her eyes are only black.

Take a picture, asshole. It'll last longer.

Your sharp white teeth digging into my shoulder, and I laid down, your bed too narrow for the both of us, but it's never stopped you before. That pain so familiar. The pain of kissing you, and in another second or two I was hard and looking for a way inside. "Reciprocal penetration," you once said. Your teeth, my cock, tit for tat, yin and yang, square pegs and round holes, and I really don't care. It made you angry when I told you that I didn't care, but almost everything makes you angry, sooner or later. I should know better than to say anything at all.

"Why so green and lonely?" the thing on the floor in front of me asks again. I spit at it, and it laughs at me.

"That's just a song I heard on the radio," I say. "It doesn't mean anything. It doesn't mean anything at all."

Your knees pressing hard against my thighs, and you sink your teeth in deeper. There's more blood now than you can swallow all at once. You'll throw these sheets out when we're done. Sometimes, I think half your paycheck goes for new sheets. But there will still be stains on the mattress. You say you know all those stains by heart. You say you keep them so you won't forget. Not all of them are mine.

And then I find my way inside, and you're so wet I can't help but think about drowning again. Past the hungry red-eyed guardians tattooed on either side of your sex, which you keep shaved or waxed or plucked or, I suspect, whatever hurts the most. Whatever keeps it smooth and bare and keeps those guardian beasts watchful.

"Kiss me," you say, and blood spills from your lips and dribbles onto my throat. I kiss you the only way I know how, deep as I can go, deep as I'm allowed to go, so deep my feet never touch bottom and deep enough to drown. You smile, your sharp teeth stained crimson, and go back to work on the new hole you've made in me.

"You don't even know where you're going," I said, flinching at the way the darkness trapped in the stairwell made my voice so much bigger than it had any right to ever be. "You don't know where these stairs lead."

"Turn back if you're afraid. I never said I couldn't do this alone."

That part's true. You never said that you couldn't do this alone. You never even asked if I'd come with you. I tagged along like a fucking puppy or a younger sibling because I didn't know what the hell else I was supposed to do. You read a book a man sold you on the internet, a book that was printed in 1906, the same year as the Great San Francisco Earthquake, you said, as if that should mean something to me, as though that might explain why we're slipping deeper and deeper below the city. No one ever dug anything this deep. I tell you that, and you think I'm making a joke. I'm following you because you're going, with or without me, and you're going, because you bought a book from a man on the internet and this is what the book's told you to do.

"She'll be hungry," she says, this thing on the floor, the woman with golden barbell pupils and then no pupils at all. "When she wakes up, she'll be very hungry."

"She's always hungry," I reply.

"Maybe you shouldn't be here," she says.

"Is that the best you can do?" you growl, grinding your hips against me, crushing me into the bed. There's pain, and I shut my eyes, wondering how much longer until I've sunk so far there's no hope of ever getting back to the surface again.

"You could have joined her," the woman says, the thing that might have been a woman—as they say—once upon a time. Back before that book of yours was printed. Before this deep place opened up like the whole wide world asking for a fucking kiss and someone hid the wound so you'd need a book to ever find it. "It would have been easier that way, easier for the both of you."

A coward dies a thousand times before his death…

I try to stand, because I want to see what they've made of you. I want to see what's left. What you're becoming, but my legs are so weak, and my head spins, and I sit right back down again. She watches while I draw a circle in the dust, as perfect a circle as I can manage with my fingers on the gritty, ancient cement floor, trying to remember all the things you ever taught me about casting circles, north, south, the four fucking quarters, and she laughs at me again.

"Your head is filled with music," she says. She sounds delighted.

"There's always a siren," I tell her, spitting the words like pebbles, "singing you to shipwreck." And I'm wishing there were magic in the words, magic like the mess they've made of you. Alchemy. Transformation. Something that changes one thing into something else entirely.

We were halfway to the bottom before it occurred to me to start counting the steps.

You sat up straight, some trick you'd learned, and those secret muscles inside you tightened around me until I gasped and clenched my teeth. Your breasts smeared with my blood, my blood trickling thick down your chin, dripping onto my belly. You licked your lips clean and grinned. "I could tear it off," you say. "I could always find another play pretty. Someone who isn't such a goddamn pussy."

Inside my circle, mock safe inside my circle, and all the sea pressing down on me. There are things that are born into darkness and live their entire lives in darkness, in deep places, and they've learned to make whatever light they need. It sprouts from them, lanterns of flesh to dot the abyss like yellow-green stars. Stars like bare bulbs strung on electrical cords, and I wish that I could make my own light here at the bottom of the vaults of the earth.

"I see a stairway," the demon thing says to me, "so I follow it down into the belly of a whale."

"They're only songs," I tell her again.

"I built the shadows here," it says, as though it understands. "I built the growl in the voice I fear..."

"Did you?" I ask. "Did you really?" and then she laughs that laugh that reminds me just how much darker dark can be, if it has a mind to stop fooling around and be done with me once and for fucking all.

"I could always find someone else," you said, in case I hadn't heard you the first time. And then you shut up and make another hole in me.

She kissed you, the way you'd always asked *me* to kiss you. She kissed you, and your eyes rolled back. Your lips moved, but the noises from the ceiling, the excited rustle of wings and the *clack clack clack* of all those claws against concrete and the suckling sounds, all of that to mask whatever you were saying to her or to me or to whatever ravenous gods a stone cold bitch like you deigns to get down on her knees for.

She *folded* you, and I could never even have dreamt such a geometry, such a fine and terrible origami of flesh and bone and blood. A paper flower budding from nothing at all but the flatness of you. A butterfly. A scorpion of planes and angles and nightmares, and before she was finished, you'd begun to sweat the way she sweats. She'd gone deeper into you than I could ever have gone, a hundred times deeper, a thousand thousand times deeper, down stairs I had never even glimpsed. You sweated milk-white droplets that pooled at your bare feet, your whole body bleeding itself dry of your soul, of the humanity you'd spent your life hating and wanting someone to cut away. And then something grew from the pool, from the sweat that spoiled in an instant, going to tar or India-ink tendrils that slithered greedily around your ankles and up your long pale legs and twined themselves about you until there was no more of you left to see.

"Why so green and lonely?" she asks.

"Will she even remember me?" I ask back.

"It would have been easier for both of you," the woman says and shrugs, and then spreads her wings. It makes me think of some great lazy animal stretching itself after a nap, and the light shines through the webbing between the supporting struts of those fingers grown so impossibly long and thin. I can see veins and capillaries like a satellite photograph of rivers from outer space, Mother Ganges, the Mekong Delta, the mighty, muddy Mississippi from five hundred miles up.

That's you in there, I think and begin retracing the protective, delusory circumference of my circle. *Those are rivers of you, stolen rivers winding through her flesh.*

"I'd hold you under and drown you like a sack of kittens," you laughed as I slid out of you, trying to ignore the way my balls had begun to ache. You licked me from your fingers. You bent down and sucked my cock, taking back any stray bit of you I might have scrubbed loose. I shut my eyes and tried to lie still as your sharp, sharp teeth drew a few more drops.

"She'll know how now," the woman says, turning away from me, turning to see your cocoon, your black chrysalis glistening wetly beneath the two twenty-five watt bulbs hanging from the ceiling. "How to *drown* you, I mean," she adds, though I'd understood the first time.

I'm a small thing dropped overboard and lost at the bottom of the sea. I'm a man slit open, stem to stern, and there are bricks and lead and ballast stones where my guts should be.

I sit within the confines of my circle and wonder how long it would take me to cross the concrete room to the foot of the stairs leading back up to the subbasement and the basement and abandoned warehouse and the city and the surface of the sea. I try to remember how many steps I counted on the way down, because twice that number might tell me how many there were altogether, and I pretend that I could ever have the courage to leave whatever you've become. I tell myself I'll go. I tell myself that I could find the way back alone and you wouldn't try to follow me. I pretend I wouldn't see you every time I shut my eyes.

The chrysalis ripples and begins to split apart.

You licked roughly at the tip of my penis and told me to open my eyes and stop being such a baby. "I haven't bitten it off yet," you said.

"Kiss me," the demon sighs and folds its wings away.

And I'm only a stone or a penny or an empty, discarded bottle.

And I have no light of my own.

Bridle

It's not a wild place—not some bottomless, peat-stained loch hidden away between high granite cliffs, and not a secret, deep spring bubbling up crystal clear from the heart of a Welsh or Irish forest where the Unseelie host is said to hold the trees always at the dry and brittle end of autumn, always on the cusp of a killing winter that will never come. It's only a shallow, kidney-shaped pool in a small, neglected city park. No deeper than a tall man's knees, water the color of chocolate milk in a pool bordered by crumbling mortar and mica-flecked blocks of quarried stone. There are fountains that seem to run both night and day, two of them, and I suppose one might well imagine *this* to be some sort of enchantment, twin rainstorms falling always and only across the surface directly above submerged, disgorging mechanisms planted decently or deceitfully out of sight. In daylight, the water rises from the cloudy pool and is transformed, going suddenly clean and translucent, a fleeting purity before tyrant gravity reasserts itself and the spray falls inevitably back into the brown pool, becoming once again only some part of the murky, indivisible whole. There are gnarled old willows growing close together, here and there along the shore, trees planted when my grandmother was a young woman. They lean out across the pool like patient fishermen, casting limp green lines leaf-baited for fish that have never been and will never be.

No one much comes here anymore. Perhaps they never did. I suspect most people in the city don't even know the park exists, steep-sided and unobtrusive, hidden on three sides behind the stately Edwardian-era houses along Euclid Avenue, Elizabeth Street, and Waverly Way. The fourth side, the park's dingy north edge, is bordered by an ugly redbrick apartment complex built sometime in the seventies, rundown now and completely at odds with everything else around it. I wonder how many grand old houses were sacrificed to the sledgehammers and bulldozers to make room for that eyesore. Someone made a lot of money off it once, I suppose. But I'm already letting myself get distracted. Already, I'm indulging myself with digressions that have no place here. Already, I'm trying to look away.

Last spring, they found the boy's body near the small stone bridge spanning one end of the pool, the end farthest from the brick apartment complex. Back that way, there are thick bunches of cattails and a few sickly water lilies and other aquatic plants I don't know names for. I've seen the coroner's report, and I know that the body was found floating face up, that the lungs were filled with water, that insects had done a lot of damage before someone spotted the corpse and called the police. No one questioned that the boy had drowned, and there was no particular suspicion of foul play. He had an arrest record—shoplifting, drugs and solicitation. To my knowledge, no one ever bothered to ask how he might have drowned in such shallow water. There are ways it could happen, certainly. He slipped and struck his head. It might have been as simple as that.

No one mentioned the hoofprints, either, but I have photographs of them. The tracks of a large unshod horse pressed clearly into a patch of red mud near the bridge, sometime before the boy's body was pulled from the pool. You don't see a lot of horses in this part of town. In fact, you don't see any. I'm writing this like it might be a mystery, like I don't already know the answers, and that's a lie. I'm not exactly a writer. I'm a photographer, and I don't really know how one goes about this sort of thing. I'm afraid I'm not much better with confessions.

I could have started by explaining that I happen to own one of those old houses along Euclid, passed down to me from my paternal grandparents. I could have begun with the antique bridle, which I found wrapped in a moth-eaten blanket, hidden at the bottom of a steamer trunk in the attic, or…I could have started almost anywhere. With my bad dreams, for example, the things I only choose to call my bad dreams out of cowardice. The dreams—no, the *dream*, singular, which has recurred too many times to count, and which is possibly my shortest and most honest route to this confession.

(No, I didn't *kill* the boy, if that's what you're thinking. I'm no proper murderess. It'll never be so simple as that. This is a different sort of confession.)

In the dream, I'm standing alone on the little stone bridge, standing there stark naked, and the park is washed in the light of a moon that is either full or very near to full. I have no recollection of getting out of bed, or of having left the house, or of the short walk down to the bridge. I'm cold, and I wonder why I didn't at least think to wear my robe and slippers. I'm holding the bridle from the trunk, which is always much heavier than I remember it being. Something's moving in the water, and I want to turn away. Always, I *want* to turn away, and when I look down I see that the drowned boy floating in the water smiles up at me and laughs. Then he sinks below the surface, or something unseen pulls him down, and that's when I see the girl, standing far out near the center of the pool, bathing in one of the fountains.

A week ago, I laid the pen down after that last sentence, and I had no intention of ever picking it up again. At least, not to finish writing this. But there was a package in the mail this afternoon—a cardboard mailing tube addressed to me—and one thing leads to another, so to speak. The only return address on the tube was Chicago, IL 60625. No street address or post-office box, no sender's name. And I noticed almost immediately that the postmark didn't match the Chicago zip. The zip code on the postmark was 93650, which turns out to be Fresno, California. I opened the tube and found two things inside. The first was a print of a painting I'd never seen before, and the second was a note neatly typed out and paper-clipped to a corner of the print, which read as follows:

A blacksmith from Raasay lost his daughter to the *Each Uisge*. In revenge, the blacksmith and his son made a set of large hooks, in a forge they set up by the lochside. They then roasted a sheep

33

and heated the hooks until they were red hot. At last, a great mist appeared from the water and the *Each Uisge* rose from the depths and seized the sheep. The blacksmith and his son rammed the red-hot hooks into its flesh and, after a short struggle, dispatched it. In the morning there was nothing left of the creature apart from a foul jelly-like substance. (*More West Highland Tales*; J. F. Campbell, 1883)

The print was labeled on the back, with a sticker affixed directly to the paper, as *The Black Lake* by Jan Preisler, 1904. It shows a nude young man standing beside a tall white horse at the edge of a lake that is, indeed, entirely black. The horse's mane is black, as well, as is its tail and the lower portions of its legs. The young man is holding some black garment I can't identify. The sticker informed me that the original hangs in the Nárdoni Gallerie in Prague. I sat and stared at it for a long time, and then I came back upstairs and picked up this pen again.

These are only words. Only ink on paper.

I had the dream again tonight, and now it's almost dawn, and I'm sitting in my study at my desk, trying to finish what I started.

And I am standing on the stone bridge in the park, standing naked under the full moon, and I can hear the fountains, all that water forced up and then spattering down again across the pool, which, in my dream, is as black as the lake in Preisler's painting. The girl's wading towards me, parting the muddy, dark water with the prow of her thighs, and her skin is white and her long hair is black, black as ink, the ink in this pen, the lake in a picture painted one hundred and two years ago.

Her eyes are black, too, and I can read no expression in them. She stops a few yards from the bridge and gazes up at me. She points to the heavy bridle in my hands, and I hold it out for her to see. She smiles, showing me a mouthful of teeth that would be at home in the jaws of some devouring ocean thing, and she holds both her arms out to me. And I understand what she's asking me to do, that she wants me to drop the bridle into the pool. I step back from the edge of the bridge, moving so slowly now I might as well be mired to the ankles in molasses; she takes another quick step towards me, and her teeth glint in the moonlight. I clutch the bridle more tightly than before, and the bit and curb chains jingle softly.

I found this online an hour or so after I opened the mailing tube and copied it down on a Post-It note, something from a website, "Folklore of the British Isles"—*There was one way in which a Kelpie could be defeated and tamed; the Kelpie's power of shape shifting was said to reside in its bridle, and anybody who could claim possession of it could force the Kelpie to submit to their will.*

One thing leads to another.

In my dream, I have lain the bridle in the fallen leaves gathered about the base of a drinking fountain that hasn't worked in decades, setting it a safe distance from the water, and she's standing at the edge of the pool, waiting for me. I go to her, because I can't imagine what else I would ever do. She takes my hand and leads me down into the cold black water. She kisses me, presses her thin, pale lips to mine, and I taste what any drowning woman might taste—silt and algae, fish shit and all the fine particulate filth that drifts in icy currents and settles, at last, to the bottoms of lakes that have no bottoms. Her mouth is filled with water, and it flows into me like ice. Her piranha's teeth scrape against my cheek, drawing blood. She laughs and whispers in a language I can't understand, a language that I can somehow only vaguely even *hear*, and then she's forcing me down into the muck and weeds beneath the bridge. She cups my left breast in one hand, and I can see the webbing between her fingers.

And then…

Then we are riding wild through the midnight streets of the city, her hooves pounding loud as thunder on the blacktop, and no one we pass turns to look. No one sees. No one would dare. I tangle my fingers in her black mane, and the wind is a hurricane whisper in my ears. We pass automobiles and their unseeing drivers. We pass shops and restaurants and service stations closed up for the night. We race along a railroad track past landscapes of kudzu and broken concrete, and the night air smells of creosote and rust. I think the ride will surely never end. I *pray* that it will never end, and I feel her body so strong between my legs.

Beneath the stone bridge, she slides her fingers down and across my belly, between my legs. The mud squelches beneath us, and she asks me for the bridle, stolen from her almost two hundred years ago, when she was tricked into leaving her lake. She promises no harm will ever come to me, at least no harm from her, if only I will return the bridle, a bewitched and fairie thing that is rightfully hers and which I have no conceivable use for.

Her hooves against the streets seem to rattle the stars above us, seem to loosen them from their places in the firmament. I beg her to let the ride never end. I promise her everything, *except* the old bridle.

In the fetid darkness beneath the bridge, away from the glare of the moon, her eyes blaze bright as burning forests, and she slips two fingers deep inside me. More words I can't understand, and then more that I do, and I imagine myself crawling back to the spot where I left the bridle lying next to the broken drinking fountain. I imagine myself giving it to her.

Her hooves are thunder and cyclones, cannon fire and the splintering of bedrock bones deep within the hearts of ancient mountains. I am deaf and blind and there is nothing remaining in the universe except her. In another instant, my soul will flicker out, and she will consume even the memory of me.

And then I see the dead boy watching me, standing near the bridge and watching as she fucks me, or he's watching from a street corner as we hurry past. Holes where his eyes once were, holes the hungry insects and birds have made, but I know that he can see us, nonetheless. One does not need eyes to see such things. Indeed, I think, eyes only blind a woman or a dead boy to the truth of things as terrible as the white woman leaning over me or the black horse bearing me along deserted avenues. And he is a warning, and I see him dragged down and down into depths only the kelpie can find in a knee-deep pool in a city park. The air rushes from his lungs, bleeds from his mouth and nostrils, and streams back towards the surface. I see him riding her all the way to the bottom, and I push her away from me.

The night is filled with the screams of horses.

And I come awake in my bed, gasping and sweat-drenched, sick to my stomach and fumbling for the light, almost knocking the lamp off the table beside my bed. My skin is smeared with stinking mud, and there's mud on the white sheets and green-grey bits of weed caught in my wet hair. When I can walk, I go to the shower and stand beneath the hot water beating down on me, trying to forget again, and afterwards, I take the soiled sheets down to the washing machine in the basement. Again. And, the last part of this ritual, I find a flashlight and go to the trunk in the attic to be sure that the bridle is still there, wrapped safe inside its wool blanket.

For One Who has Lost Herself

1.

The woman stands across the street from the little shop on Columbus Avenue, almost a whole week now and she still hasn't found the nerve to simply walk across the street and go inside. She's tall and thin, a bit too thin, some would say, and almost pale as the snow that fell two days before and hasn't all melted away. Her eyes are a little too large for her face, and the irises are so big and black that the pupils are all but invisible and almost nothing of the white sclerae can be seen around their broad periphery. Her hands are long and slender, but her nails have been chewed down to stubs and her cuticles are red and raw. She's wearing a tattered grey wool coat with fur stitched about the collar and lapels, and about the cuffs, as well. Catching a glimpse of her (because hardly anyone looks directly at this woman), someone might be struck by how poorly the coat seems to fit her, perhaps a size too large, or two sizes two small. She can't recall where she got the coat, but thinks it might have been a gift. On her feet, she wears green galoshes, and she can't quite recall where those came from, either. Her ash blonde hair reaches down past her shoulders, a tangled, unkempt mane to frame her pale face.

A city bus growls past, belching diesel fumes and trailing soot, and the woman steps nervously back from the curb. She dislikes the Manhattan traffic, but she dislikes the huge buses most of all. She's thought of warning the people she sees climbing into them, and the people climbing out, but she knows enough of human beings to understand that none of them would listen.

From the other side of Columbus Avenue, the little shop beckons, the sight of it calling her like a foghorn or a ship's bell, or the lament of harpooned and dying whales. She knows that she only has to go to the corner and wait for the light to change, that she only has to walk across the street and place her hand upon the brass knob of the green door and go inside. She has only to step across the threshold, pass beneath the broad black-and-white placard hung above the entrance—GREYE'S ANATOMY (SINCE 1962)—and her journey will be all but over. She's come such a long way already, has crossed more than three thousand miles and almost a decade since she started out from the red sandstone beaches of Veantro Bay and Shapinsay Island. Leaving the Orkneys behind and wandering the Scottish Highlands, following rumours and hearsay west over the Atlantic to the shores of Iceland and Greenland, then on to America, to St. John's and Halifax, Winter Harbor and Gloucester, a hundred other fishing villages and smoky industrial towns whose names she's already forgotten. And finally, all the way down to this terrible city, this canyon of steel and glass and electricity which is always moving and crackling and muttering in its countless languages, always awake and watching her with its innumerable, unseeing human eyes.

The light at the corner turns red again, and the traffic comes to a sudden, reluctant, grumbling halt. A moment or two more and there are people streaming hurriedly across the street, some of them moving towards her from the other side and many others moving away, walking towards *that* side and the little shop with its cluttered display windows and black-and-white sign and mocking green door.

"Is there something over there you fancy, Miss?" someone asks, an old man's voice, rough but patient, like sand polishing driftwood smooth. She turns quickly around, startled because the people in this city hardly ever speak to her. The old man is barely half her height, peering out at her from behind a pair of spectacles that sit crookedly on the bridge of his wide nose. His skin's dark brown and wrinkled, almost the same color as his overcoat, and there's not a hair left on his bald head. He grins up at her, flashing a mouthful of perfectly spaced false teeth, and she sees that he's not really an old man at all. He's really someone like her, one thing pretending to be another, hiding out in plain sight where this rush and press of mortal men and women will never pause to recognize him for what he is.

"Oh, I'm not gonna *tell* anybody, if that's what you're worrying about," he says. "I got better things to do than waste my days telling these poor, dumb beasts secrets what they won't believe," and then he motions dismissively towards the cars and bright yellow taxis and all the people crossing Columbus Avenue.

"I've come a great distance," she says, though that doesn't answer the question he's asked her. And she thinks how it's been days since she's heard the sound of her own voice. No, not her *own* voice, but the voice she's had so long now that it's starting to seem like the only voice she's ever had, the voice she was born with and the voice she'll die with.

"Me, I pass this way almost every day," the old man says. "And I've seen you standing here, pretending you're one of them and staring at that place. Greye's Anatomy. I'll wager my toenails someone thought himself a right witty bastard, coming up with that one. Anyhow, I'm not so far gone I can't put one thing up against another, rub them together and see the sense of it."

She turns back towards the shop and chews at her lower lip a moment, then asks, "Did they steal something of yours, too?"

"Well, maybe. In a manner of speaking," he replies, "but then it's nothing I couldn't take right back, if ever the mood were to strike me I *wanted* it back. Is that how it is with you, Miss?"

"I think so," she says, not taking her eyes off the green door and the placard and all the dead things stuck up in the shop window. "It's been so long now, I'm not quite certain anymore."

"Then, if you don't mind my saying so, maybe it would be best if you didn't squander too many more days standing here in the cold, just watching."

"I don't mind the cold," she tells him.

"That's not what I was getting at, and you know it," he says, and makes a dry, coughing sound.

"It might not be there."

"You won't be sure until you look."

"But I'm so tired of looking," she says, and stuffs her hands into the deep pockets of the wool coat, which are bulging with an assortment of shells and pebbles she's gathered over the years, a withered mermaid's purse and a gold coin that's a full century older than the oldest parts of this city. She moves her fingers anxiously among these souvenirs, searching for comfort that isn't there to find. "It seems like I've been looking forever."

"Mind the difference between the way things *seem* and the way things *are*," the old man says, and when she turns to reply, to ask him what he means, he's gone, and she's alone again with these people and their clattering automobiles and the roaring, smoldering buses.

2.

In the end, it was such a simple thing. As simple a thing as waiting for the light to change and crossing the busy street. As simple as following the sidewalk to the place where it ends beneath the black-and-white placard that reads GREYE'S ANATOMY. And as simple a thing as pausing only a moment or two to take in the morbid disarray of the window dressings before she opens the green door, trading the bitter, bright day for the musty warmth and shadows of the shop.

3.

When she dreams, which she doesn't do as often as she once did, the tall woman with ash blonde hair and her nails chewed down to their quicks always dreams the same dream, which is the dream of the wide clean beach and the high cliffs, the sand and sky and red-brown boulders at the edge of the sea. She's playing alone in the surf and hears music, a merry, lilting sort of music, clear and crystal notes tumbling one against the next and carried along on the salty wind. And, being a curious creature, the music draws her up and out of herself, out of the waves, finally even out of her skin, and she stands in the brilliant morning sunlight. The boy is seated cross-legged on one of the larger boulders, so intent upon the positions of his fingers, upon their quick, precise movements and the sounds they are coaxing from his instrument, that he doesn't notice her at first. So she stands very still, with the saltwater lapping at her bare ankles, and listens.

She's seen human boys before, of course, on the decks of the fishing boats and ferries that come and go between the small rocky islands, but she's never seen one half so handsome, and never once did she imagine they might be capable of making such beautiful music. His hair is long and black, as black as the slender stick he's pressing to his lips, the black stick with silver keys that he's using to make the music, some sort of pipe, some strange man-made thing. When she takes another step towards him, he stops playing and looks up at her.

"Hello," he says and smiles.

She doesn't answer him, even though she understands and even though she knows well enough how to speak in all the tongues of men. She stands very still, watching and waiting for him to finish staring at her and go back to making his music.

"Aren't you cold?" he asks and points at her with his black and silver pipe.

"I don't mind the cold," she says, speaking loudly enough to be heard above the wind, and she takes a hesitant step or two nearer the boulder where he's seated. She knows to be wary of men, because her mother has told her stories about the slaughter of seals, about the wooden clubs and steel knives and stolen hides, and she's seen the rotting carcasses and the bleached white bones to prove all the stories true.

"No," he says, and winks his left eye at her. "I don't suppose you do," and then the boy presses the pipe to his lips and brings the music back again. It flows over her and through her and fills her in some way that she's never been filled before, satiating some terrible hunger she's never even known she had. It makes her want to dance, and she laughs and spins about and kicks at the sea. She tries to catch each note and hold it, freeze it forever in her memory before it's gone and replaced by the next and then the next after that. But it's like trying to hold a warm summer wind or the flickering shafts of sunlight slanting down through kelp into the deep places between the islands. *No*, she thinks. *It's like trying to capture time*, and the thought makes her sad, so she pushes it away and tries hard to think of nothing but the human boy's beautiful, sweet music moving all about her like the arms of the sea.

And what happens next is never quite the same thing twice, as though the truth of that day is more than she can bear to remember exactly and whole, so in her sleep she can only whisper less monstrous variations, a shifting torrent of falsehoods that she's spun to stand in for the day itself. No more or less true than her pale face reflected in still water or a looking glass, and what's the difference, when the dreams all end the same way? How can the details ever matter, if the conclusion is inescapable?

This happens, or this, or this other thing, and then the music stops and the boy has come down off his rock. He's standing on the beach, and in one hand he holds his piccolo (which, she's since learned, is what men call the black stick with silver keys) and in the other he holds her empty skin. He's still smiling, but this is another sort of smile. This is the smile of a shark or a hungry eel or the men who murder seals to steal their fur. This is a hard, triumphant smile, a smile to say he has what he came for. A smile so she can never forget she's been tricked.

"I hadn't thought it would be so easy," he says, and she begs him to give it back to her, weeps and pleads and goes down on her knees before he stops smiling and turns and walks away towards the cliffs. At first, she's too frightened to follow, remembering the old tales of stolen skins and her sisters and grandmothers who were forced to marry human men and bear their children and grow old and die and be buried in the stony earth like potatoes. She climbs up onto his boulder, naked and human to anyone without the eyes to see her true self trapped there inside. She doesn't take her eyes from him, and after a time the boy's only a small speck where the land turns green at the top of the cliffs, and then, a moment later, he's nothing at all.

4.

She imagined that it would smell like death inside the little shop—GREYE'S ANATOMY (SINCE 1962)—and is surprised when there's only the smell of dust and old books and a very faint hint of jasmine incense. There's a single aisle leading from the door back to the cash register, a narrow aisle lined with glass-fronted wooden museum cases filled with skulls and skeletons that stare sightlessly out at her. There are pickled things floating in jars of formalin—lizards from tropical rainforests, bats from Mexican caves, salamanders from icy Chinese streams. There are brilliant rainbows of butterflies and enormous iridescent beetles and hairy tarantulas sealed up tight inside shadow-box coffins. There's a bowl heaped with pigs' teeth, a necklace strung from the vertebrae of a boa constrictor, bracelets made from the wiry hair of an elephant's tail, a paperweight fashioned from a chunk of petrified wood. The door jingles shut behind her, and the tall, thin woman gazes back at the flat acrylic eyes of a taxidermied bobcat, its jaws permanently set into a snarl or a hiss. Behind it are shelves crowded with fossil bones and pyritized brittle stars on oily slabs of black German slate, the skull of a small dinosaur brought here from the deserts of Mongolia, and the delicate carbonized imprints of feathers and leaves and insects. All around her, the stuffed, pickled, silicified captives of this silent menagerie seem to be warning her she should turn back now, that she should run, before she finds herself drifting in a corked bottle or pinned down flat or stuffed with sawdust.

The man sitting behind the counter looks up from his newspaper and smiles.

"If there's anything I can help you with," he says, "just let me know."

"Yes," she replies, her voice breathless and unsteady, and she manages to look away from the bobcat, but there's no place safe for her dark eyes to linger, no corner of the little shop that doesn't hold some terrible artifact or lifeless husk. She spies the skeleton of a dodo bird, wired together and held upright with metal rods, and she reads the brass plaque on its oak stand: The Dodo (*Raphus cucullatus*), Family Raphidae, Island of Mauritius, Indian Ocean.

"Is this real?" she asks the man, and he stops reading his newspaper again, glances up at her and shakes his head. His hair is auburn, and there's a small patch of auburn beard on his chin, auburn stubble on his cheeks. His eyes are blue, the easy, disarming blue of late summer skies above the skerries.

"Are you a collector?" he asks.

45

She thinks of the shells and pebbles in her coat pockets, the bits and pieces of here and there she's gathered in her travels. "Yes," she says. "After a fashion."

The blue-eyed man lays his newspaper on the counter and rubs at his forehead. "Well, some of the spinal column's actual bone, and the right femur. That's real, too. But the rest is resin, cast from bones in a Dutch museum. It's a very accurate restoration. We're quite picky about our merchandise."

She looks at him a moment, then turns back to the dodo skeleton, a few precious bones the color of charcoal and all the rest only deceitfully painted scraps of plastic. There's a price tag dangling from the bird's left wing, and she reads it aloud. "Is that a fair price?" she asks the man, and he shrugs.

"Well, I figure fair's in the eye of the beholder, or at least in the depth of the beholder's pockets. It's one of a kind, top-notch craftsmanship. Our preparators are some of the best. And you won't easily find another like it outside an auction house."

"I wouldn't want to," she says, and thinks again about retracing her steps back to the shop's green door, and then back across Columbus Avenue, and maybe she'd keep going until the city was far behind her.

"So, is there something else you'd like to see?" the man asks. "You said you're a collector. What exactly is it that you fancy?" And the second question reminds her of the brown old man who wasn't an old man, the spectacles perched on his nose, his ratty overcoat.

Mind the difference between the way things seem *and the way things* are...

"I am looking for something," the woman says, and she turns to face the man behind the counter. "Something very dear to me. I've come a long way to find it. But I don't see it here anywhere."

The man chews at a thumbnail a moment, watching her, his expression gone suddenly uncertain and guarded, and she suspects he's about to ask her to leave. Perhaps, he thinks that she's insane. Perhaps, he only thinks she's wasting his time and wants to get back to his paper, if she doesn't intend to buy the dodo bird. But then he nods his head very slowly and motions to the curtain behind him, heavy green cloth almost the same shade as the door.

"This is just the showroom," he says. "Perhaps we have what you're looking for in the back. If you told me a little more—"

"A sealskin," she says, and her voice seems to fall like ice from her lips. She can almost hear those three syllables striking the hardwood floor of Greye's Anatomy and shattering. She swallows back the cold and waits for whatever the man will say next.

"I'm sorry. We're not a furrier. But if you—"

"It would have come from Scotland, originally," she tells him, and takes another step along the aisle towards the counter. "From Shapinsay in the Orkney Islands. It was...*collected* there, almost a decade ago. To your eyes, it would seem only the hide of any common seal.

"*Phoca vitulina*," the man says, and the Latin sounds like an incantation, something meant to drive her away from the little shop, a spell to banish her like a troublesome ghost or an autumn gale.

"To *your* eyes," she says again.

The auburn-haired man scratches at his neck, at a spot just beneath his left ear, not taking his eyes off the tall, thin woman in her dingy coat and green galoshes.

"Like I said, we're not a furrier. Who needs all that crazy PETA crap, right? Fuckers flinging red paint at people and all that shit. But...it just so happens, today might just be your lucky day."

"And why is that?" she asks him, speaking very softly now. She's come much too far to ever allow herself to hope. She will not dare to think she's found it, not after all these years, to imagine that there's anything waiting for her behind that green curtain but disappoint and another dead end.

"You're not a cop, right? Sorry, but I have to ask you that."

"No," she says. "I'm not a cop. It was a family heirloom, that's all. It was my mother's, before me," and the man nods his head, then he smiles again and folds his newspaper away before leading her through the green curtain to the shadowy place beyond.

5.

"I know it's back here somewhere," the man says, and then he lifts a heavy stack of antique books and folios from a rusty metal folding chair and puts them down on the floor. "You have a seat, and I'll bring it to you...if I can remember where I last saw the damned thing."

She nods her head and sits, trying hard to keep her eyes trained on the bare concrete at her feet. If anything, it's worse back here than it was in the front of the shop. There's no sunlight on this side of the green curtain, only stark and colorless fluorescence from a fixture hung on chains by four hooks set into the high ceiling, light that's hardly real light at all. She starts to shut her eyes, then decides the darkness would be even worse.

"I swear I saw it just the other day," the man tells her. "I was moving some stock around to make room for a new shipment and came across it. So, yeah, it can't have gotten far," and he laughs to himself.

There's a long table beneath the light fixture, jumbled with unfinished taxidermies and more old books, gooseneck lamps, and the shattered fragments of an enormous fossilized tortoise shell that's only been half reassembled. The man's standing on the far side of the table now, shifting crates and boxes about and mumbling to himself.

"Why did you want to know if I was a cop?" she asks him, and he stops and looks over his shoulder at her.

"You can never be too careful," he replies. "We've had cops show up before. FBI, customs agents, US Fish and Wildlife, all sorts. Not that anything back here's illegal, not strictly speaking, but it's best to keep the badges in the showroom, unless they've got warrants. Of course, that's happened, too. Fuckers seem to think any place with human skulls in the window must be up to *something* illicit."

"People should always mind the difference between the way things seem and the way things are," she says, wishing that the brown man had crossed the street and come into the shop with her, wishing that she'd thought to ask him if he would.

"Ain't *that* the goddamned truth," the red-headed man says. And then he squats down out of sight, vanishing below the edge of the table and all its curious burdens. "Ah-ha! *There* you are," he says, and she's about to get up from the rusty folding chair to see what he's found, if it can possibly be what she doesn't dare hope it is, when he stands up again. He has his arms wrapped about a small chest, wood almost as dark as chocolate, rotting leather straps and one of the latches broken off, and he's straining to lift it onto an edge of the table that is only piled with papers and anatomical diagrams.

"But I'm not looking for a chest," she says, already disappointed, because clearly the man hasn't understood. "A sealskin. I'm looking for a sealskin."

But he shakes his head and tells her to be patient, then flips up the one remaining latch. There's a dull *thap* of iron against hollow wood, and the hinges creak loudly as he lifts the lid. "This belonged to a cousin of mine, on my father's side," he tells her. "He died a couple of years ago. AIDS, complications from AIDS. I'm not sure what they put on the death certificate. We were friends when I was a kid."

"And this belonged to him?" she asks, and now she does stand up, though she still can't see what's inside the trunk because the open lid is obscuring her view.

"This and a whole lot of other useless crap. He was a trust-fund baby, and he was also a packrat, which always makes for an interesting combination."

"I'm not looking for a chest," she says again. "I have no *need* of a chest."

"Yeah," the man sighs, and he glances up at her. "I *know* that. But what was it you said just a moment ago? That people need to know the difference between the way things appear and the way things really are?" And then he raises one eyebrow and motions for her to walk around the table and see for herself.

"Truth be told," he says, "I've almost thrown this thing out once or twice. Thought about taking the flute to a pawnshop, but figured I couldn't get much for it. You're fortunate that I'm the sentimental sort, and a bit of a packrat myself."

And then she's standing next to the man, gazing down at the chest and refusing to believe what she sees there. A velvety pelt, fur that's all the gentle colors of storm clouds, darker and lighter shades of grey, shot through with small patches of pure black, a sealskin, rolled into a tight bundle and filling the bottom of the chest. And on top of the pelt, there's a piccolo.

"It's not a flute," she says.

"Whatever. I'm not a musician. In the will, Garrison said he thought maybe I could get a few bucks for it. For the skin, I mean, because I'd loaned him money a couple times and he'd never paid me back. But I'm afraid it's not in very good shape, and, like I said, I'm not a furrier. Supposedly, he picked it up somewhere in Scotland, back in the nineties, but I never knew if that part was true or not. He always liked to embellish, when it came to his odd bits of junk."

"I've traveled *so far*," she whispers, and then has to close her eyes, her head filled suddenly with the roar of wind rushing around the headlands and out across the sea, with the crash of breakers against the beach, the raucous cries of the guillemots and gulls soaring overhead. She can smell the sunshine and the salt and seaweed, and she can feel the cold water flowing all about her, taking her back, taking her down to her lost sisters and brothers, to submarine canyons of sand and silt and the broken masts of sunken ships. Behind her eyelids, there are darting seal shadows and the silver-scale flash of a school of herring moving quickly through gently swaying forests of kelp, and the thin woman gasps at the sweet and living taste of a codfish on her tongue.

"Are you okay?" the man asks, and he sounds concerned, but she doesn't open her eyes. "Should I get the chair? You're not about to go and faint on me, are you?"

"No, I'm fine," she assures him, which is true. For the first time in ten years, for the first time since she heard the piccolo that brilliant morning at Veantro Bay and allowed the sound of it lure her from the water and even from her skin, she *is* fine.

"And you're telling me this is what you were looking for?" the man asks, and she can hear the skepticism in his voice and that, finally, makes her open her eyes. "The heirloom? This nappy old sealskin belonged to your mother, and you've come all the way from Scotland just to find it?"

"Yes," she says, and reaches into the chest, expecting the pelt to vanish before her fingers can reach it. But it doesn't vanish, and she stands stroking the short, soft fur, only half believing that she isn't still standing on the other side of Columbus Avenue, only imagining that she'll ever find the courage to cross the street and open the green door beneath the black-and-white sign.

"Well," the man says. "Then I guess the next question would be the price."

"The price?" she asks, and presses her hand deeper into the folds of the pelt. "You'd ask me to pay you for what's already rightfully mine?"

"What you *say* is already yours," he replies. "I mean, nothing personal, right, but I'm running a business here, and this chest belonged to my cousin, who, I will remind you, is now deceased."

"I don't want the chest," she says, not taking her eyes off the sealskin. "Or the piccolo."

"Okay, then I'll only *charge* you for the sealskin. And I'll keep the rest. That works for me."

"It doesn't work for me," she tells him, and reluctantly withdraws her hand from inside the chest. "I don't have any money. I have never had any money."

The man takes a deep breath and lets it out very slowly. He rubs at the scruff of his auburn beard and shakes his head. "Then we have a problem. I'm sorry, lady, but I can't just *give* you this. I've got bills to pay."

The woman takes a step back from the edge of the table, and she wonders if she's still strong enough to murder a human being, if she's ever been that strong, and if it would count as murder if she killed this man, who makes his living selling things which should have been decently returned to the earth or sea or sky, or simply left there in the first place, this man who will never know and can never understand the theft of one's true shape. There's a small hammer lying on the table, between the chest and the scattered pieces of the fossil tortoise's carapace. She imagines how it would feel in her hand.

"Nothing personal," he says again.

She puts both her hands into her deep coat pockets, because it *would* be so easy to reach for the little hammer, because she's still fast, and he doesn't expect she would do such a thing, that the sealskin could possibly mean so much to her that she'd kill him for it. She worries with the shells and pebbles filling her pockets, limpets and mussels and polished granite, all her souvenirs, and they make their familiar, soothing, clacking noises between her fingers.

She can still hear the wind calling her home again, the voice of the sea speaking from the old chest.

"I could hold it for you," he says. "I could hold onto it for, say, six months. That's the best I can promise."

And then her fingers brush something that isn't shell or stone, something smooth and cold, and she remembers the old coin she's carried all the way from Prince Edward Island. She found it one evening, half buried in the mud of a tidal flat, glinting faintly in the setting sun. She removes it from her coat pocket and lays it on the table in front of the man. "I have this," she says. "It *is* money, isn't it? It is gold."

"Yeah, that's what it looks like," he says, and gives her a quick sidewise glance; she can see surprise and suspicion in his easy blue eyes. "Can I hold it? Do you mind"

"I found it, a long time ago. You can have it, for the chest."

"But you said you didn't want—"

"It *is* gold," she says again, raising her voice slightly.

He picks up the coin and rubs at it with his thumb, then holds it up to the light. "It's Roman, I think," he tells her. "But I don't know much about coins, so I can't say what it might be worth. I'd have to show it to someone. I know a numismatist over on—"

"It's worth an old wooden chest and a piccolo," she interrupts and licks her dry lips. "It's worth a nappy, moth-eaten sealskin that you're ashamed to put in your shop window. It's worth *that* much, at least," and then she turns and looks directly at him for the first time since the man opened the chest. And there's a flash of something like fear in his eyes, something like awe or horror, and she thinks perhaps he's glimpsed some dim sliver of the truth. Maybe he's beginning to understand what manner of being she is, and what he's let follow him alone into the back room of his shop.

"Yeah," he says, his voice grown flat and cautious. "I expect it's worth at least that much."

"Then we have a deal?" she asks, though the words come out sounding less like a question than she'd meant them to sound.

"Jesus, you're a weird one," he says, and at first she thinks he means the old Roman coin, which he's holding up the fluorescent light again. "Do you want a bill of sale for that? Should I sign somewhere in blood? At any rate, it's yours now."

"It was always mine," she replies, and she takes the sealskin out of the chest, leaving it empty except for the piccolo. "But I should thank you, for keeping it safe until I found it again."

"Well, then you're very fucking welcome," he says, squinting at the coin so he doesn't have to look at her. "I'm thinking you can show yourself out. You're a big girl."

"I'm sorry about your cousin," she tells him, even though it isn't true. She'd always meant to kill the piper who stole her skin, and some part of her feels cheated that a disease has beaten her to it. She's dreamt his death many times, how she might separate him from out *his* skin before the end.

"Don't bother. He really was an asshole. It was always only a question of which would kill him first, his cock or his mouth or the liquor."

"You won't see me again," she says, and slips the bundle of sealskin beneath her grey coat, holding it there against bare flesh, and already it feels a part of her once more.

"All I got to say is this better not fucking go up in a great puff of pink smoke when you're gone," he says, and mutters something else under his breath and squints more intently at the coin. So she leaves him there with the trunk and the piccolo and all his other hoarded treasures, retracing her steps to the green curtain and down the shop's narrow, death-haunted aisle. The green door jingles loudly, and then she's across the threshold and out in the sun again, and there's only the indifferent noise of the taxis and buses, only the busy city streets, between her and the sea and home.

Ode to Edvard Munch

I find her, always, sitting on the same park bench. She's there, no matter whether I'm coming through the park late on a Thursday evening or early on a Monday evening or in the first grey moments of a Friday morning. I play piano in a martini bar at Columbus and 89th, or I play *at* the piano, mostly for tips and free drinks. And when I feel like the long walk or can't bear the thought of the subway or can't afford cab fare, whenever I should happen to pass that way alone in the darkness and the interruptions in the darkness made by the lampposts, she's there. Always on that same bench, not far from the Ramble and the Bow Bridge, just across the lake. They call that part of the park Cherry Hill. The truth is that I haven't lived in Manhattan long enough to know these things, and, anyway, I'm not the sort of man who memorizes the cartography of Central Park, but she *told* me it's called Cherry Hill, because of all the cherry trees growing there. And when I looked at a map in a guidebook, it said the same thing.

You might mistake her for a runaway, sixteen or maybe seventeen; she dresses all in rags, or clothes so threadbare and dirty that they may as well be rags, and I've never seen her wearing shoes, no matter the season or the weather. I've seen her barefoot in snow. I asked her about that once, if she would wear shoes if I brought her a pair, and she said no, thank you, but no, because shoes make her claustrophobic.

I find her sitting there alone on the park bench near the old fountain, and I always ask before I sit down next to her. And always she smiles and says of course, of course you can sit with me. You can always sit with me. Her shoulder-length hair has been dyed the color of pomegranates, and her skin is dark. I've never asked, but I think she may be Indian. India Indian, I mean. Not Native American. I once waited tables with a girl from Calcutta, and her skin was the same color, and she had the same dusky brown-black eyes. But if she is Indian, the girl on Cherry Hill, she has no trace of an accent when she talks to me about the fountain or her favorite paintings in the Met or the exhibits she likes best at the Museum of Natural History.

The first time she smiled...

"You're a vampire?" I asked, as though it were the sort of thing you might ask any girl sitting on a park bench in the middle of the night.

"That's an ugly word," she said and scowled at me. "That's a silly, ugly word." And then she was silent a long moment, and I tried to think of anything but those long incisors, like the teeth of a rat filed down to points. It was a freezing night near the end of January, but I was sweating, nonetheless. And I had an erection. And I realized, then, that her breath didn't fog in the cold air.

"I'm a daughter of Lilith," she said.

Which is as close as she's ever come to telling me her name, or where she's from, or anything else of the sort. *I'm a daughter of Lilith*, and the *way* she said it, with not even a trace of affectation or humor or deceit, I knew that it was true. Even if I had no idea what she meant, I knew that she was telling me the truth.

That was also the first night that I let her kiss me. I sat with her on the bench, and she licked eagerly at the back of my neck. Her tongue was rough, like a cat's tongue.

She smelled of fallen leaves, that dry and oddly spicy odor which I have always associated with late October and jack-o'-lanterns. Yes, she smelled of fallen leaves, and her own sweat and, more faintly, something which I took to be woodsmoke. Her breath was like frost against my skin, colder even than the long winter night. She licked at the nape of my neck until it was raw and bleeding, and she whispered soothing words in a language I could neither understand nor recognize.

"It was designed in 1860," she said, some other night, meaning the fountain with its bluestone basin and eight frosted globes. "They built this place as a turnaround for the carriages. It was originally meant to be a drinking fountain for horses. A place for thirsty things."

"Like an oasis," I suggested, and she smiled and nodded her head and wiped my blood from her lips and chin.

"Sometimes it seems all the wide world is a desert," she said. "There are too few places left where one may freely drink. Even the horses are no longer allowed to drink here, though it was built for them."

"Times change," I told her and gently touched the abraded place on my neck, trying not wince, not wanting to show any sign of pain in her presence. "Horses and carriages don't much matter anymore."

"But horses still get thirsty. They still need a place to drink."

"Do you like horses?" I asked, and she blinked back at me and didn't answer my question. It reminds me of an owl, sometimes, that slow, considering way she blinks her eyes.

"It will feel better in the morning," she said and pointed at my throat. "Wash it when you get home." And then I sat with her a while longer, but neither of us said anything more.

She takes my blood, but never more than a mouthful at a time, and she's left me these strange dreams in return. I have begun to think of them as a sort of gift, though I know that others might think them more a curse. Because they are not entirely pleasant dreams. Some people would even call them nightmares, but things never seem so cut and dried to me. Yes, there is terror and horror in them, but there is beauty and wonder, too, in equal measure— a perfect balance that seems never to tip one way or the other. I believe the dreams have flowed into me on her rough cat's tongue, that they've infected my blood and my mind like a bacillus carried on her saliva. I don't know if the gift was intentional, and I admit that I'm afraid to ask. I'm too afraid that I might pass through the park late one night or early one morning and she might not be waiting for me there on her bench on Cherry Hill, that asking would break some brittle spell which I can only just begin to comprehend. She has made me superstitious and given to what psychiatrists call "magical thinking," misapprehending cause and effect, when I was never that way before we met. I play piano in a martini bar, and, until now, there's never been anything in my life which I might mistake for magic. But there are many things in her wide sienna eyes which I might mistake for many *other* things, and now that uncertainty seems to cloud my every waking thought. Yet I believe that it's a small price to pay for her company, smaller even than the blood she takes.

I thought that I should write down one of the dreams, that I should try to make mere words of it. From this window beside my bed, I can see Roosevelt Island beyond the rooftops, and the East River and Brooklyn and the hazy blue-white sky that can mean either summer or winter in this city. It makes me think of her, that sky, though I'm at a loss to explain why. At first, I thought that I would write it down and then read it to her the next time I see her. But then I started to worry that she might not take it the way I'd intended, simply as reciprocation, my gift to repay hers. She might be offended, instead, and I don't think I could bear the world without her. Not after all these nights and mornings and all these dreams.

I'm stalling. Yes, I am.

There's the silhouette of a city, far off, past the sand and smoke that seem to stretch away in all directions except that one which would lead to the city. I know I'll never go that far, that going as far as that, I'd never again find my way home. The city is for other beings. I know that she's seen the city, that she's walked its streets and spoken all its dialects and visited its brothels and opium dens. She knows the stink of its sewers and the delicious aromas of its markets. She knows all the high places and all the low places. And I follow her across the sand, up one dune and down another, these great waves of wind-sculpted sand which tower above me, which I climb and then descend. In this place, the jackals and the vultures and the spiny black scorpions are her court, and there is no place here for thirsty horses.

Sometimes I can see her, through stinging veils of sand. And other times it seems I am entirely alone with the wailing Sirocco gale, and the voice of that wind is a thousand women crying for their men cut down on some Arabian battlefield a thousand years before my birth. And it is also the slow creep of the dunes across the face of the wasteland, and it is my heart pounding loudly in my ears. I'm lost in the wild, and I think I'll never see her again, but then I catch a glimpse of her through the storm, crouched in the lee of ruins etched and defaced by countless millennia of sand and wind and time. She might almost be any animal, anything out looking for its supper or some way to quench its thirst.

She waits there for me in the entrance to that crumbling temple, and I can smell her impatience, like dashes of turmeric. I can smell her thirst and her appetite, and the wind drives me forward.

She leads me down into the earth, her lips pressed to my ear, whispering so I can hear her over the storm. She tells me the name of the architect who built the fountain on Cherry Hill, that his name was Jacob Wrey Mould, and he came to New York in 1853 or 1854 or 1855 to design and build All Soul's Church. He was a pious man, she tells me, and he illustrated Thomas Grey's "Elegy in a Country Church-Yard" and "Book of Common Prayer." She says he died in 1886, and that he too was in love with a daughter of Lilith, that he died with no other thought but her. I want to ask where she learned all these things, if, perhaps, she spends her days in libraries, and I also want to ask if she means that she believes that I'm in love with her. But then the narrow corridor we've been following turns left and opens abruptly on a vast torch-lit chamber.

"Listen," she whispers. "This is one of my secrets. I've guarded this place for all my life."

The walls are built from great blocks of reddish limestone carved and set firmly in place without the aid of mortar, locking somehow perfectly together by a forgotten masonic art. The air reeks of frankincense, and there is thick cinnamon-colored dust covering everything; I follow her down a short flight of steps to the floor. It occurs to me that we've gone so deep underground that the roar of the wind should not still be so loud, but it is, and I wonder if maybe the wind has found its way *inside* me, if it's entered through one of the wounds she leaves on my throat.

"This was the hall of my mother," she says.

And now I see the corpses, heaped high between the smoky braziers. They are nude, or they are half-dressed, or they've been torn apart so completely or are now so badly decomposed that it's difficult to tell whether they're clothed or not. Some are men and others are women and not a few are children. I can smell them even through the incense, and I might cover my nose and mouth. I might begin to gag. I might take a step back towards the stairs leading up to the long corridor and the bloodless desert night beyond. And she blinks at me like a hungry, watchful owl.

"I cannot expect you to understand," she says.

And there are other rooms, other chambers, endless atrocities that I can now only half recall. There are other secrets which she keeps for her mother in the deep places beneath shifting sands. There are the ghosts of innumerable butcheries. There are demons held in prisons of crystal and iron, chained until some eventual apocalypse; their voices are almost indistinguishable from the voice of the wind.

And then we have descended into some still greater abyss, a cavern of sparkling stalactite and stalagmite formations, travertine and calcite glinting in the soft glow of phosphorescent vegetation which has never seen and will never have need of sunlight. We're standing together at the muddy edge of a subterranean pool, water so still and perfectly smooth, an ebony mirror, and she's already undressed and is waiting impatiently for me to do the same.

"I can't swim," I tell her and earn another owl blink.

If I *could* swim, I cannot imagine setting foot in that water, that lake at the bottom of the world.

"No one has asked you to swim," she replies and smiles, showing me those long incisors. "At this well, men only have to drown. You can do that well enough, I suspect." And then I'm falling, as the depths of that terrible lake rise up around me like the hood of some black desert cobra and rush over me, bearing me down and down and down into the chasm, driving the air from my lungs. Stones placed one by one upon my chest until my lungs collapse, constricting coils drawing tighter and tighter about me, and I try to scream. I open my mouth, and her sandpaper tongue slips past my lips and teeth. She tastes of silt and dying and loss. She tastes of cherry blossoms and summer nights in Central Park. She wraps herself about me, and the grey-white wings sprouting from her shoulders open wider than the wings of any earthly bird. Those wings have become the sky, and her feathers brush aside the fire of a hundred trillion stars.

Her teeth tear at my lower lip, and I taste my own blood.

This wind howling in my ears is the serpent flood risen from out that black pool, and is also icy solar winds, and the futile cries of bottled demons.

"Don't be afraid," she whispers in my ear, and her hand closes around my dick. "One must only take very small drinks. One must not be greedy in these dry times."

I gasp and open my eyes, unable to remember having shut them, and now we're lying together on the floor of the abattoir at the end of the long corridor below the temple ruins. This is the only one of her secrets she's shown me, and anything else must have been my imagination, my shock at the sight of so much death. There is rain, rain as red and sticky as blood, but still something to cool my fever, and I wrap my legs around her brown thighs and slide inside her. She's not made like other women, my raggedy girl from Cherry Hill, and she begins to devour me so slowly that I will still be dying in a thousand years.

She tells me she loves me.

There are no revelations here.

My eyes look for the night sky somewhere beyond the gore and limestone and sand, but there are only her wings, like Heaven and Hell and whatever might lie in between, and I listen to the raw and bitter laughter of the wind…

Some nights, I tell myself that I will walk around the park and never mind the distance and inconvenience. Some nights, I pretend I hope that she *won't* be there, waiting by the fountain. But I'm not even as good a liar as I am a pianist, and it hardly matters, because she's always there.

Last night, for instance.

I brought her an old sweater I never wear, a birthday present from an ex-girlfriend, and she thanked me for it. I told her that I can bring her other things, whatever she might need, that she only has to ask, and she smiled and told me I'm very kind. My needs are few, she said and pulled the old sweater on over whatever tatters she was already wearing.

"I worry about you," I said. "I worry about you all the time these days."

"That's sweet of you," she replied. "But I'm strong, stronger than I might seem." And I wondered if she knows about my dreams, and if our conversation were merely a private joke. I wonder if she only accepted the sweater because she feels sorry for me.

We talked, and she told me a very funny story about her first night in the park, almost a decade before I was born. And then, when there were no more words, when there was no longer the *need* for words, I leaned forward and offered her my throat. Thank you, she said, and I shut my eyes and waited for the scratch of her tongue against my skin, for the prick of those sharp teeth. She was gentle, because she is always gentle, lapping at the hole she's made and pausing from time to time to murmur reassurances I can understand without grasping the coarser, literal meaning of what she's said. I get the gist of it, and I know that's all that matters. When she was done, when she'd wiped her mouth clean and thanked me again for the sweater, when we'd said our usual good-byes for the evening, I sat alone on the bench and watched as she slipped away into the maze of cherry trees and azaleas and forsythia bushes.

I don't know what will become of these pages.

I may never print them. Or I may print them out and hide them from myself.

I could slip them between the pages of a book in the stacks at NYU and leave them there for anyone to find. I could do that. I could place them in an empty wine bottle and drop them from the Queensboro Bridge so that the river would carry them down to the sea. The sea must be filled with bottles...

The Cryomancer's Daughter
(Murder Ballad No. 3)

I.

"A nd then," she says, as though she still imagines that I've somehow never heard this story before, "the demons tried to carry the looking glass all the way up to Heaven, that they might even mock the angels." *But it shattered*, I cut in, trying to sound sober, and she smiles a vitreous sort of smile for me. I catch a glimpse of her uneven bluish teeth, set like mismatched pegs of lazulite into gums the colour of a stormy autumn sky. If I were but a stronger woman—a woman of uncommon courage and resolve—I might now use all my geologist's rambling vocabulary to describe the physical and optical properties of that half-glimpsed smile, to determine its electron density and Fermion index, the axial ratios and x-ray diffraction, diaphaneity, fracture, and etc. and etc., and on and on and on. I would take up my fountain pen and put it all down on paper, and there would be no mention anywhere of her tiresome fairy stories or my deceitful, subjective desires. I would reduce her to the driest of crystallographies. And then she says, as though I never interrupted her, "Every tiny sliver of the broken looking glass retained the full power of the whole, and they rained down over the entire world." *I'm tired*, I say. *I'm very tired, and now I want to sleep.* So she sighs, exasperated, impatient, exhaling the very breath of Boreas, and a ragged bouquet of frost blooms across the tiny window looking down on the nub end of Gar Fish Street. I've never seen her sleep. Not even once in the long three weeks since she came to the decrepit boarding house where I live, bearing a peculiar stone and a threadbare carpetbag and asking after me. Oh, sometimes she yawns, or her eyes flutter in a way as to suggest the dimmest memory of sleep. Her eyes flutter, and those pale lashes scatter snowflakes across my bed, but I've never seen her asleep. Perhaps she sleeps only when *I'm* asleep; I can't prove otherwise. "Most of the bits of the looking glass were so small they were like dust or grains of sand," she says, still gazing down at the dim and gas-lit cobblestones. "But there were a few fragments large enough to be found and polished flat and smooth and fashioned into windowpanes." It sounds like a threat, the way she puts it, and also the way she's staring at the window, and then she turns her pretty head and looks at me, instead. "I should never have come to this terrible old house," she tells me. "I should have gone to some other town, farther inland, over and across the Klamath Mountains, and we should never have met." But I know this is a game, not so different from the stories she tells again and again, and I don't reply. I roll over and bury my face in my pillow. "It's a wicked, filthy place, this town," she continues, "a sodden ghetto, fit only for leprous fishmongers and ten-cent Jezebels and—" *And what?* I ask her, my words muffled by the pillow. So here I am playing after all. Here I am dancing for her, and I know without turning to see that she's wearing that smug lazulite smile again. *Just what else is this filthy old town fit for?* She doesn't answer me right away, because now I'm dancing, and so she has all the time she needs. I open my eyes and stare at the wall, the peeling ribbons of pin-striped wallpaper, the books stacked high on my rented chifforobe. I put out the lamp some time ago, so the only light in the room is coming from the window, and now she's gone and blocked half that with the frost from her sigh. "My father," she says, beginning this *other* lie, "he said that I should find you, that I must seek out the Sapphic professor, so recently disgraced and duly dismissed from her lofty post at University, fallen low and holed up in this squalid abode, drinking herself halfway to death and maybe then back again. He said you know all the deepest secrets of the earth, the mysteries of the ages, and that you even speak with her, the earth, in your dreams. He said I should show you the stone, that only you would know it for what it is." *But you have no father*, I say, playing the good and faithless heretic, stumbling through my part like the puppet she's made of me. *You're merely another wandering war orphan, an urchin whoring her way down the coast. And that precious rock of yours is nothing more than a cast-off ballast stone which you picked up on the beach the morning you crawled off that tramp steamer and first set foot in this wicked, filthy place. You're an orphan, my dear, and the rock is no more than a gastrolith puked forth from the overfull craw of some whaling ship or another.* She listens silently. She has never interrupted me, as that would be not so very different from interrupting herself. I can remember when there was some force behind these words, before I caught on. Before I wised up. I can remember when they had weight and anger. When I meant them, because I mistakenly believed that they were my own.

"My father..." she begins, then trails off, and I feel the temperature in my dingy little fourth-floor room at the end of Gar Fish Street plummet ten or fifteen degrees.

—was likely a Russian foot soldier, I continue for her on cue, *bound for some flea-ridden Kamchatkan hellhole, when he met up with whichever Koryak witch-sow you would have called your mother, had she ever given you the chance.* And yes, these are words from my mouth, spoken by my tongue and passing between my lips, but still they are always *her* words. I shut my eyes, willing silence upon myself (which is easy, as this particular soliloquy has come to its end), and she reaches out and brushes frozen fingertips across the space between my shoulder blades. I gasp, and at least it is *me* gasping, an *honest* gasp at the pain and cold flowing out of her and into me. All the breath driven from my lungs in that instant, and now I must surely look like some gulping, fish-eyed thing hauled up from the briny sea, my lips going a cyanotic tint and my mouth opening and closing, closing and opening, suffocating on this thin air I coughed out and can't seem to remember how to breathe back in. Then she presses her palm flat against my back, and the chill doubles, trebles, expands ten-fold and tenfold again between one gasp and the next. She draws the warmth from me, because she can manufacture none of her own. Because, she says, she has been cursed by her own father, a man who conjures blizzards from clear summer skies and commands the grinding courses of mighty glaciers. A wizard king of snow and ice who has so condemned his own daughter because she would not be his consort in some unnatural and incestuous liaison. It's as good an explanation as

any for what she is and what she's done to me, again and again and again, though I can believe it no more than I can believe that six and three are ten or that the sun and moon move round about the Earth. I am unaccustomed and unreceptive to phantasia and make-believe, even when I find myself trapped hopelessly within it. Perhaps my disbelief can be a prison as surely as this room, as surely as her wintry hand pressed against my spine, but I've little enough remaining of my former life, those vanished years when there was still camaraderie and purpose and dignity. By all the gods in which I have never sought comfort I will cling to Reason, no matter how useless it may prove before she is done with me. She leans near, and her breath spills across my face like Arctic waters. "I am alone," she says sweetly, and with a brittle edge of loss. "I have no one now but you, no one and nothing, only you and that damned stone. You will love me. You will love me as you have never comprehended love before. And your love will be the furnace to finally melt the sorcery that binds me." I would laugh at her, at these preposterous lines she might have ripped from the pages of some penny dreadful or stolen from a bit of low burlesque, but my throat has frozen over. I might as well be stone now. She has made of me the very thing I've spent my life researching and cataloging, for what is ice but water assuming a solid mineral form? I am made her petrifaction, and she leans nearer still and kisses me upon my icy lips. I wish that she'd at least allowed me to shut my eyes this time, just this once, that I would not now be forced to *see* her, to stare back into the daemon lover who is staring into me. That too-round china-doll face and the wild, tumbling cataract of hair as white as snow spun into silk, her bitter lazulite grin, her own eyes the colour of a living oyster pulled from out its bivalve shell. In this moment, I could almost believe her tales of broken mirrors and snow queens, lost children and cruel magician fathers. And then she touches me, her hands seeking out the frigid gash of my sex, and I am no longer even granted the tethered freedoms of a marionette. I am at best a chiseled pagan idol to polar bears and hungry killer whales, a statue upon which she will prostrate herself, stealing from me such pleasures as she might wish and can yet endure.

II.

Later, long hours later, after she's grown bored with me and after dawn and sunrise and after my blood has thawed to slush and I'm left shivering and fevery, I sit naked at the foot of the bed in the boarding-house room on Gar Fish Street and sip the cheapest available gin from a tin cup. She's gone out. I cannot say with any certainty *where* she goes, but she disappears from time to time. It's not unusual if she doesn't return for days, and I can not help but to imagine that she must have other unfortunates trapped in other dingy rooms scattered throughout the city. I stare back at my reflection, watching myself from the cracked mirror mounted crookedly on the dressing table. Perhaps, I think, she is gathering to her an *army* of puppets, and at the last she will have us take up flaming brands and march against her wizard father, locked in his palace of ice and baling wire. I raise the cup to my lips, and the woman in the mirror obligingly does the same. I've seen corpses floating in the harbour that looked more alive than her, more alive than me. I could have aged ten years in these few weeks. My lover has stolen more from me than simple warmth, of that I *am* certain. She's diminished me with every successive freeze and thaw, and this reflection is little more than a ghost of the woman who arrived here from San Francisco last summer. I came to hide and drink and maybe die, for there would never be any return to that former life of privilege and reward which had been so hastily, so thoughtlessly, traded for hurried trysts with one of my first-year students, a yellow-haired girl whose name I can hardly now recollect. I only came here to be a drunkard and, in time, a suicide, to drift farther and farther away from the world which would have no more of me. I thought surely that would be penance enough for all my sins. I never dared conceive of any punishment so sublime as the wizard's daughter. No, I do not believe she is the daughter of a wizard, but how else would I name her? One night, I tried to make a game of guessing at some other appellation, whether Christian or heathen, but she waved away every suggestion I made. Hundreds or thousands of names dismissed, and there was never anything in her wet oyster eyes but truth. But I may be a poor, poor judge of truth, and we should keep that in mind. After all, remember, some fraction of me *believed* the yellow-haired girl in San Francisco when she promised that she'd never so much as whisper even the most nebulous hint of our nights together to another living soul. Indeed, I may be no fit judge of truth at all. The woman in the mirror who looks exactly like my corpse takes another sip of gin, realizes the cup is almost empty, and reaches for the quart bottle on the floor. She fills my cup halfway, and I thank her for such boundless generosity. The wizard's daughter, she won't ever deign to drink with me, though she sometimes returns from her disappearances with the gift of a fresh bottle—gin or rye whiskey or the peaty brown ale they brew down by the waterfront. She says she doesn't drink with anyone or alone, so I don't take it personally.

"Aren't you a sorry sight," the woman in the mirror says to me. "A shame the way you've let yourself go. Can you even remember the last time you bathed? Or took a comb to your hair, perhaps?" And so I tell her to go fuck herself.

Then there are footsteps in the hallway, and I listen, expecting them to stop outside my door, expecting the dry rattle of a key in the lock, and then the cut-glass knob will turn and—

"The Tolowa Indians have a story about a crazy woman who talks to her reflection—"

Shut up, I hiss at my own face in the dressing-table mirror and almost drop the tin cup, my heart pounding and hands shaking so badly that no small measure of gin splashes over the rim and darkens the grimy floor at my feet. *Such a waste,* I think, *such a pointless, goddamned waste,* and by then the footsteps in question have come and gone, and it isn't the wizard's daughter, after all. Only another lodger or someone else, a prostitute or sneak thief or a dutiful officer of the law, coming to call upon another lodger. I reach for the gin bottle before the woman in the mirror does it for me. *She gives me dreams,* I say and, having refilled my cup, shove the cork firmly back into the mouth of the bottle. I can not afford another spill today, for I am in no condition to dress myself and descend the stairs to the smoky lobby and the narrow street beyond and still have to walk the two blocks (uphill) from the boarding house on Gar Fish Street to the Gramercy Digs Saloon on the corner of Muskie and Walleye. And I have no guarantee that she will bring me another bottle, either, as her small mercies and smaller kindnesses are, at best, capricious and wholly unpredictable. *She gives me dreams,* I say again, because I do not think the mirror woman heard me the first time.

"Does she?" the doppelgänger asks. It's grinning at me now, only that is not *my* grin, those rotting lazulite pegs in swollen stormy gums, but its is still my face. "I was until this moment quite unaware that any among the Oneiroi concealed a cunt between its legs."

I shut my eyes, praying to no one and nothing that I'll stop shaking and my teeth with stop chattering, wishing for warmth and sunlight and wishing, too, that I had even half the strength I'd need to get to my feet and stand and walk the five or six steps to the three-legged chair where my overcoat and gloves are lying in a careless heap. But I am too sick and much too drunk to try. I would wind up on the floor, and that's where she would find me when she returns. I would rather suffer this chill in my veins and my bones than have her find me sprawled naked upon the floor, unconscious in a pool of spilled gin and my own piss. Behind my eyelids, the dreams she has given unfold like flickering cinematograph projections. And I keep my eyes tightly closed, lest these Lumière images escape from out the windows of my blighted soul and fall upon the silvered glass, for I have no mind to share them with that grinning fiend behind the mirror. The wizard's daughter has given them to me, and so they are mine and mine alone—this clouded, snow-dimmed sky spread wide above a winter forest of blue spruce and fir and pine, the uneasy shadows huddled beneath the sagging boughs. I have been walking all my life, it seems, or, more precisely, all my *afterlife,* those many long months since my abrupt departure from San Francisco. The howling, wolf-throated wind stings my bare face, and I stumble blindly forward through snow piled almost as high as my knees. I cannot feel my feet. I am become no more or less than a phantom of frostbite and rags, lost and certain that I will never again be anything but lost. I know what lies ahead of me, what she brings me here to see, again and again and again. It was only a surprise that first time I walked these woods, and also the second time, as I've never suffered from recurring dreams. My lungs ache, filled as they are with the thin air which seems heavy and thick as lead, and then I've reached the place where the trees end, opening onto a high alpine meadow. In summer, the ground here would be resplendent in green and splashed with the gay blooms of black-eyed susans and Joe-Pye weed, columbine and parry clover. But this is a dead month, a smothered month—December or January, the ending or beginning of the year—and perhaps all months are dead here. Perhaps every word she's told me is the truth, plain and simple, and this *is* truly a blasted land which will never again know spring grasses, nor the quickening hues of wildflowers. *Do not show me this,* I plead, but I cannot ever say whether these are words spoken or merely words thought. Either way, they tumble from me, silently or whispered from my cracked and bleeding lips. *Do not show me this. Don't make me see. I know, I know already what happened here, because I've seen it all before, and there is no profit in seeing it ever again.* She does not answer me. Only the wind speaks to me here, as it rushes down from the raw charcoal-coloured peaks, the sky's breath pouring out across splintered metamorphic teeth and over the meadow. And this is what I behold: a great crimson sleigh with gilded rails and runners drawn by Indian ponies, like something a red-skinned Father Christmas might command; a single granite standing stone or menhir of a sort not known to exist in the Americas—there are glyphs or pictographs graven upon the stone, which I can never quite see clearly; and in the lee of the menhir, there is an enormously obese man wrapped in bearskin robes and a naked girl child kneeling in the snow at his feet. The man holds a four-gallon metal pail over her, and the furs which the girl must have worn only moments before are spread out very near the crimson sleigh. The man and the girl can not be more than fifty feet away from me, and every time I have tried to cry out, to draw his attention towards myself, to forestall what I know is coming next. And I have tried, too, to leave the shelter of the treeline and cross the meadow to the spot where he stands and she kneels and the granite menhir looms threatfully above them both. From the first time I beheld it with my dreaming eyes, I have understood that there is more to this awful standing stone than its constituent molecules, far more than mere chemistry and mineralogy can fathom. It is an evil thing, and the man in the bearskin robes is somehow in its service or its debt. It has stood a thousand years, perhaps, demanding offerings and forfeiture—and no, it matters not that I do not even now believe in the existence of evil beyond a shorthand phrase for the cruelties and insanity of human beings. It matters not in the least, for in the dream, the menhir, or something trapped within the stone, *glances* towards the edge of the forest, and it *sees* me there. And I can feel its delight, that there is an audience to this atrocity. I feel its perfect hatred, deeper and blacker than the submarine canyons out beyond the harbour. "Are you cold, my darling?" the enormous man growls, and then he spits on the shivering girl at his feet. "Would you have me build for you a lovely roaring fire to chase the frostnip from your toes and fingertips?"

But she was not the same girl, my reflection calmly professes from its place behind the dressing table. *Not the same girl as your visitor.*

She was, I reply through gritted teeth and without opening my eyes. *She was that very same girl.*

But the girl in your dream—her hair is red as a sunset, and her eyes blue as lapis lazuli. So, you see, she cannot possibly be your pale companion.

The Tolowa Indians have a story about a crazy woman who talks to her reflection, I say, and at that the mirror falls silent again, but I know it wears a smirking satisfaction on its borrowed face. And there in the high meadow, the man wrapped in bearskins slowly pours water from his pail over the naked body of the red-haired girl. She screams, but only once, and makes no attempt whatsoever to escape. Her cry startles the ponies, and they neigh and stamp their hooves. "Is that better?" the man asks her, and already the water has begun to freeze on her skin, before the pail is even empty. "Are you warmer now?" I can hear the menhir laughing behind his back, an ancient, ugly sound which I could never hope to describe, the laughter of granite which isn't granite at all. For a moment it seems somehow less solid, and in my horror I imagine the menhir bending down low over the man and the dying girl. "See there?" the fat man cackles and tosses his pail away. "You are *mine*, child. You were mine from the start, from the day you slithered from twixt your momma's nethers, and you'll never be anyone else's." But she can no longer hear him. I am certain of that, for the cold mountain air has turned the water solid, sealing and stealing her away, and I cannot help but think of the fossils of prehistoric flies and ants which I've seen encased in polished lumps of Baltic amber. The man spits on her again, spits at the crust of new ice concealing her, and then he turns and trudges away through the snow to the sleigh and the two waiting ponies. "Let her lie there till the spring," he bellows, taking up the leather reins and giving them a violent shake. "Let her lie there seven winters and another after that!" And then the sleigh is racing away, those golden runners not slicing through the snow, but seeming instead to float somehow an inch or so above it. And then I feel the ground fall away beneath my feet, in this nightmare which she has given to me, that I might witness her desecration and murder a hundred hundred times. The day vanishes and I drop feet-first into an abyss, through the hollow, rotten heart of the world, and for a time I am grateful my eyes can no longer see, and that the only sound is the air rushing past my ears as I fall.

III.

She comes back early the next morning, shortly after I have risen and had my first drink of the day and managed to dress in my slovenly, mannish best, feeling just a little more myself for her time away from me. The night before, I hardly slept, tossing and turning, starting awake at every sound, no matter how far off or insignificant it might have been. Towards dawn there was a foreboding, melancholy sort of dream in which I watched a waxing quarter moon sinking into the sea and the sun coming up over the town where it huddles at the crumbling edge of the continent. This cluttered grotesquerie of winding lanes and leaning clapboard cottages, chimneys and cisterns and rusting corrugated tin roofs, and the few brick-and-mortar buildings so scabbed with mosses and ferns and such other local flora that one might easily mistake them for some natural part of the landscape, only lately and incompletely modified to the needs of men. The morning washed away the night, finishing off the drowning moon, and the motley assortment of boats and small ships moored along the wharves seemed no more than bobbing toys awaiting the hands of children. The morning light snagged in their sails and rigging, and a grey flock of gulls arising from the narrow, mussel-littered beach screeched out her name, which I heard clearly, but knew I would forget immediately upon waking. It was a peaceable scene, in its way, and I thought perhaps this is as good a place to lie down and die as any other. But, even so, I could not shake the sense that something immeasurably old and malign watched the town from the redwood forests crowding in on every side. Something that had trailed her here, possibly. Or something that had been here all along, something that was already here aeons before the mountains were heaved up from a sea swarming with great reptiles and ammonites and archaic species of gigantic predatory fish. Either way, they were in league now, the wizard's wayward daughter and this unseen watcher in the trees, and I alone knew of their alliance. The dream ended as a velvet curtain was drawn suddenly closed to hide what I realized had only been the most elaborate set arranged upon a theatre stage, a cleverly lit and orchestrated miniature to fool my sleeping eyes, and then there was vaudeville, and then opera, and I woke to Verdi from a phonograph playing loudly across the hallway from my room.

"We should go for a walk together," she says and half fills my tin cup with gin. "Hand in hand, yes? Brazen in our forbidden love for one another."

I don't love you, I tell her. *I have never loved you,* but I can see from the knowing glimmer in her oyster eyes that she recognizes my lie at once. *Besides,* I add, *nothing which is properly depraved or deviant is forbidden here, unless it be some arcane offence to the patron saints of kelp and syphilitic mariners which I've yet to stumble upon. Why else would we be so tolerated here, you and I?* And, at that, she puts the cork back into the bottle and scowls at me. "Speak for yourself," she says. "I go where I like. I do as I wish." I laugh at her and sip my gin. She stands up, her petticoats rustling like snowy boughs, and I wonder what the townspeople descry when they look at her. Do they see her breath fog on balmy summer afternoons? Do they notice the scum of frost left behind on anything she's touched? Do they ever detect the faint auroral flicker from her pupils, a momentary glint of brilliant reds or greens or blues from her otherwise lifeless eyes? Or are they so accustomed to minding their own affairs—for I *am* convinced this town is a refuge for the damned and cast-away—that they see only some shabby girl too plain for even the most unpretentious sporting house? I'll never know, for I'll never have the courage to ask them. Secretly, I fear I am the only one who can see her, and I am possessed of no pressing desire to have this irrational dread confirmed. "Oh, they see well enough," she says, and I am not surprised. Puppets have no private thoughts. She lingers before the dressing-table mirror, straightening the folds of her skirt. "They see and stay awake nights, wishing they could forget the sight of me." This seems to please her, and so she smiles, and I have another drink from my dented tin cup. "Or they long for my embrace," she continues. "They pine for my attentions. They can think of naught else save the torment of my cold hand about their prick or pressed tight to their windward passage. Some have been driven nigh unto *seppuku* or have learned to tie a hangman's noose, should the longing grow more than merely unbearable." And I reply that I can believe that part, at least, though myself I would prefer a bullet in the brain. "No, that's a *real* man's death," she says and turns to face me. "Now, have you figured out my stone? Last night, a magpie found me behind the livery and brought word from my father who wishes me home at the earliest possible date. But *not* without your learn'd observations, my sweet professor." I stare silently into my cup for a moment, my stomach sour and cramping, and I tell that her I'm in no mood for the game today. Tomorrow, maybe. Maybe the day after, and, in the meantime, she should haunt some other poor bitch or bastard. "But the magpie was quite insistent," she says. "You know by now that my father is not a patient man, even at his best, and he has long since tired of waiting on your verdict." And she holds the peculiar stone out to me as she has done so many times before. *But what of the curse?* I ask her, resigned that there will be no allowances today for hangovers and sour stomachs. I know all these lines by heart. *What of winning my love, the furnace to finally melt the sorcery that binds you? Has someone gone and changed the rules? Do you begin to miss the old man's cock between your legs?* She smiles her vitreous smile once more to flash those bluish pegs she wears for teeth, and closes her fingers around the stone resting in her palm. "Surely you didn't take me *seriously*?" she scoffs. "My father is a proud man, a man of principles and lofty morals, and he would *never* permit me to take a lesbian dipsomaniac for my husband."

You have no father, I remind her, because I know all these lines by heart, and she would have me say nothing more or less. *You were born into a brothel but a few miles farther up the coast, the albino child of a half-nigger whore and a chink from a medicine show. Fortunately, your mother sold you to a kind-hearted merchant marine for two pints and a black pearl broach, saving you from a life spent peddling pussy and Clark Stanley's snake oil liniment. Sadly, though, your adoptive father soon perished at sea when his ship was pulled down by the arms of a giant cephalopod.* She smiles again, licks her lips, and asks eagerly, "The Kraken of Norwegian legend?" *One and the same, I have no doubt about it. But you survived,* and I pause to drain and then refill my cup. *You were discovered in a leaky wicker basket one midsummer eve, carried in on the high tide.* And she tells me she'd almost forgotten that story, but I know that she's lying, that it's her most-favored of the lot. "That's so much better than the one in which I'm a Cossack's illegitimate daughter on the run from Czarist spies, or the other one, where we're actually half sisters, but I have been stricken with an hysterical amnesia beyond the curative powers of even the most accomplished alienist." Her voice rattles inside my skull like dice, like razor shards of ice. It is slicing apart my brain, and soon my thoughts will be little more than tatters. No, they were tattered long ago, if truth be told. I place three fingers against the soft spot at my left temple, as if this mere laying on of hands would alone be enough to still the mad somersault of her words. "Though I was only an infant," she says, "I can almost recall my valiant, grief-stricken father swaddling me in his pea jacket and placing me inside that basket as the sea monster wailed and gnawed at the bowsprit." *No,* I reply, *you never had a father,* and for the briefest fraction of a moment I see (or only *wish* I'd see) the dull gleam of disappointment in her damp oyster eyes, as though she'd begun to believe (or at least *wishes* to believe) in her own canard. "No matter," she sighs. "As I was saying, the snowflakes grew bigger and bigger until they resembled nothing so much as fat white geese." *That's not what you were saying,* I tell her. *You were reminding me of the stone and your father's impatient need to know its provenance.* But she ignores me, already deep into the middle of a story she's told so many times it hardly matters where she begins the tale. "The big sled stopped, and the child saw then that it was driven by a tall and upright lady, all shining white—the Snow Queen herself. 'It is cold enough to kill one,' she said. 'Creep inside my bearskin.'" *But you've never had a mother, either,* I say, and then, before she can reply or withdraw any deeper into that moth-eaten narrative, Kay and Gerda and the Snow Queen, the demons and their grinning looking glass, I ask to see the stone.

"Again? But I should think you'd have the damned thing memorized by now."

I stop rubbing at my aching head and hold out my left hand to her. *Give it to me,* I say, and she narrows her grey eyes suspiciously, as I've never once before *asked* to see the stone, and it isn't like me to deviate from the confines of the events and dialogue which she has scripted so meticulously. Possibly, she begins to suspect the unthinkable, rebellion from her wooden puppet, and must wonder if she's allowed me too much string, too much slack upon my tethers. I half expect her to turn away again, to seek such refuge as might be had in the cracked dressing-table mirror, or to walk out the door and leave me alone in my dingy room. Instead, she nods her head and places the peculiar stone into my outstretched hand.

…and there would be no mention anywhere of her tiresome fairy stories or my deceitful, subjective desires.

I would reduce her to the driest of crystallographies.

The stone is not quite round and is somewhat flattened side to side, the approximate colour of licorice, and I tell her what I've already told her before, that it's only a beach cobble, a bit of Mesozoic slate fallen from the headlands or the high cliffs surrounding the harbour, then polished smooth by time and the ocean. I describe its mineral composition for her—muscovite and quartz, with small quantities of biotite, pyrite, and hematite, and perhaps also traces of kaolin and tourmaline. But I have said repeatedly that it is a *peculiar* stone, have I not, and none of these things make it peculiar in the least. "What else?" she asks. A flurry of minute snowflakes escapes her lips, borne upon her voice and blown towards me on her Siberian breath, and they look nothing at all like fat white geese. "What is there about it that I *couldn't* learn from the pages of one of your schoolbooks?" It grows so heavy in my hand then, her stone, as though it has suddenly trebled or quadrupled in size while appearing just exactly the same as always. *It is a sympathetic stone,* I say to her, surprising myself, and she takes a quick step backwards and bumps hard against a corner of the dressing table. *What?* I ask. *Did you believe we'd never get this far?* But she only looks afraid and doesn't answer me. And I understand now, at last, that the wizard's daughter is as surely a puppet as am I. She is frozen to her core, kneeling in an alpine meadow, trapped forever in the icy shadow of an old man's despite. It does not matter whether these things are literally true or only figurative. It does not matter, either, what I can and cannot believe, or whether I am sane. *A sympathetic stone,* I say again, and the snow from her lips settles in my hair and on the harsh angles of my face. *These markings scratched into its surface, I can't read those, but I suspect that's not important. It isn't what we can see in this stone, but what this stone can see in us. Are you following me?* She licks her lips nervously, and they sparkle with the thinnest sheen of frozen saliva. *That's its genius, you see. It truly is a looking glass.* She rubs at her hip where it struck the dressing table, and laughs the driest, most unconvincing laugh that I have ever heard. "You think me simple, an imbecile, is that it? Do you think you might gain the upper hand, and your freedom, too, with only a quick-witted riddle and a straight face? My father—" *But that was such a very long time ago,* I say, interrupting her. *Long ago and far away, in a country I have never visited outside your dreams.*

"One day, the old hobgoblin invented a mirror," she says, and those cold auroral fires burn brightly in the twin voids of her pupils. Red, then blue, then green, and then back to red again; I can plainly hear them crackle in the sky above the boarding house on Gar Fish Street. "A mirror with this peculiarity—that every good thing reflected in its surface shrank away almost to nothing."

I set the tin cup down upon my bed, and for the third time I say to her, *It is a sympathetic stone,* as I have always heard there is magic contained within the number three. In my palm, the licorice-coloured cobble quivers and transforms into a crude sort of dagger. Many days or nights later, when these grim and fabulous events have run their course and I have weighted her corpse with an anvil and a burlap bag filled with rusted horseshoes, I shall ponder the question of her relationship with the stone. Or the stone's relationship with her. If, for instance, it is as Coleridge's murdered albatross, some cross she has been condemned to bear in penance for all eternity, acting out this marionette performance down countless centuries. I will draw no conclusions to satisfy me, nor will I find any sense in any fraction of it, but, still, I will lay awake nights, turning the question over and over in my persistent, gin-addled mind. But I think, in contradiction to the evidence of her fear, the tremble in her snowy voice, the northern lights blazing in her eyes, that she was *glad* when we were done. Perhaps she was permitted some brief period of oblivion between one haunting and the next, and so I'd granted her exhausted spirit an interval of rest, a respite from the trails and horrors of her damnation. Without speaking another word, I rose from the bed and drove the stone dagger deep into her chest just beneath the sternum, then twisted it sharply up and to the right, that the blade might find and pierce her heart. Her lips parted, and a trickle of something dark, which was not blood, leaked from her mouth and spattered on my hand and the floor between us. In her grey eyes, the polar fires were extinguished, and she did not so much seem to fall at my feet as *flow* downward, as though her body had never been anything more substantial than water held forever but one degree below freezing. In my hand, the stone was only a stone again, still bearing those indecipherable runes or glyphs, the same ones I might have glimpsed, dreaming, carved into a granite menhir. And for the first time since she came to me, all those months ago, I felt warm, genuinely warm. But it is late, and the candle by which I have put down on paper these strange occurrences—being possibly nothing greater than a confession or the ramblings of a lunatic—has melted to little more than a puddle of beeswax and a guttering scrap of blackened wick. So I will not trouble myself with the details of how it was I removed her body from my room and the boarding house. However, I will add that I placed the peculiar, *sympathetic* stone inside her mouth, which was then sewn shut with a needle and thread I borrowed from the wife of my landlord. I told her simply that my socks had worn almost through and needed darning. I have considered leaving this place, before I am utterly bereft of even the price of a train ticket. I've looked at my maps and considered traveling north to Coos Bay, or inland to Salem or Pendleton. I might even go so far as Seattle. I have thought, too, that I might find gainful employment as a geologist in a mining camp. In the wild places, men are not so concerned with a woman's indiscretions, or so I have been led to believe.

A Child's Guide
to the Hollow Hills

Beneath the low leaf-litter clouds, under endless dry monsoons of insect pupae, strangling rains of millipede droppings and noxious fungal spores, in this muddy, thin land pressed between soil and bedrock foundations, the fairie girl awakens in the bed of the Queen of Decay. She opens her violet eyes and sees, again, that it was not only some especially unpleasant dream or nightmare, her wild descent, her pell-mell tumble from light and day and stars and moonshine, down, down, down to this mouldering domain of shadow walls and knurly taproot obelisks. She is *here*, after all. She is *still* here, and slowly she sits up, pushing away those clammy spider-spun sheets that slip in and tangle themselves about her whenever she dares to sleep. And what, she thinks, is sleep, but admitting to myself this is no dream? Admitting that she has been snared and likely there will be no escape from out this unhappy, foetid chamber. Always she has been afraid of falling, deathly frightened of great heights and holes and wells and all the very deep places of the world. Always she has watched so carefully where fell her feet, and never was she one to climb trees or walls, not this cautious fairie girl. When her bolder sisters went to bathe where the brook grows slow and wide beneath drooping willow boughs, she would venture no farther in than the depth of her ankles. They laughed and taunted her with impromptu fictions of careless, drowning children and hungry snapping-turtle jaws and also an enormous catfish that might swallow up any careless fairie girl in a single lazy gulp of its bristling, barbeled lips. *And you only looked beneath a stone,* the Queen sneers, reminding her that she is never precisely alone here, that her thoughts are never only *her* thoughts. *Your own mother, she told you that your sisters were but wicked liars, and there was no monster catfish or snapping turtles waiting in the brook. But, she said, do not go turning over stones.* And the fairie girl would shut her violet eyes now, but knows too well she'd still hear that voice, which is like unto the splintering of granite by frost, the ceaseless tunneling noises of earthworms and moles, the crack of a goblin's whip in air that has never once seen the sky. *Don't you go looking under stones,* the Queen says again and smiles to show off a hundred rusted-needle teeth. *In particular, said she—your poor, unheeded mother—beware the great flat stones that lie in the oldest groves, scabbed over with lichens and streaked with the glinting trails of slugs, the flat stones that smell of salamanders and moss, for these are sometimes doorways, child.* The Queen laughs, and her laughter is so terrible that the fairie girl cringes and *does* close her eyes. *Disobedient urchin, you knew better.* "I was following the green lizard," she whispers, as though this might be some saving defence or extenuation, as if the Queen of Decay has not already heard it from her countless times before. "The green lizard crawled beneath the stone—"—*which you knew damn well not to lift and look beneath. So, here now. Stop your whimpering. You were warned; you knew better.* "I wanted only to find the lizard again. I never meant to—" *You only came knocking at my door, dear sweet thing. I only answered and showed you in. You'd have done well not to entrust your well-being to a fascination with such lowly, squamous things—serpents and lizards and the dirty, clutching feet of birds.* The fairie girl opens her eyes again, trying not to cry, because she almost always cries, and her tears and sobs so delight the Queen. She sees herself staring back with watery sapphire eyes, reflected in the many mirrors hanging from these filthy walls, mirrors which her captor ordered hung all about the chamber so that the girl might also witness the stages of her gradual dissolution. The fracturing and wearing away of her glamour, even as water etches at the most indurate stone. Her eyes have not yet lost their colour, but they have lost their inner light. In the main, her skin is still the uncorrupted white of fresh milk caught inside a milkmaid's pail, but there are ugly, parchment splotches that have begun to spread across her face and arms and chest. And her hair, once so full and luminous, has grown flat and devoid of lustre, without the sympathetic light of sun or moon, wilting even as her soul wilts. She is drinking me, the girl thinks, and, *Yes*, the Queen replies. *I have poured you into my silver cup, and I am drinking you down, mouthful by mouthful. You have a disagreeable taste upon my tongue, but it is a sacred duty, to consume anything so frail as you. I choke you down, lest your treacle and the radiance of you should spread and spoil the murk.* And all around them the walls, wherever there are not mirrors, twitch and titter, and fat trolls and raw-boned redcaps with phosphorescent skins and hungry, bulging eyes watch the depredations of their queen. This is rare sport, and the Queen is not so miserly or selfish that she will not share the spectacle with her subjects. *See*, she says, *but do not touch. Her flesh is deadly as cold iron to the likes of us. I alone have the strength to lay my hands upon so foul a being and live.* In the mirrors hung on bits of root and bone and the fishhook mandibles of beetles, the fairie girl sits on the black bed far below the forest floor, and the Queen of Decay moves across her like an eclipse of the sun. *Do not go looking under stones, your poor mother said. I have heard from the pill bugs and termites that she is a wise woman. You'd have done well to heed her good advices.* It is hard for the girl to *see* the Queen, for she is mostly fashioned of some viscous, shapeless substance that is not quite flesh, but always there is the dim impression of leathery wings, as if from some immense bat, and wherever the Queen brushes against the girl, there is the sensation of touching, or being touched by, matted fur and the blasted bark of dying, lightning-struck trees. The day she chased the quick green lizard through the forest, she was still whole, her maidenhead unbroken, the task of her deflowering promised— before her birth—to a nobleman, an elfin duke who held his court on the shores of a sparkling lake and was long owed a considerable debt by her father. The marriage would settle that account. Would *have* settled that account, for the Queen took the fairie girl's virginity almost at once. *We'll have none of that here*, she said, slipping a sickle thumb between the girl's pale thighs and pricking at her sex. Only as much pain as she'd always expected, and hardly any blood, but the certain knowledge, too, that she had been undone, ruined, despoiled, and if ever she found some secret stairway leading up and out of the Queen's thin lands, her escape would only bring shame to her family. *Better a daughter lost and dead and picked clean by the ants and crows*, the Queen of Decay told her, *than one who's given herself to me, who's soiled my bedclothes with her body's juices and played my demimondaine.* "Nothing was given," replied the fairie girl, and how long ago *was* that? A month? A season? Only a single night? There is no time in the land of the Queen of Decay. There is no *need* of time when despair would serve so well as the past and all possible futures. Mark it all the present and be done. *What next?* the Queen asks, mocking the laws of her own timeless realm. *Have you been lying here, child, asking yourself, what is next in store for me?* "No," said the girl, refusing to admit the truth aloud, even if the Queen could hear it perfectly well unspoken. "I do not dwell on it," the girl lies. "You will do as you will, and neither my fear nor anticipation will stay your hand or teach you mercy." And then the Queen swelled and rose up around her like a glistening, alveolate wreath of ink and sealing wax, and the spectators clinging to the walls or looking out from their nooks and corners held their breath, collectively not breathing as though in that moment they had become a single beast divided into many bodies. *I only followed the lizard,* the fairie girl thinks, trying not to hear the wet and stretching noises leaking from the Queen's distorted form, trying not to think what will happen one second later, or two seconds after that. *It was so pretty in the morning sun. Its scales were a rainbow fashioned all of shades of green, a thousand shades of green,* and she bows her head and strains to recall the living warmth of sunlight on her face. *Show me your eyes, child,* growls the Queen of Decay. *We will not do this thing halfway.* And, reminded now of details she'd misplaced, the girl replies, "*Its* eyes were like faraway red stars twinkling in its skull. I'd never before seen such a lizard—verdant, iridian, gazing out at me with crimson eyes." The moldy air trapped within the chamber seems to shudder then, and the encircling mesh that the Unseelie queen has made of herself draws tighter about the girl from the bright lands that are ever crushing down upon those who must dwell below. *I have not taken everything,* she says. *Not yet. We've hardly begun,* and the fairie girl remembers that she is not chasing a green lizard with red eyes on a summer's morning, that she has finally fallen into that abyss—the razor jaws of a granddaddy snapping turtle half buried in silt and waterlogged poplar leaves, or the gullet of a catfish that has waited long years in the mud and gloom to make a meal of her. There is always farther to fall. This pool has no bottom. She will sink until she at last forgets herself, and still she will go on sinking. She glances up into the void that the Queen of Decay has not bothered to cover with a mask, and something which has hidden itself under the black bed begins to snicker loudly. *You are mine, daughter,* says the Queen. *And a daughter of loam and toadstools should not go about so gaudily attired. It is indecent,* and, with that, her claws move swiftly and snip away the girl's beautiful dragonfly wings. They slip from off her shoulder, falling from ragged stumps to lie dead upon the spider sheets. "My wings," the girl whispers, unsurprised and yet also disbelieving, this new violation and its attendant hurt seeming hardly more real than the bad dreams she woke from some short time ago (if there *were* time here). "You've taken my wings from me," and she reaches for them, meaning to hide them away beneath a pillow or within the folds of her stained and tattered shift before any greater harm is done to those delicate, papery mosaics. But the Queen, of course, knows the girl's will and is far faster than she; the amputated wings are snatched up by clicking, chitinous appendages which sprout suddenly from this or that dank and fleshy recess, then ferried quickly to the sucking void where a face should be. The Queen of Decay devours the fairie girl's wings in an instant, less than half an instant. And there below the leaf-litter clouds and the rustling, grub-haunted roof of this thin, thin world, the Queen, unsated, draws tight the quivering folds of her honeycomb skin and falls upon the screaming, stolen child...

...and later, the girl is shat out again, or vomited—that indigestible, fecal lump of her which the Queen's metabolism has found no use for. Not the fairie girl, but whatever *remains* when the glamour and magick have been stripped away by acid and cruel enzymes and a billion diligent intestinal cilia. This dull, undying scat which can now recall only the least tangible fragments of its life before the descent, before the fall, before the millennia spent in twisting, turning passage through the Queen's gut, and it sits at one of the mirrors which its mistress has so kindly, so thoughtfully, provided and watches its own gaunt face. On the bed behind it, there is a small green lizard with ruby eyes, and the lizard blinks and tastes the stale, forest-cellar air with a forked tongue the colour of ripe blackberries. *Perhaps,* thinks the thing that is no longer sprite or nymph or pixie, that is only this naked stub of gristle, *perhaps you were once a dragon, and then she swallowed you, as she swallowed me, and all that is left now is a little green lizard with red eyes.* The lizard blinks again, neither confirming nor denying the possibility, and the thing staring back at itself from the mirror considers conspiracy and connivance, the lovely little lizard only bait to lead her astray, that she might wander alone into a grove of ancient oaks and lift a flat, slug-streaked stone and…fall. The thing in the mirror is only the wage of its own careless, disobedient delight, and with one skeletal hand, it touches wrinkled fingertips to the cold, unyielding surface of the looking glass, reaching out to that *other* it. There is another green lizard, trapped there inside the mirror, and while the remains of the feast of the Queen of Decay tries to recall what might have come before the grove and the great flat stone and the headlong plunge down the throat of all the world, the tiny lizard slips away, vanishing into the shadows that hang everywhere like murmuring shreds of midnight.

The Ammonite Violin
(Murder Ballad No. 4)

If he were ever to try to write this story, he would not know where to begin. It's that sort of a story, so fraught with unlikely things, so perfectly turned and filled with such wicked artifice and contrivances that readers would look away, unable to suspend their disbelief even for a page. But he will never try to write it, because he is not a poet, or a novelist, or a man who writes short stories for the newsstand pulp magazines. He is a collector. Or, as he thinks of himself, a Collector. He has never dared to think of himself as *The* Collector, as he is not without an ounce or two of modesty, and there must surely be those out there who are far better than he, shadow men, and maybe shadow women, too, haunting a busy, forgetful world that is only aware of its phantoms when one or another of them slips up and is exposed to flashing cameras and prison cells. Then people will stare, and maybe, for a time, there is horror and fear in their dull, wet eyes, but they soon enough forget again. They are busy people, after all, and they have lives to live, and jobs to show up for five days a week, and bills to pay, and secret nightmares all their own, and in their world there is very little *time* for phantoms.

He lives in a small house in a small town near the sea, for the only time the Collector is ever truly at peace is when he is in the presence of the sea. Even collecting has never brought him to that complete and utter peace, the quiet which finally fills him whenever there is only the crash of waves against a granite jetty and the saltwater mists to breathe in and hold in his lungs like opium fumes. He would love the sea, were she a woman.

And sometimes he imagines her so, a wild and beautiful woman clothed all in blue and green, trailing sand and mussels in her wake. Her grey eyes would contain hurricanes, and her voice would be the lonely toll of bell buoys and the cries of gulls and a December wind scraping itself raw against the shore. But, he thinks, were the sea but a women, and were she his lover, then he would *have* her, as he is a Collector and *must* have all those things he loves, so that no one else might ever have them. He must draw them to him and keep them safe from a blind and busy world that cannot even comprehend its phantoms. And having her, he would lose her, and he would never again know the peace which only she can bring.

He has two specialties, this Collector. There are some who are perfectly content with only one, and he has never thought any less of them for it. But he has two, because, so long as he can recall, there has been this dual fascination, and he never saw the point in forsaking one for the other. Not if he might have them both, and yet be a richer man for sharing his devotion between the two. They are his two mistresses, and neither has ever condemned his polyamorous heart. Like the sea, who is *not* his mistress, but only his constant savior, they understand who and what and *why* he is, and that he would be somehow diminished, perhaps even undone, were he forced to devote himself wholly to the one or the other. The first of the two is his vast collection of fossilized ammonites, gathered up from the quarries and ocean-side cliffs and the stony, barren places of half the globe's nations. The second are all the young women he has murdered by suffocation, *always* by suffocation, for that is how the sea would kill, how the sea *does* kill, usually, and in taking life he would ever pay tribute and honor that first mother of the world.

That first Collector.

He has never had to explain his collecting of suffocations, of the deaths of suffocated girls, as it is such a commonplace thing, and a secret collection, besides. But he has frequently found it necessary to explain to some acquaintance or another, someone who thinks that she or he *knows* the Collector, about the ammonites. The ammonites are not a secret and, it would seem, neither are they commonplace. It is simple enough to say that they are mollusks, a subdivision of the Cephalopoda, kin to the octopus and cuttlefish and squid, but possessing exquisite shells, not unlike another living cousin, the chambered nautilus. It is less easy to say that they became extinct at the end of the Cretaceous, along with most dinosaurs, or that they first appear in the fossil record in early Devonian times, as this only leads to the need to explain the Cretaceous and Devonian. Often, when asked that question, *What is an ammonite?*, he will change the subject. Or he will side-step the truth of his collection, talking only of mathematics, and the geometry of the ancient Greeks, and how one arrives at the Golden Curve. Ammonites, he knows, are one of the sea's many exquisite expressions of the Golden Curve, but he does not bother to explain that part, keeping it back for himself. And, sometimes, he talks about the horns of Ammon, an Egyptian god of the air, or, if he is feeling especially impatient and annoyed by the question, he limits his response to a description of the Ammonites from the *Book of Mormon*, how they embraced the god of the Nephites and so came to know peace. He is not a Mormon, of course, as he has use of only a single deity, who is the sea and who kindly grants him peace when he can no longer bear the clamor in his head or the far more terrible clamor of mankind.

On this hazy winter day, he has returned to his small house from a very long walk along a favorite beach, as there was a great need to clear his head. He has made a steaming cup of Red Zinger tea with a few drops of honey and sits now in the room that has become the gallery for the best of his ammonites, oak shelves and glass display cases filled with their graceful planispiral or heteromorph curves, a thousand fragile aragonite bodies transformed by time and geochemistry into mere silica or pyrite or some other permineralization. He sits at his desk, sipping his tea and glancing occasionally at some beloved specimen or another—*this* one from South Dakota, or *that* one from the banks of the Volga River in Russia, or one of the *many* that have come from Whitby, England. And then he looks back to the desktop and the violin case lying open in front of him, crimson silk to cradle this newest and perhaps most precious of all the items which he has yet collected in his lifetime, the single miraculous piece which belongs strictly in neither one gallery nor the other. The piece which will at last form a bridge, he believes, allowing his two collections to remain distinct, but also affording a tangible transition between them.

The keystone, he thinks. *Yes, you will be my keystone.* But he knows, too, that the violin will be something more than that, that he has devised it to serve as something far grander than a token unification of the two halves of his delight. It will be a *tool,* a mediator or go-between in an act which may, he hopes, transcend collecting in its simplest sense. It has only just arrived today, special delivery, from the Belgian luthier to whom the Collector had hesitantly entrusted its birth.

"It must done be *precisely* as I have said," he told the violin-maker, four months ago, when he flew to Hotton to hand-deliver a substantial portion of the materials from which the instrument would be constructed. "You may not deviate in any significant way from these instructions."

"Yes," the luthier replied, "I understand. I understand completely." A man who appreciates discretion, the Belgian violin-maker, so there were no inconvenient questions asked, no prying inquiries as to *why,* and what's more, he'd even known something about ammonites beforehand.

"No substitutions," the Collector said firmly, just in case it needed to be stated one last time.

"No substitutions of any sort," replied the luthier.

"And the back must be carved—"

"I understand," the violin-maker assured him. "I have the sketches, and I will follow them exactly."

"And the pegs—"

"Will be precisely as we have discussed."

And so the collector paid the luthier half the price of the commission, the other half due upon delivery, and he took a six a.m. flight back across the wide Atlantic to New England and his small house in the small town near the sea. And he has waited, hardly daring to *half* believe that the violin-maker would, in fact, get it all right. Indeed—for men are ever at war with their hearts and minds and innermost demons—some infinitesimal scrap of the Collector has even *hoped* that there *would* be a mistake, the most trifling portion of his plan ignored, or the violin finished and perfect but then lost in transit, and so the whole plot ruined.

For it is no small thing, what the Collector has set in motion, and having always considered himself a very wise and sober man, he suspects that he understands fully the consequences he would suffer should he be discovered by lesser men who have no regard for the ocean and her needs. Men who cannot see the flesh and blood phantoms walking among them in broad daylight, much less be bothered to pay tithes which are long overdue to a goddess who has cradled them all, each and every one, through the innumerable twists and turns of evolution's crucible, for three and a half thousand million years.

But there has been no mistake, and, if anything, the violinmaker can be faulted only in the complete sublimation of his craft to the will of his customer. In every way, this is the instrument the Collector asked him to make, and the varnish gleams faintly in the light from the display cases. The top is carved from spruce, and four small ammonites have been set into the wood—*Xipheroceras* from Jurassic rocks exposed along the Dorset Coast at Lyme Regis—two inlaid on the upper bout, two on the lower. He found the fossils himself, many years ago, and they are as perfectly preserved an example of their genus as he has yet seen anywhere, for any price. The violin's neck has been fashioned from maple, as is so often the tradition, and, likewise, the fingerboard is the customary ebony. However, the scroll has been formed from a fifth ammonite, and the Collector knows it is a far more perfect logarithmic spiral than any volute that could have ever been hacked from out a block of wood. In his mind, the five ammonites form the points of a pentacle. The luthier used maple for the back and ribs, and when the Collector turns the violin over, he's greeted by the intricate bas-relief he requested, faithfully reproduced from his own drawings—a great octopus, the ravenous devilfish of a so many sea legends, and the maze of its eight tentacles makes a looping, tangled interweave.

As for the pegs and bridge, the chinrest and tailpiece, all these have been carved from the bits of bone he provided the luthier. They seem no more than antique ivory, the stolen tusks of an elephant, or a walrus, or the tooth of a sperm whale, perhaps. The Collector also provided the dried gut for the five strings, and when the violin-maker pointed out that they would not be nearly so durable as good stranded steel, that they would be much more likely to break and harder to keep in tune, the Collector told him that the instrument would be played only once and so these matters were of very little concern. For the bow, the luthier was given strands of hair which the Collector told him had come from the tail of a gelding, a fine grey horse from Kentucky thoroughbred stock. He'd even ordered a special rosin, and so the sap of an Aleppo pine was supplemented with a vial of oil he'd left in the care of the violin-maker.

And now, four long months later, the Collector is rewarded for all his painstaking designs, rewarded or damned, if indeed there is some distinction between the two, and the instrument he holds is more beautiful than he'd ever dared to imagine it could be.

The Collector finishes his tea, pausing for a moment to lick the commingled flavors of hibiscus and rosehips, honey and lemongrass, from his thin, chapped lips. Then he closes the violin case and locks it, before writing a second, final check to the Belgian luthier. He slips it into an envelope bearing the violin-maker's name and the address of the shop on the rue de Centre in Hotton. The check will go out in the morning's mail, along with other checks for the gas, telephone, and electric bills, and a handwritten letter on lilac-scented stationary, addressed to a Brooklyn violinist. When he is done with these chores, the Collector sits there at the desk in his gallery, one hand resting lightly on the violin case, his face marred by an unaccustomed smile and his eyes filling up with the gluttonous wonder of so many precious things brought together in one room, content in the certain knowledge that they belong to him and will never belong to anyone else.

The violinist would never write this story, either. Words have never come easily for her. Sometimes, it seems she does not even think in words, but only in notes of music. When the lilac-scented letter arrives, she reads it several times, then does what it asks of her, because she can't imagine what else she would do. She buys a ticket, and the next day she takes the train through Connecticut and Rhode Island and Massachusetts until, finally, she comes to a small town on a rocky spit of land very near the sea. She has never cared for the sea, as it has seemed always to her some awful, insoluble mystery, not so very different from the awful, insoluble mystery of death. Even before the loss of her sister, the violinist avoided the sea when possible. She loathes the taste of fish and lobster and of clams, and the smell of the ocean, too, which reminds her of raw sewage. She has often dreamt of drowning, and of slimy things with bulging black eyes, eyes as empty as night, that have slithered up from abyssal depths to drag her back down with them to lightless plains of silt and diatomaceous ooze or to the ruins of haunted, sunken cities. But those are *only* dreams, and they do her only the bloodless harm that comes from dreams, and she has lived long enough to understand that she has worse things than the sea to fear.

She takes a taxi from the train depot, and it ferries her through the town and over a murky river winding between empty warehouses and rotting docks, a few fishing boats stranded at low tide, and then to a small house painted the color of sunflowers or canary feathers. The address on the mailbox matches the address on the lilac-scented letter, so she pays the driver, and he leaves her there. Then she stands in the driveway, watching the yellow house, which has begun to seem a disquieting shade of yellow, or a shade of yellow made disquieting because there is so much of it all in one place. It's almost twilight, and she shivers, wishing she'd thought to wear a cardigan under her coat, and then a porch light comes on and there's a man waving to her.

He's the man who wrote the letter, she thinks. *The man who wants me to play for him,* and for some reason she had expected him to be a great deal younger and not so fat. He looks a bit like Captain Kangaroo, this man, and he waves and calls her name and smiles. And the violinist wishes that the taxi were still waiting there to take her back to the station, that she didn't need the money the fat man in the yellow house had offered her, that she'd had the good sense to stay in the city where she belongs. *You could still turn and walk away,* she reminds herself. *There's nothing at all stopping you from just turning right around, and walking away, and never once looking back, and you could still forget about this whole ridiculous affair.*

And maybe that's true, and maybe it isn't, but there's more than a month's rent on the line, and the way work's been lately, a few students and catch-as-catch-can, she can't afford to find out. She nods and waves back at the smiling man on the porch, the man who told her not to bring her own instrument because he'd prefer to hear her play a particular one that he'd just brought back from a trip to Europe.

"Come on inside. You must be freezing out there," he calls from the porch, and the violinist tries not to think about the sea all around her or that shade of yellow, like a pool of melted butter, and goes to meet the man who sent her the lilac-scented letter.

The Collector makes a steaming-hot pot of Red Zinger, which the violinist takes without honey, and they each have a poppy-seed muffin, which he bought fresh that morning at a bakery in the town. They sit across from one another at his desk, surrounded by the display cases and the best of his ammonites, and she sips her tea and picks at the muffin and pretends to be interested while he explains the importance of recognizing sexual dimorphism when distinguishing one species of ammonite from another. The shells of females, he says, are often the larger, and so are called macroconchs by paleontologists. The males may have much smaller shells, called microconchs, and one must always be careful not to mistake the microconchs and macroconchs for two distinct species. He also talks about extinction rates, and the utility of ammonites as index fossils, and *Parapuzosia bradyi*, a giant among ammonites and the largest specimen in his collection, with a shell measuring slightly more than four and a half feet in diameter.

"They're all quite beautiful," she says, and the violinist doesn't tell him how much she hates the sea and everything that comes from the sea, or that the thought of all the fleshy, tentacled creatures that once lived stuffed inside those pretty spiral shells makes her skin crawl. She sips her tea and smiles and nods her head whenever it seems appropriate to do so, and when he asks if he can call her Ellen, she says yes, of course.

"You won't think me too familiar?"

"Don't be silly," she replies, half charmed at his manners and wondering if he's gay or just a lonely old man who's grown a bit peculiar because he has nothing but his rocks and the yellow house for company. "That's my name. My name is Ellen."

"I wouldn't want to make you uncomfortable, or take liberties that are not mine to take," the Collector says and clears away their china cups and saucers, the crumpled paper napkins and a few uneaten crumbs, and then he asks if she's ready to see the violin.

"If you're ready to show it to me," she tells him.

"It's just that I don't want to rush you," he says. "We could always talk some more, if you'd like."

And so the violinist explains to him that she's never felt comfortable with conversation, or with language in general, and that she's always suspected she was much better suited to speaking through her music. "Sometimes, I think it speaks for me," she tells him and apologizes, because she often apologizes when she's actually done nothing wrong. The Collector grins and laughs softly and taps the side of his nose with his left index finger.

"The way I see it, language is language is language," he says. "Words or music, bird songs or all the fancy, flashing colors made by chemoluminescent squid, what's the difference? I'll take conversation, however I can wrangle it." And then he unlocks one of the desk drawers with a tiny brass-colored key and takes out the case containing the Belgian violin.

"If words don't come when you call them, then, by all means, please, talk to me with this," and he flips up the latches on the side of the case and opens it so she can see the instrument cradled inside.

"Oh my," she says, all her awkwardness and unease forgotten at the sight of the ammonite violin. "I've never seen anything like it. Never. It's lovely. No, it's much, *much* more than lovely."

"Then you will play it for me?"

"May I touch it?" she asks, and he laughs again.

"I can't imagine how you'll play it otherwise."

Ellen gently lifts the violin from its case, the way that some people might lift a newborn child, or a Minoan vase, or a stoppered bottle of nitroglycerine, the way the Collector would lift a particularly fragile ammonite from its bed of excelsior. It's heavier than any violin she's held before, and she guesses that the unexpected weight must be from the five fossil shells set into the instrument. She wonders how it will affect the sound, those five ancient stones, how they might warp and alter this violin's voice.

"It's never been played, except by the man who made it, and that hardly seems to count. You, my dear, will be the very first."

And she almost asks him why *her*, because surely, for what he's paying, he could have lured some other, more talented player out here to his little yellow house. Surely someone a bit more celebrated, more accomplished, someone who doesn't have to take in students to make the rent, but would still be flattered and intrigued enough by the offer to come all the way to this squalid little town by the sea and play the fat man's violin for him. But then she thinks it would be rude, and she almost apologizes for a question she hasn't even asked.

And then, as if he might have read her mind, and so maybe she should have apologized after all, the Collector shrugs his shoulders and dabs at the corners of his mouth with a white linen handkerchief he's pulled from a shirt pocket. "The universe is a marvelously complex bit of craftsmanship," he says. "And sometimes one must look very closely to even begin to understand how one thing connects with another. Your late sister, for instance—"

"My *sister?*" she asks and looks up, surprised and glancing away from the ammonite violin and into the friendly, smiling eyes of the Collector. There's a cold knot deep in her belly, and an unpleasant pricking sensation along her forearms and the back of her neck, goose bumps and histrionic ghost-story clichés, and all at once the violin feels unclean and dangerous, and she wants to return it to its case. "What do you know about my sister?"

The Collector blushes and peers down at his hands, folded there in front of him on the desk. He begins to speak and stammers, as if, possibly, he's really no better with words than she.

"What do *you* know about my sister?" Ellen asks again. "*How* do you know about her?"

The Collector frowns and licks nervously at his chapped lips. "I'm sorry," he says. "That was terribly tactless of me. I should not have brought it up."

"How do you know about my sister?"

"It's not exactly a secret, is it?" the Collector asks, letting his eyes drift by slow, calculated degrees from his hands and the desktop to her face. "I do read the newspapers. I don't usually watch television, but I imagine it was there, as well. She was murdered—"

"They don't *know* that. No one knows that for sure. She is *missing*," the violinist says, hissing the last word between clenched teeth.

"She's been missing for quite some time," the Collector replies, feeling the smallest bit braver now and beginning to suspect he hasn't quite overplayed his hand.

"But they do not know that she's been murdered. They don't *know* that. No one ever found her body," and then Ellen decides that she's said far too much and stares down at the fat man's violin. She can't imagine how she ever thought it a lovely thing, only a moment or two before, this grotesque *parody* of a violin resting in her lap. It's more like a gargoyle, she thinks, or a sideshow freak, a malformed parody, or a sick, sick joke, and suddenly she wants very badly to wash her hands.

"Please forgive me," the Collector says, sounding as sincere and contrite as any lonely man in a yellow house by the sea has ever sounded. "I am unaccustomed to company. I forget myself and say things I shouldn't. Please, Ellen. Play it for me. You've come all this way, and I would so love to hear you play. It would be such a pity if I've gone and spoiled it all with a few inconsiderate words. I so admire your work—"

"No one *admires* my work," she replies, wondering how long it would take the taxi to show up and carry back over the muddy, murky river, past the rows of empty warehouses to the depot, and how long she'd have to wait for the next train to New York. "I still don't even understand how you found me."

And at this opportunity to redeem himself, the Collector's face brightens, and he leans towards her across the desk. "Then I will tell you, if that will put your mind at ease. I saw you play at an art opening in Manhattan, you and your sister, a year or so back. At a gallery on Mercer Street. It was called…damn, it's right on the tip of my tongue—"

"Eyecon," Ellen says, almost whispering. "The name of the gallery is Eyecon."

"Yes, yes, that's it. Thank you. I thought it was such a very silly name for a gallery, but then I've never cared for puns and wordplay. It was at a reception for a French painter, Albert Perrault, and I confess I found him quite completely hideous, and his paintings were dreadful, but I loved listening to the two of you play. I called the gallery, and they were nice enough to tell me how I could contact you."

"I didn't like his paintings, either. That was the last time we played together, my sister and I," Ellen says, and she presses a thumb to the ammonite shell that forms the violin's scroll.

"I didn't know that. I'm sorry, Ellen. I wasn't trying to dredge up bad memories."

"It's not a *bad* memory," she says, wishing it were all that simple and that were exactly the truth, and then she reaches for the violin's bow, which is still lying in the case lined with silk dyed the color of ripe pomegranates.

"I'm sorry," the Collector says again, certain now that he hasn't frightened her away, that everything is going precisely as planned. "Please, I only want to hear you play again."

"I'll need to tune it," Ellen tells him, because she's come this far, and she needs the money, and there's nothing the fat man has said that doesn't add up.

"Naturally," he replies. "I'll go to the kitchen and make us another pot of tea, and you can call me whenever you're ready."

"I'll need a tuning fork," she says, because she hasn't seen any sign of a piano in the yellow house. "Or if you have a metronome that has a tuner, that would work."

The Collector promptly produces a steel tuning fork from another of the drawers, and slides it across the desk to the violinist. She thanks him, and when he's left the room and she's alone with the ammonite violin and all the tall cases filled with fossils and the amber wash of incandescent bulbs, she glances at a window and sees that it's already dark outside. *I will play for him,* she thinks. *I'll play on his violin, and drink his tea, and smile, and then he'll pay me for my time and trouble. I'll go back to the city, and tomorrow or the next day, I'll be glad that I didn't back out. Tomorrow or the next day, it'll all seem silly, that I was afraid of a sad old man who lives in an ugly yellow house and collects rocks.*

"I will," she says out loud. "That's exactly how it will go," and then Ellen begins to tune the ammonite violin.

And after he brings her a rickety old music stand, something that looks like it has survived half a century of high-school marching bands, he sits behind his desk, sipping a fresh cup of tea, and she sits in the overlapping pools of light from the display cases. He asked for Paganini; specifically, he asked for Paganini's Violin Concerto No. 3 in E. She would have preferred something contemporary—Górecki, maybe, or Phillip Glass, a little something she knows from memory—but he had the sheet music for Paganini, and it's his violin, and he's the one who's writing the check.

"Now?" she asks, and he nods his head.

"Yes, please," he replies and raises his tea cup as if to toast her.

So Ellen lifts the violin, supporting it with her left shoulder, bracing it firmly with her chin, and studies the sheet music a moment or two more before she begins. *Introduzione, allegro marziale*, and she wonders if he expects to hear all three movements, start to finish, or if he'll stop her when he's heard enough. She takes a deep breath and begins to play.

From his seat at the desk, the Collector closes his eyes as the lilting voice of the ammonite violin fills the room. He closes his eyes tightly and remembers another winter night, almost an entire year come and gone since then, but it might only have been yesterday, so clear are his memories. His collection of suffocations may indeed be more commonplace, as he has been led to conclude, but it is also the less frequently indulged of his two passions. He could never name the date and place of each and every ammonite acquisition, but in his brain the Collector carries a faultless accounting of all the suffocations. There have been sixteen, sixteen in twenty-one years, and now it has been almost one year to the night since the most recent. Perhaps, he thinks, he should have waited for the anniversary, but when the package arrived from Belgium, his enthusiasm and impatience got the better of him. When he wrote the violinist his lilac-scented note, he wrote "at your earliest possible convenience" and underlined "earliest" twice.

And here she is, and Paganini flows from out the ammonite violin just as it flowed from his car stereo that freezing night, one year ago, and his heart is beating so fast, so hard, racing itself and all his bright and breathless memories.

Don't let it end, he prays to the sea, whom he has faith can hear the prayers of all her supplicants and will answer those she deems worthy. *Let it go on and on and on. Let it never end.*

He clenches his fists, digging his short nails deep into the skin of his palms, and bites his lip so hard that he tastes blood. And the taste of those few drops of his own life is not so very different from holding the sea inside his mouth.

At last, I have done a perfect thing, he tells himself, himself and the sea and the ammonites and the lingering souls of all his suffocations. *So many years, so much time, so much work and money, but finally I have done this one perfect thing.* And then he opens his eyes again, and also opens the top middle drawer of his desk and takes out the revolver that once belonged to his father, who was a Gloucester fisherman who somehow managed never to collect anything at all.

Her fingers and the bow dance wild across the strings, and in only a few minutes Ellen has lost herself inside the giddy tangle of harmonics and drones and double stops, and if ever she has felt magic—*true* magic—in her art, then she feels it now. She lets her eyes drift from the music stand and the printed pages, because it is all right there behind her eyes and burning on her fingertips. She might well have written these lines herself and then spent half her life playing at nothing else, they rush through her with such ease and confidence. This is ecstasy, and this is abandon, and this is the tumble and roar of a thousand other emotions she seems never to have felt before this night. The strange violin no longer seems unusually heavy; in fact, it hardly seems to have any weight at all.

Perhaps there is no violin, she thinks. *Perhaps there never was a violin, only my hands and empty air, and that's all it takes to make music like this.*

Language is language is language, the fat man said, and so these chords have become her words. No, *not* words, but something so much less indirect than the clumsy interplay of her tongue and teeth, larynx and palate. They have become, simply, her *language*, as they ever have been. Her soul speaking to the world, and all the world need do is *listen.*

She shuts her eyes, no longer needing them to grasp the progression from one note to the next, and at first there is only the comfortable darkness there behind her lids, which seems better matched to the music than all the distractions of her eyes.

Don't let it stop, she thinks, not praying, unless this is a prayer to herself, for the violinist has never seen the need for gods. *Please, let it be like this forever. Let this moment never end, and I will never have to stop playing, and there will never again be silence or the noise of human thoughts and conversation.*

"It can't be that way, Ellen," her sister whispers, not whispering in her ear, but from somewhere within the Paganini concerto, or the ammonite violin, or both at once. "I wish I could give you that. I would give you that, if it were mine to give."

And then Ellen sees, or hears, or simply *understands* in this language which is *her* language, as language is language is language, the fat man's hands about her sister's throat. Her sister dying somewhere cold near the sea, dying all alone except for the company of her murderer, and there is half an instant when she almost stops playing.

No, her sister whispers, and that one word comes like a blazing gash across the concerto's whirl. Ellen doesn't stop playing, and she doesn't open her eyes, and she watches as her lost sister slowly dies.

The music is a typhoon gale flaying rocky shores to gravel and sand, and the violinist lets it spin and rage, and she watches as the fat man takes four of her sister's fingers and part of a thighbone, strands of her ash blonde hair, a vial of oil boiled and distilled from the fat of her breasts, a pink-white section of small intestine—all these things and the five fossils from off an English beach to make the instrument he wooed her here to play for him. And now there are tears streaming hot down her cheeks, but still Ellen plays the violin that was her sister, and still she doesn't open her eyes.

The single gunshot is very loud in the room, and the display cases rattle, and a few of the ammonites slip off their Lucite stands and clatter against wood or glass or other spiraled shells.

And finally she opens her eyes.

And the music ends as the bow slides from her fingers and falls to the floor at her feet.

"No," she says, "please don't let it stop, please," but the echo of the revolver and the memory of the concerto are so loud in her ears that her own words are almost lost to her.

That's all, her sister whispers, louder than any suicide's gun, soft as a midwinter night coming on, gentle as one unnoticed second bleeding into the next. *I've shown you, and now there isn't any more.*

Across the room, the Collector still sits at his desk, but now he's slumped a bit in his chair, and his head is thrown back so that he seems to be staring at something on the ceiling. Blood spills from the black cavern of his open mouth and drips to the floor.

There isn't any more.

And when she's stopped crying and is quite certain that her sister will not speak to her again, that all the secrets she has any business seeing have been revealed, the violinist retrieves the dropped bow and stands, then walks to the desk and returns the ammonite violin to its case. She will not give it to the police when they arrive, after she has gone to the kitchen to call them, and she will not tell them that it was the fat man who gave it to her. She will take it back to Brooklyn, and they will find other things in another room in the yellow house and so have no need of the violin and these stolen shreds of her sister. The Collector has kindly written everything down in three books bound in red leather, all the names and dates and places, and there are other souvenirs, besides. And she will never try to put this story into words, for words have never come easily to her, and like the violin, the story has become hers and hers alone.

The Lovesong of Lady Ratteanrufer

1.

In the stories she tells herself late at night, there were rats even before the world began. There were fat, hungry rats that waited huddled together in the void, the endless nowhere place where there were not yet stars or planets or gods or angels, but only the nothingness before creation and only the rats. Lying on her dirty mattress on long summer nights when it's too hot to sleep, or longer winter nights when it's too cold to do anything much but shiver, she's watched the blue-black sky draped low above the city and whispered to herself, and to anything else that might be listening, how the rats finally grew bored and tired of always being hungry, and so from their droppings they made the heavens and all the worlds that have ever been. They chewed tiny holes in the darkness to let in starlight, and then they pissed out all the rivers and oceans and the bright spatter of the Milky Way so that they wouldn't have to go on being thirsty any longer. In her story, the rats made men and women, too, and every other sort of animal and plant. Like all her stories, it's a secret. Like her coins and the eyeless doll and the pennywhistle she found one day in a weedy cemetery near the river. Dull and dented brass with six holes punched out along its length, a black plastic fipple for her thin lips, and a garish bit of scarlet dabbed partway down the tube, but most of the paint was already scratched away when she found it. In her secret story, the first rats made themselves a brass pennywhistle, dabbed with red paint, and when they played it, their droppings became the universe. She keeps the whistle wrapped up in a swatch of denim, tucked into a wooden box hidden beneath a loose floorboard. She can't remember where exactly, or when exactly, she found the wooden box, but for a while it played pretty music whenever she opened its lid. Then she dropped it one day, bump to the floor, and now she only gets music from the pennywhistle she keeps inside the wooden box. In her story, this is the very same pennywhistle the rats played to make the stars and planets and moons and animals from the primordial void. And it has fallen upon her to keep it safe until the day when they need it again, because, in her story, the rats *will* need their whistle again, when history is finally over and they've grown bored with all the things they made to gnaw and keep their bellies full and the time has come to *unmake* the world. But, until then, they don't mind that she plays it. That's why the rats left it there in the cemetery among the moss and dandelions, the broken headstones and toadstools, that she would find it one day and teach herself songs that no one else had ever heard before because in learning how to play them she also created them. That is the peculiar magic of this pennywhistle, that it blithely weaves creation in rolls and slides and vibrato embellishments, in the practiced dance of fingertips and the press of lips and tongue and the living breath that spills in through its mouthpiece and out the other end. But she also knows that it must be a deadly, perilous thing, for death is the shadow of creation, and to court one is always to invite its familiar. There are other things in the wooden box with the pennywhistle and the swatch of denim: a striped sock filled with the coins she's found, scraps of paper printed with words that she mostly can't read, a green marble, rocks, buttons, a die, a piece of white lace, rubber bands, spools of thread, the discarded husks of bugs and wasps and cicadas, three odd wooden tiles with the letters A, Y, and T on them, the feathers of blue jays and mockingbirds, a tiny ceramic animal that looks sort of like a white dog but isn't, and an old pair of spectacles she sometimes wears when she's in a rut and wants to see things differently. But she knows that of all these treasures, only the pennywhistle really matters. Only the pennywhistle must be kept safe. Rats have almost no use at all for rubber bands and spools of thread. In the story, the rats have a word for music, and it's the same word they use for *yesterday* and *today* and *tomorrow*, and the same word that means *now*, too.

2.

She lives in a mostly empty redbrick building not far from the river, because looking out a window and seeing the wide gray-green river winding past usually makes her feel safe whenever she's frightened and can't think of a story to tell herself. Hardly anyone else lives in the building, as it's very damp so close to the water, and the air often stinks of mold and mud and dead fish and the oily rainbow sheen that floats along on top of the river. There's tall grass and crooked trees and all sorts of briars and bushes growing around the redbrick building, and she likes to think these things were planted to conceal her from the street and curious eyes and any people who might be passing by, the people who usually keep to the city and hardly ever come down to the river. But sometimes they *do* come, to stand out there on the bridge that spans the river and drop things into the water, or shoot their guns at the sky, or get drunk and fight among themselves. In one of her stories, the people from the city worship an enormous snake that lives at the bottom of the river below the bridge, and the things she's seen them dropping into the water are offerings to the snake god. Long ago, after the rats made the world, but ages before she was born, the snake slithered up out of the oily river and vomited fire and lightning bolts, burning the city and killing almost everyone but these crazy men with their guns and liquor and their scabby fists. The fire seared their minds and boiled their eyes and made them insane—the few it didn't simply kill—but not so blind or crazy that they didn't understand that now they had to keep the snake content unless they wanted it rising from the river to spit fire at them all over again. The rats and the snake are ancient, mortal enemies. Maybe the rats made the whole universe, but they *didn't* make the snake or all the countless wriggling children of the snake. The snake came here from somewhere else. Some other universe, perhaps, some place else where it wasn't welcome, and there's a story she tells herself where the brave rats fought the snake after it had burned down all the cities in the world. The rats drove the snake back down into the murky water beneath the bridge, and it has stayed there ever since, because the crazy men bring it offerings of whiskey and wine, and sing it gunpowder songs and hurt one another, bleeding to keep it happy and to keep it asleep. But today there are no men on the bridge, and she can sit alone in her room and play the magic pennywhistle for the rats who live in the walls of the redbrick building. Sometimes, they even come peeping out of the holes in the plaster and sit very still, listening to the music she makes for them. Not today, but sometimes they do. They come to hear her songs and to see that they've not made a mistake trusting her to keep the pennywhistle safe. If the snake were ever to get it, they've told her time and again, he would immediately begin to play the secret backwards song that would undo the universe, and only the rats can say when it's time for all things to end. She plays them pretty songs and sad songs and songs that don't mean much of anything at all, songs that are only music. Once, on a night when the moon was full and tinted an angry yellow and staring threatfully in through her window, the rats came to her, a hundred or two hundred of them all at once. They sat and listened while she played a story about looking for crayfish and mussels along the banks of the river, about picking blackberries and pricking her fingers on the thorns. When she was done, they made small and approving rat noises, and a few even came right up to the edge of her mattress so she could stroke their fur with her fingers, the same fingers that drew stories out of the magical pennywhistle. And from that night on, she understood that the rats all watched over her and kept her safe from the moon and the fire-breathing snake sleeping beneath the bridge and from all the drunken, crazy men, just as she kept their whistle hidden safely inside her mute wooden box beneath the loose floorboard.

3.

The night that the God of all Rats comes to see her, the moon is only an ashen sliver, and the night is not so cold that she can't keep warm with the yellow fleece blanket she found hanging in a tree the summer before. She is dreaming about a delicious stew she's made from crayfish and bullfrogs and fat white grubs, onions and ground-fall apples. And then something wakes her, but there's only the thin slice of moon and the distant twinkling stars and the sky right outside her window, only the disappointment that she won't likely be getting a second bowl of the stew. She doesn't notice him at first, doesn't realize that it was the God of all Rats who woke her from the dream. Then he says her name, which she hears so infrequently that there are times when she almost forgets she has one. The God of all Rats says her name, and she rolls over on her blanket to find him standing nearby, watching her with his intense black rat eyes. He is very tall, this god, and she doesn't know if he always looks this way, like a tall man covered in the dark pelt of a rat, a man with the head and tail and sharp claws of a rat, or if this is just how he wants *her* to see him.

"Have I done something wrong?" she asks him, startled by the sound of her own voice, which she hears almost as infrequently as her name.

"Why would you ask me that?" the God of all Rats replies. "You have kept the pennywhistle safe, and ever have you been a friend to my people."

"I know who you are," she says and rubs at her eyes; the rat god nods his head and takes a step nearer the mattress.

"I thought perhaps you would. I did not think I would need to explain myself to you. You have played the pennywhistle, and you know the true stories. You are not like other human women, and you are not like human men, either."

"Do you want to hear me play?" she asks. "Is that why you're here?"

"I have heard you play a hundred times. You play so beautifully, but that is not why I have come to you tonight."

"Do you want me to tell you a story?"

"Perhaps, daughter, I have come here to tell *you* a story, one you do not yet begin to suspect."

At that, she sits up and yawns and rubs her eyes again. The God of all Rats sits down cross-legged on the floor next to her mattress and stares at her.

"But I already know so many stories," she tells him. "Are you hungry? I have a little food and—"

"I am not hungry," replies the God of all Rats. "I have sharp teeth and sharp claws and can find my own food when I am hungry."

"You want to tell *me* a story," she says, confused, still smelling the bubbling dream stew, still only just half awake and beginning to wonder if she even wants to know the sort of story a god might have for her.

"I want to teach you something and give you a gift, to show my gratitude and the gratitude of all my people for keeping the pennywhistle safe from the serpent who lives below the bridge. It will seem like a story to you."

"I know the difference," she says. "I can tell what is a story and what isn't. I'm not a child. I hope you don't think I'm a child, or that I'm insane, like the men from the city." And she pulls the yellow blanket up tight about her arms and shoulders, because there's something about the black, unblinking gaze of the God of all Rats that makes the night seem much colder than it actually is.

"No, you are not like them," the rat god agrees. "But neither are you entirely sane. If you were, I doubt we would be able to speak like this, you and I. If you were sane, you would have never found the pennywhistle in the cemetery, and I would never have come to you."

"I'm not crazy," she says, pressing herself flat against the wall beneath the window, frightened now and wishing this were only a dream she could wake from, only a story she could stop telling herself. She looks away, no longer wanting to see the eyes of the God of all Rats, not wanting to feel them on her. "If someone told you I'm crazy, they were lying."

Somewhere in the wild tangle of branches and vines that has grown up all around the redbrick building, an owl cries out— *hoo, hoo-oo, hoo, hoo*—and now she feels like a hunted thing, like whatever it is the owl must be stalking through the tall grass and ragweed, only a trembling rabbit or a vole, a mouse...or a rat.

"Please do not be afraid of me," the God of all Rats says and sniffs at the air. "I did not come all this way to frighten you."

"You might not *mean* to," she says, keeping her eyes on the loose floorboard, trying to think about the pennywhistle and not the owl prowling outside her window. "You might not mean to *hurt* me, either, but things don't always happen the way we want them to."

"I will not hurt you," he says again, and again he says her name, speaking those two familiar, half-forgotten syllables, and it seems like music on his tongue. "You have my word I will not harm you, ever. Nor will I ever allow another to harm you, if I can prevent it. I am in your debt, daughter."

"I am not *your* daughter," she says, wanting to believe him, wishing the owl would fly far, far away, all the way down to the sea, and not spend the night perched outside her window.

"Will you accept my gift?" the God of all Rats asks, and she can tell that he's growing impatient with her.

"Do I have a choice?"

"You do. Otherwise, I would not call it a gift."

Slowly, she turns back to face the god, who is kneeling now before her, down on his knees and his head bowed, and suddenly she wants to cry, even though she can't remember ever having cried before. The owl calls out again, and she wonders what sort of god the owls and hawks and ravens pray to.

"I'm sorry," she says. "I shouldn't have said those things. I should know better."

"Then will you accept my gift?" he asks her once more, and she tells him yes, she will. And so the God of all Rats takes her in his velvet arms and presses his wet nose to her right ear and whispers new secrets and shows her new worlds, and before the sun rises again, he slips himself in between her legs, and she shuts her eyes and thinks this must be the most wonderful night of her life. While the God of all Rats makes love to her, the room fills with his children—two hundred pairs of twitching whiskers, four hundred dewy eyes—and they watch and wait and wonder what will happen next.

4.

And in the weeks that follow, there do not seem to be quite as many hours when she feels alone or afraid, and it is easier to sleep without telling herself stories. She often climbs the stairwell up to the roof of the redbrick building so she has the best view of the river, and she sits there and plays the pennywhistle and hopes that the God of all Rats is somewhere nearby, listening. An emptiness inside her has gone away, some terrible hollow that she only ever half suspected and then understood not as an *absence*, but simply an intrinsic, inescapable part of being alive. The snows come, but they do not seem to bring with them as much cold or as much desolation as in all the years past. She uses the pennywhistle to find a new song in which she and the God of all Rats go down to his underground kingdom miles below the redbrick building, where there is always enough food, and never any ice or frost or freezing winds, and never the need to hide. She becomes his queen, the lost queen for whom he has spent half an eternity searching, and she spends her days in great caverns playing the pennywhistle for all their assembled court, all the creatures who live in the world's deep, dark spaces—the moles and fat pink earthworms, the beetles and the bats and such a gathering of rats that their numbers are beyond counting. The God of all Rats gives her a ring spun from the blackness before creation so that she will never have to die, and she gives him a litter of beautiful children with eager grey eyes and restless pink noses. *This is the best song I have ever found*, she tells herself and wishes that he would come back to her, even though he said that he never would. She watches the comforting river and the blue sky and the bare, craggy branches of the trees and hopes that maybe he was mistaken or that he'll change his mind, because even gods can change their minds, and one night she'll be dreaming about a bubbling pot of stew or a summer day or maybe finding a new blanket, and there will be a sudden, unexpected sound that breaks the dream and wakes her. And it will be him, standing there in the room, and the only thing she will miss about this place is the sight of the river. But she knows that these are only fancies, and that they cannot be more than that does not lessen the peace that the God of all Rats has given her in exchange for keeping his pennywhistle safe from the snake sleeping beneath the bridge.

5.

The plague finds the city in the raw, dead heart of winter, in a bleak month, a grim and disheartening month when dawn and twilight seem to come with nothing in between, nothing there to divide night from day but half-light and clouds. There are only fleeting glimpses of a pale and indifferent sun, and when she asks the pennywhistle if the sun will ever be warm again, it won't answer her. She rarely leaves the redbrick building anymore, because of the things she hears in the night and the madness of the dying men and women and their children, all lost in fever and turned out to roam the streets by those in the city who have not yet fallen ill. She stops going up to the roof and must make do with what she can see of the river from her window. And then she stops looking at the river altogether, too frightened by all the frail and raggedy people clustered along its icy banks or drowning themselves in waters that have gone the color of a very bad bruise. The pennywhistle knows a song about the plague, and it tells her that the sick people believe the river can cool them and drive away the fever. But they've forgotten about the snake below the bridge, and they do not know that it waits there to pull them down, one by one by one, feasting and stoking its infernal belly with the very same fever they pray the river will relieve. She cannot help them. She can only huddle beneath her blankets and think of the God of all Rats, who surely has not forgotten her. There is very little food, and most of what there is has gone over, so she tries not to eat. She nibbles snow from the windowsill to quench her thirst. And then one night the city begins to burn, staining the undersides of the clouds with angry, flickering shades of red and orange, and she starts to think that this must be the end of everything, and soon the rats will ask her to return their pennywhistle so they can begin to play the backwards song that will undo the universe they created. She doesn't know if the serpent has crawled out of the river and started the fire, or if the people have started it themselves. It hardly seems to make much difference, one way or another. Fire is fire. Maybe, she thinks, the fire is another part of the plague, that, in the grip of their fevers, the men and women of the city have begun to sweat these flames. She takes out the wooden box from its place beneath the loose floorboard and unwraps the pennywhistle from the swatch of denim and plays a desperate, keening song that is only *Come back for me, come back for me* over and over again. But if the God of all Rats hears her, he does not answer, and he does not come back for her. By morning—that lighter shade of night that has come to *pass* for morning—the sky is consumed by billowing clouds of charcoal smoke and heavy rains of black ash and soot that ruin the white snow. The wind blowing in through her window stinks of everything that is burning, and she drags her mattress across the room and out into the fourth-floor hallway, as far from the window as she dares to go. It *must* be the end of time, when men sweat fire and even the sky falls, and she almost breaks the pennywhistle so the backwards song can never be played upon it and the snake will have to sleep forever in its nest beneath the bridge. She squeezes her eyes tightly shut and holds it in her hands, meaning to snap it in half, meaning to make of it something twisted and ruined and ugly, a thing that can never play another note for anyone or anything or tell another story. But she is not that brave, even if she has been a god's lover, and if she destroys the whistle she will be utterly alone forever, for all her life, and there will only be the stories that words can make. If she destroys the pennywhistle, she'll have betrayed the rats' trust and there will be no hope that the God of all Rats will *ever* come back for her. So she sits there shivering in the hallway, wrapped in her yellow blanket and humming a tuneless story about the river, unable to keep her eyes off the drab smudge of daylight, and the low winter clouds, and the smoke filling up her window, and the place where the sky used to be.

6.

Three nights after the beginning of the fire, she's dozing in the hallway, not really sleeping, and certainly not dreaming, only dozing, because she's too scared and hungry to truly sleep. And then she hears stomping feet and drums, people shouting and singing, all their many voices joined and singing the same song together—more or less together—which is something she's never heard before. It must be a sort of celebration, she thinks, because there's something *triumphant* in the song they're singing. And if it's a celebration, maybe that means the plague is over, or the fire consuming the city has finally burnt itself out, so it's not the end of the world after all. But when she looks from the hallway across her wide, empty room to the window, the night sky is still smeared with the colors of burning. She gets to her feet, wrapped in the yellow blanket, and goes to the window to find out what has happened. Through the bare branches of the trees growing beside the redbrick building, she can see that the street is *filled* with people. Never before has she seen so great a congregation of them, all in one place and at one time. Many of them are carrying torches, and so she guesses that maybe they're trying to empty the city of fire by hauling it away at the ends of these long guttering brands. Some of the people have drums and some flattened pieces of metal that they're banging with sticks or hammers or spoons or just their bare hands. Their song fills the night, though she'd have thought there was no room left anywhere for anything else, what with all the cold and the smoke and the falling ash, the light from the burning city, the wind, the filthy snow, and the low, glowing clouds pushing down from above. It's not a song she's ever heard before, not a pennywhistle song, and it seems to be built mostly of words and the banging, thumping, clanging sounds the people are making. *Help me, O Lord, My strength and rock; Lo, at the door I hear death's knock. Uplift thine arm, once pierced for me, that conquered death.* And she's delighted at this commotion, so much noise and movement, delighted at these strange new lyrics and the mystery of their meaning, and so she does not see everything there is to see, or remember how dangerous the city people are. She leans a little farther out, bracing herself against the snow and ice and soot-encrusted windowsill, trying to catch all the words and catch their meanings, too. *And set me free. Yet, if thy voice, in life's midday, recalls my soul, then I obey. In faith and hope Earth I resign, secure of heaven, for I am thine. My pains increase; haste to console; for fear and woe seize body and soul. Death is at hand.* But then she sees that the men and women are carrying something besides their drums and torches. There are tall poles strung with the limp bodies of dead rats. There are huge reed baskets filled with dead rats. There are wheelbarrows, and a metal cart drawn by an old mule, and bulging burlap sacks, all filled to overflowing with the corpses of rats. There are children, and they gaily dance in and out of the procession, swinging dead rats by their tails. And even as she comprehends *what* she sees, she also understands *why* they are doing this awful thing, that this must be the sacrifice that the snake beneath the bridge has demanded of them, and in return he has promised that there will be an end to the fire and the plague. For a moment, there's only silent horror at what they've done, at this senseless massacre and the desecration of all the murdered rats, so many of them that she wonders if any are left alive in all the world. Perhaps they've even managed to slay the God of all Rats. Perhaps they found the way down to his palace underground, and his beautiful body has been carved up and tossed into one of those burlap sacks or the pieces strung from a pole. They dance and sing that strange song and whack at their drums and sheets of corrugated tin, and when at last she finds her voice it is barely even a hoarse whisper above the noise of the mob. Nothing they will ever hear, no way she can ever stop them and whatever it is they've marched all this way to do. No way that she can fight something so cruel and clever as the snake, and now it is too late to even try. The rats are already dead. They died while she dozed on her mattress in the hallway, oblivious to the slaughter. Caught in steel traps or bludgeoned with mallets, crushed beneath bricks and stones or poisoned with arsenic or lye or anything else that was handy, at least a thousand easy ways for a man to kill a rat, and watching the delirious, torch-lit spectacle, she imagines all of them. Even over the noise, she can hear their dying screams and squeals, can see the blood-flecked jaws and the sea of shattered bodies, the scrabbling paws and broken bones caught between the merciless teeth of cats and dogs, those feckless, mercenary servants of man. And now the people at the front of the procession have reached the bridge, and they begin setting the dead rats afire and tossing them over the side into the river, flinging them down into *her* comforting river, her river that has been spoiled forever now. The swirling, traitorous waters open wide, accepting the dead and dragging them all straight down to the waiting snake, who must surely be watching this all from somewhere far below, smiling his wicked, scaly smile, pleased that they have done exactly as he has asked. Smiling that men may be bent to his will with so simple a thing as fear, with such a common thing as death, and smiling, too, because after countless millennia he's been avenged, the tables turned, and his old enemy has been laid low. She knows *all* these things, and she closes her eyes because she cannot stand the sight of it any longer. She sinks to the floor beneath the window, whispering futile prayers to a dead god, and she wonders how long it will be until the snake sends them to find her and take the pennywhistle. Not long, not long at all. Just as soon as the feast is done. She covers her ears, trying not to hear their wicked, wicked song of adulation, their hymn to the serpent below the bridge, but it slips in between her fingers: *My God! My Lord! Healed by the hand. Upon the earth once more I stand. Let sin no more rule over me; my mouth shall sing alone to thee. Though now delayed, my hour will come.* And then the room seems to sway and tilt beneath her, and there's only a moment of nausea before there's merciful silence and blackness and nothing more.

7.

When she wakes, the room is still dark, so either it's not yet morning, or the snake has used its magic and the blood of a million murdered rats to steal away the daylight for good. She isn't certain if she's actually awake or just dreaming, because there's only the sound of the wind and dry branches scraping against the walls of the redbrick building. The singing and drumming and shouting have stopped, though the air continues to reek of burning. She sits with her back to the plaster wall, counting heartbeats, and when she has reached one hundred, she gets slowly to her feet, ignoring the aches and cramps of stiff muscles, the numbness in her fingers and toes, the rumble in her belly. And, peering fearfully over the windowsill, she sees that the people from the city, exhausted by the murder they have done, by their celebration and the pilgrimage from the city, are all lying together asleep on the bridge. Some of their torches have been wedged into cracks in the masonry or tied to now-empty carts, and so there is still that wavering, wind-lashed light washing dimly across their sleeping faces. *Why have they not come for me?* she thinks. *Why has the snake not sent someone to kill me and take the pennywhistle so the backwards song can be played?* And then she wonders if maybe someone *has* already come, if one of them slipped in while she was asleep and discovered her secret hiding place beneath the loose floorboard. It may well be as simple as that, and the snake ordered them not to harm her, to leave her alive, the queen of the God of all Rats, that she will have to hear the backwards song and witness the end of all things. And then she scrambles across the freezing floor and pulls up the loose board to find that the wooden box is still there where she left it; opening the lid and looking inside, she sees that the pennywhistle is still there, too. So it is only the snake's arrogance that has spared her, believing he has won and now he can take the pennywhistle from her whenever he chooses, so there's still plenty of time to sleep off his gluttony, time enough to savor the victory before he sends someone, or slides up from the river to take it for himself. She glances over her shoulder at the window, and the clouds are still bloody with firelight. If the snake did promise the men and women that he would extinguish the fire in their city, he has lied to them. It occurs to her then that maybe they aren't sleeping at all, that possibly the snake has killed them, just as they killed the rats. Perhaps they all died screaming with his venom blazing in their veins, because he had no more use of them. She crawls back to the window and looks out again, and she can't believe that she ever found the river soothing, that it was ever anything but the black grave it has become. And then she sits down again and puts the pennywhistle to her lips. "Will you accept my gift?" the God of all Rats asked her all those many weeks ago, and she had. "And now," she whispers, "will you accept mine?" And she begins to play, something that starts out low and mournful, remembering the time *before* time, acknowledging that age when there was only the void and the rats. But then her fingers warm and loosen with movement and the effort of playing the pennywhistle, and the song and the story tumble along, chasing one another, rushing ahead and spilling their wild magic into the night. With this old brass whistle, the rats created all that is, all that has ever been, and she knows that it still holds within it the power to create, to make something where there was before nothing at all. She has learned its ways and has wielded it to fashion the tales that have kept her company and given her joy and a few scraps of courage against the endless string of days and nights, against the yawning sky and the biting cold, against hunger and her fear of the men and women of the city. And so she plays a healing song, an awakening song, her gift to the God of all Rats, which is a song and a story that will call the murdered rats back from the murky prison of death. *Come back to me, come back for me, come back to me,* and without looking she knows that the water below the bridge has begun to seethe and roil, and already she can hear the angry, cheated howl of the snake as rat souls and mangled rat bodies slide free of his suffocating coils. She wants to look, to be *sure,* wants to *see* their resurrection with her own eyes, but then she might miss a note or only half a note, or the tune might fall flat, the story faltering as she fumbled some indispensable bit of the song. One mistake and the pennywhistle's magic could yet be defeated and undone. So she sits on the floor, and she plays. She plays as she has never played before, as she has never believed she *could* play. When her chapped lower lip splits open, her blood is blown out through the whistle and spatters on the floor, but she understands that this only makes the pennywhistle stronger. Outside the redbrick building, through the trees and weeds and down the street past sooty drifts of snow and dangling icicles and burnt-out, discarded torches, the river opens a second time, breached like clouds parting after a thunderstorm. The river splits wide, even as her lip has split, and it bleeds rats. And still she plays, because she has found a verse that will seal the snake away forever, snaring it in the water-logged roots of a willow tree that fell and sank into the river years and years ago. She plays until there is no hope the snake will ever escape, and now she can hear the rats scrambling through the mud and muck and rushes and over cobblestones, flowing like a furious living wave across the bridge and the men and women and children whom she'd only imagined were dead. Because now they've begun to shriek and curse as the wet rats fall upon them, and *still* her fingers move, faster and faster, racing up and down the pennywhistle, as sure of herself as any god has ever been. Knowing now exactly how the story ends, she plays on and on and on, finishing what she's started.

Metamorphosis A

Though she asked, and though she asked me three times, no, I would not go down with her. I would not follow, tagging along like Orpheus or Dante or Hermód or some other dumb son of a bitch walking into Hell. Not down those slick black November side streets and the narrow alleys and empty warehouses and steep, winding stairwells leading never up, but always and only *down*, through oases of incandescent glare, through dust and musty vales of shadow; warped doors hanging loose on bent and rusted hinges—if there were ever any doors at all—opening at last into basements and subbasements, cellars waiting above sub-cellars, a mile or so of old train tunnel, various abandoned excavations, sewers gone dry and littered with a century or two of mummified shit and rat carcasses, caverns constructed by the hand of man three or four hundred years ago. All of those forgotten, barren places beneath our feet that would serve as the necessary stations of her crucifixion.

She was gone a long time. Longer than I'd expected. I just sat at the window and watched a dirigible burning above the river, smoking cigarettes and wondering if that was the last I'd ever see of her, the last of us, too. The dirigible seemed to take hours to fall, which can't be right, and it drifted like a wounded demon, dripping liquid fire and wreckage and charred bodies. I might have felt guilt, that I'd allowed her to go alone. But it might have only been disgust at myself, and maybe apprehension, maybe dread. I know I am a coward, and I know that she's insane. It's not a good combination, and by the time the dirigible finally gave up the ghost and fell like a broken, battle-weary angel, by then I'd begun to think it would be better for us both, and perhaps a few other people, if she *didn't* come back.

Which is not the same thing as not caring what had happened to her, or wishing she were dead. It's not the same thing at all.

And then I heard footsteps in the hallway, your key rattling in the lock, and so I lit another cigarette and kept my eyes on the window. Another hour or so and it would finally be dawn, and I was no more prepared for that cold morning light than I was for the sight of whatever the descent and the long, long climb back up to the world had made of you.

You don't say a word to me, which, I suppose is more than I deserve. I sit and smoke my cigarette and listen to you doing something in the kitchen. I think that I hear silverware and the refrigerator door open and shut. I look at the clock for the first time since you left, and it seems impossible that only a little more than six hours have passed. I think that I might hear you crying, a very brittle sound I'd rather not be hearing, and I get up and go to the bathroom because I have to piss, and I don't want to be sitting here listening to you sobbing in the fucking kitchen. I don't want to sit here trying to figure out what I'll say when you walk through the bedroom door, or what I'll see, or what you'll say to me. In the bathroom, I run cold water in the sink and splash it on my face. I look like shit. I might have shaved two days ago. There are circles beneath my eyes the color of bruised apples. My lips are so chapped they've been bleeding. There's a speck of dried blood on my chin.

I flush the toilet, and for a few seconds there's only the urine-stained water swirling round and round the rust-stained porcelain, convenient gravity and PVC plumbing there to take away my body's waste and spit it out somewhere faraway or far below where I'll never have to look at it again.

I keep waiting for you to call my name.

I *keep* waiting.

I finish my cigarette and drop the butt into the toilet, where it hisses briefly before I flush again.

When I give up and open the bathroom door, you're lying naked on the bed. You've pushed all the blankets off onto the floor, so there's just the pillows and dingy white sheets that hardly ever get washed or changed, and you're lying there on your back, staring up at the ceiling. You don't say a word, and you don't turn your head to look at me, either. Your long legs are spread so I can see your cunt, your knees bent, your feet braced flat against the sheet, all of it to make me think of a pregnant woman trying to push out something wet and helpless and squalling, something parasitic that's been carried for nine months, but enough's enough. I don't need you to tell me I've got it all backwards. But then I always have.

"Does it hurt?" I ask, because I can't stand the silence any longer, and for a moment or two I think you're not going to answer me.

"No," you say, and there's nothing the least bit different about your voice. I'd thought that there would be, that surely it would have changed somehow, but it's only your voice. You sound tired. You sound like you've been crying. And that's when I notice the aluminum canister lying on the bed beside you. It's not much larger than a thermos. There are runes or some sort of Egyptian hieroglyphics etched into it, and droplets of condensation have formed on the metal.

"Are you going to watch?" you ask me, but you're still staring at the ceiling. Your eyes are far away, and I think maybe they're still down *there* somewhere, that, possibly, whatever it was you saw at the end of all those stairs and cellars and tunnels, it wasn't the sort of thing you can ever *stop* seeing.

"Is that what you want?" I ask.

"It doesn't matter anymore. But you watch, if you want. I'm not afraid to be alone, but if you want to watch, it won't make any difference."

Your bare feet are black with soot or dirt or whatever filth you've tracked back up from the deep places below the city. There are long scrapes on your legs, like maybe you ran into a patch of brambles along the way. And then I notice the welt beneath your chin, flesh gone puffy and purple and already turning necrotic. I might think it was only a bad spider bite, if I didn't know better. If I didn't know about the stingers and the venom, the kiss of Athena to switch off your immune system. To make you receptive to what's still to come.

"My throat's sore," you tell me. "That's all. I'm tired, and my throat's a little sore."

"I could call an ambulance," I say, taking one hesitant step nearer the bed. "There might still be time."

And then you do turn your head, and you look straight look at me, and I know that it's much, much too late for ambulances and doctors and whatever they can or cannot do. Too late for intervention. I think your eyes must have drowned down there; I think this is only a corpse that has floated back up to me.

"You may watch," you tell me again, your voice turned hard and sharp as ice. I pretend that's not your voice at all (though it is), that they've already hollowed you out, and this thing on our bed is hardly more than a puppet, a crumpled marionette of flesh and *papier-mâché* with your face and your drowned blue eyes.

"I'll just sit by the window," I reply. "If you need anything, I'll do what I can."

You nod and then go back to staring at the ceiling, but your expression, your puppet's sneer is there to say so much more, to remind me that I've missed my chance, so fuck me. I let you go down to the abyss alone, down to those hungry, patient whisperers huddled in places where it is never anything but night. I waited up here and stared out a goddamn window at the city lights and the night sky and a burning dirigible. I can't help you, not now, and I deserve to see everything that's coming. I deserve to sit here in my chair and watch and know that there's absolutely nothing I can do to help.

I know what to expect, more or less, like almost anyone these days would know what to expect. I sat through one of those interminable films the WHO or CDC or whoever it is that thinks they're monitoring this mess keeps cranking out. That was months ago, because it was still summer. It was summer, a hundred plus in the shade but not a tree in sight, and I'd only gone into the theater because I thought it would be air-conditioned, but then it wasn't. No luck, buddy. The AC's busted, on the fritz, kaput, been busted for weeks now; so I sat there in the muggy darkness with half a dozen or so strangers and watched the screen through the grey haze of other people's cigarette smoke. I had a warm bottle of beer from the concession stand, and so I sipped my beer and tried to ignore some guy one row in front of me and a few seats to my left who started masturbating as soon as the lights went down. Everyone else ignored him, too.

The film was narrated by someone pretty. I can't even recall if it was a man or a woman, just that they were clean and well-dressed and didn't look sick or hungry or scared. I suppose the world must still be filled with people like that, even if I never see them anymore.

The masturbating man kept whispering to himself or his dick or someone that he only imagined was there, someone only he could see. A woman a few rows farther down turned around twice and told him to shut up, but I don't think he heard her. I don't think he was listening.

I remember thinking how much the warm beer tasted like a mixture of soda water and cornflakes and then wondering how long it had been since I'd last eaten a bowl of cornflakes.

Up on the screen, the pretty, clean, healthy, well-dressed person was sitting at a table with a black man in a white lab coat, a very nervous-looking man whom I could tell didn't want to be sitting there answering the questions he was being asked, saying the things that he was saying, most of which were probably lies, anyway. He talked about the gold mines in South Africa and Siberia, the biology of extremophiles, endoliths, and cryptoendoliths, contaminated core samples, virulence, infectivity, and on and on and on. He said something like, "Epidemiology is concerned with the incidence of disease in a given population or populations, but it doesn't address questions of the *cause* of any particular individual's disease." Talking smaller and smaller circles round himself, as though words could form some protective mandala. The pretty narrator smiled a lot. The man in the lab coat never even smiled once.

There was a warning, disclaimer sort of thing then, the following footage contains graphic images not suitable for anyone under the age of whatever, eighteen, twenty-one, I don't know. The management assumes no responsibility. Etc. and etc. and so forth. The masturbating man made an excited, eager sort of noise, and I thought about getting up and moving to another seat near the back of the theater. Most of the seats were empty, after all. But I didn't move. I kept my seat and sipped my warm beer and watched.

The narrator kept referring to the thing onscreen as a "typical patient," but there wasn't much left that could have passed for human. It was locked inside some sort of isolation chamber, glovebox, airlock quarantine sort of contraption with tall plexiglas sides. There was someone in a white biohazard suit standing behind the glovebox reading a computer monitor. The thing inside, cradled in what looked like orange gelatin, quivered and shifted about in the tank while the narrator's voice-over talked about advances in treatment and serums and shit like that.

So, I know what is coming.

I know what she went down there to find, and what she found, and what is coming. More or less.

"One significant hurdle facing doctors is the apparent willingness of many people to be infected, despite these horrific consequences," the narrator said. Or they said something very similar. It was months ago, and I can't remember precisely, and it doesn't matter, anyway.

And then the film moved on to a psychologist and an anthropologist and a priest, all of them talking about the social and ethical ramifications, the "problem" of euthanasia and life termination, cognitive and neurocognitive consequences, the Lamb of God and the Seven Seals, the fourth horseman of the Apocalypse, crap like that, blah, blah, fuckity blah, and I finished my beer and set the bottle down between my feet. But I didn't leave. I'd paid to see it all—no, I'd paid for air conditioning, but I *had* paid my money, and now I was going to see it all.

And I did. I saw it all. Everything they were willing to show. And whatever they weren't, well, I'm sure I'll be seeing very soon now.

I wasn't watching when she finally opened the aluminum canister. I was fading in and out, dozing in my uncomfortable chair by the window, the winter sunlight falling warm across my face, but I *heard* it clearly, and the noise immediately brought me back around. First, a distinct *click* and then the loud *pop* when she broke the inner hermetic seal, a sucking sound like someone taking a deep breath through pursed lips as she pulled the plug and the negative pressure inside the canister quickly equalized with the pressure in the bedroom.

It's loose in the room with us.

And I have nothing whatsoever to fear, not for my own safety, my own morphological integrity (as the nervous man in the lab coat might have said). Because I have not been kissed. I did not follow her down and through those dim subterranean paths to receive the gift, to offer myself up to the devouring shadows. I want to get up and leave the room. Leave the apartment. Leave the building. Call one of the government hotlines when I'm miles and miles away from this place, and the guys in the baggy Tyvek coveralls and booties can deal with her, all those hazmat sons of bitches with their protocols and respirators and decontaminates.

But I don't leave, because I told her I'd be there if she needed anything.

I swear that I will not watch, though. I sit at the window and stare out at the early afternoon sun shining down on the slate and tarpaper rooftops and snagging in the high, bare limbs of trees, sparking on the filthy green river where no visible evidence of the fallen dirigible remains—all the world out there that may or may not have been touched by shiny aluminum canisters of their own.

"It's what I want," she says. "You have to understand that. Please—"

And I tell her to shut the hell up, that I don't want to hear that shit, and she does as I've asked.

But there are *other* sounds, which I know better than to try to put into words. There are sounds, and describing them is more than anyone can fairly ask of a confessed coward. There are *other* sounds, that's all. The noises *they* make, those busy, busy little fuckers, those industrious fiends, asleep in the gardens of Proserpine for however many hundreds of millions of years until someone breaks their stasis, someone wakes them up, and suddenly there's not another second to spare.

She gasps, and I know that it's started.

I cover my ears, because I think she's about to scream. I cover my ears, and I wait.

The sun through the windowpane is so warm, and I'm tired, not having slept the night before, and I drift away and dream of old subway tunnels winding this way and that, ending abruptly at the edge of a vast black lake somewhere far below the city. I stand on the shore, amid shattered railroad ties, gravel ballast, and buckled steel rails, and the air stinks of mold and creosote, and that water is as smooth and dark as volcanic glass. If I know that I'm dreaming, I do not *know* that I know. I've come here to find her, because I let her go alone, and I don't want her to be alone down here, this place as close to all those mythical hells as anyone will ever come, and I don't want to spend the rest of my life hating myself for not having followed.

There's a staccato *plip*, like a single pebble dropped into that still black water, and there are ripples moving slowly towards the shore.

And I have never been even half this afraid.

And I open my eyes.

The sun is low, that last and latest bit of day before twilight sets in, so I must have been asleep for hours. My neck is stiff, and my back hurts from sleeping in the chair. The bedroom stinks like…I could not have said then *what* that smell was. Those smells, plural. But now I would say it was the commingled stench of mildew and rotting vegetation, something gone ripe way at the back of the fridge, but also a meaty, bloody, metallic sort of smell. And something else, too, something like ammonia or bleach that burns my eyes and stings my nostrils and throat.

I gag and quickly cover my mouth, not wanting to vomit, become at last so fucking dainty here in the gaping jaws of madness—not like me at all—and that's when I glance over my shoulder.

I'm still so, so near the terrible dream of that place down there below, down where the subway tracks end, that endless Stygian sea stretching away into nothingness, and for a moment none of it seems like anything but some new convolution in the nightmare.

For a moment, I have the distance and the objectivity to merely *see* what you've become.

A moment for my mind to take one perfect snapshot.

I know it's you. Because I saw the film, remember? I know it's you, because what else *would* it be, lying there on our bed? But it looks more like a chrysalis spun from gossamer strands of sugar or a hundred thousand crystalline filaments. The tall interlace of twisting needle spines, translucent and glittering in the fading day, that seem to strain for the low ceiling as if seeking some new anchorage. The spines sprout from that more substantial mass curled fetal on the bed and sunk partway into the sheets and mattress. It pulsates faintly, gently, because of course you still need air. Of course you're still drawing breath. There's an iridescent, peacock-blue cleft where your vagina used to be, and it leaks a steady, viscous stream onto the ruined bedclothes. There are a few charcoal-colored swellings clustered along the hardening outer rim of that cleft, and I know what those are, too. Ejected colonies of the parasite—of course, you would never have let me use that ugly word, *parasite*—microbial colonies that have died and so now are being expelled from the womb to make way for the living. How many countless generations were conceived while I slept in my chair and dreamed of that black lake? How many were born and nurtured deep within the hive of you, and how many billions must have done their determined, busy work and perished when their time was done?

These are not sane thoughts. But I will never have sane thoughts again, so it hardly worries me.

Your face is gone, obliterated by these relentless alterations, and I think that's probably the only bit of mercy I've got coming to me. All of this, but at least I do not have to look into your blue eyes and see whatever might have been there at the end, whatever pain or loss or regret, whatever confusion or terror. Worse yet, whatever ecstasy or relief. There are two short stumps where your arms once were, and a great bloodless gash between your shoulder blades. If any part of your brain, of your *mind*, has been spared, it must have been moved elsewhere, hidden perhaps in that dark pulsating mass below the spines. There's a wet splitting sound then, and something scarlet, something like a tongue or proboscis or the grotesque parody of a penis, lolls from that bloodless gash and flops about a moment on the bed, pushing the pillows aside.

And I'm on my knees then, as if I'd worship what they have made of you, as you must have worshipped in those secret underground temples, offering your furtive prayers and supplications to ancient bacterial gods for the grace of this change, praying to shed your unwanted and unyielding humanity. I am on my knees, breathing you in and breathing them in with you, wishing now that I'd been kissed, as well. For they will have nothing of me until after the sting. Until Athena sees what I have spun, my own conceited mockeries of Zeus and his indiscretions, his bedding of Europa and Leda and Danae, and then she will bless me as she has blessed you.

And then I will receive my own silver canister.

Then, maybe, I will at last forget the film and the masturbating man, your eyes and your kisses and what I now see lying on the bed we shared, writhing with new life in the last red-orange wash of day.

The Sphinx's Kiss

Long after midnight, but still a thousand years left until dawn, and I don't know if I said that aloud or someone else did or if it's something I only thought. The air is so close, so thick with the smoke of hookahs and braziers, cigarettes and cigars, marijuana and frankincense and white sage, and my eyes burn and water. Here I am lying flat on my back on the floor, gazing up into that fuming grey atmosphere, looking for air that is still fit to breathe. The antique carpet beneath me, I think it might only be a rusty blanket of autumn leaves scattered here for the dry amusement of old men who have seen too many Octobers come and go, weary dry old men looking backwards from their Decembers. But then the smoky clouds part above me, and the boy in the fox mask and cumbersome Marie Antoinette gown crouches next to me, and the carpet does not crackle beneath his bare feet the way that autumn leaves would crackle. So it must only be a carpet after all, some priceless, threadbare Anatolian or Persian artefact, stained with piss and countless shades of alcohol, puke and cum and no few drops of blood.

The fox boy reaches between my legs and tugs playfully at my cock, and I realize I must have passed out after that last kitty flip and wonder how long I was down and if I've missed anything that matters. My head's buzzing like there's nothing left now inside my skull but wasps, only the X and Ketamine and gin and whatever else I've swallowed since sundown, but it *feels* more like red wasps and honey bees, a whole stinging hive crawling about right there behind my eyes. The fox boy bites his lip and smoke swirls about the long snout he wears because that's what he drew from the hat. A slip of yellow paper with *Vulpes* written on it in the spider's scrawl of one of the dry old men, and so he found his mask waiting among all those others yet unclaimed, there on the mahogany dining table. Sturdy painted latex and an elastic string, their stylish, grotesque guise to hide the upper half of his face, and so the night worked its casual lycanthropy upon that slender, red-headed boy, and here he is a fox. And here I am his mate for this long, long night, because my slip of yellow paper also had *Vulpes* written upon it, like most of the guests would know Latin or Greek or even care. But, conveniently, someone was standing there at the table to translate, to say what's what, so no one gets confused and takes a tiger when he's drawn *Taxidea* and is only entitled to a badger.

The fox boy leans over and laughs and teases me with the tip end of his nimble tongue. His dress rustles the way the carpet did not, so maybe *he's* the one who's really only made of leaves. And his pretty lips are painted some shade that is neither red nor orange, so there's another reason to suspect there's less to him than silk and petticoats and that black vulpine nose. I tug roughly at his skirts, managing to sit upright despite my dizzy, buzzing head, and he stops licking me and says something about the show, that I haven't missed the show, or that we'll miss the show if we don't hurry. I try hard to remember what he's talking about—the show—and I want another drink. He helps me to my feet with strong arms, and here I stand in the smoke, naked except for my fox's mask and his lipstick smeared on my dick. And I'm still blinking and squinting and rubbing at my eyes when one of the old men comes up to us in his raven's mask and tuxedo of charcoal feathers, something even prettier than my fox boy hanging on his arm. Something pale in a sleek black mask, black whiskers that almost seem to twitch, and a silicone plug up his ass to hold that bushy black tail in place.

It's a fucking mink, the fox boy whispers loudly in my ear and giggles, and the dry old man's rheumy eyes glare out past his beak. The mink pretends not to look offended, and makes a great show of playing with his tail.

"I hope you two are enjoying the festivities," says Old Man Raven. All the old men are birds—ravens and crows, owls and cranes and crested cockatoos. They know their parts and do not have to draw slips of yellow paper from the hat. Tonight, they will crown their King of Birds, and we are merely the lowly beasts of the court.

"Exquisite," the fox boy tells him, the fox boy who is not me. "Way better than last year, in my opinion."

"You think so?" asks Old Man Raven. "*Way* better? Very good, then. I was afraid that some certain something might be missing."

Their words spar and dance through the haze like the stinging insects in my head, all whirring wings and prickling legs and dripping, venomous barbs, and I see that the mink boy has stopped stroking his tail and is busy stroking his spectacularly long penis, instead. *Two tails are better than one*, I think, and maybe I laugh, too, because now the mink boy is making a face like something smells bad, and Old Man Raven is looking straight at me. His eyes are red, but I know that's only my imagination and the drugs I've taken.

"Your friend here," he says to the fox boy. "It's his first time, isn't it? Keep an eye on him. We wouldn't want him getting in over his head, would we?"

And then they leave us standing there, Old Man Raven and his sneering mink vanishing abruptly into the smoke, and my fox boy says don't you mind them, all the minks are shits, and *none* of the birds can get it up without fucking Viagra or Cialis or whatever the hell.

"Don't you sweat it, *kitsune*," he says, but right about now I'm wishing I'd stayed home, ignored the stories you hear about secret societies and parties like this, offers of free drugs and freer sex, and stayed the fuck home.

The fox boy leads me to a sofa, garish brocade upholstery the colour of cranberries, but I have to admit it's more comfortable than the floor, and we sit together as the birds and their pets come and go, filing past with the sort of stiff grace and affected majesty that mere masks and dress up cannot remedy. A waiter comes with a silver serving tray of martinis, and I snag two of them. All the waiters are bulldogs. My fox boy says the waiters are always bulldogs, except for one year when they were mice and everyone was confused all night long. I sip at my martini, and my fox boy steals my olive and puts it into his own glass.

"Not much longer until the show," he says, lapping at his drink. And now, if I squint, I can make out a sort of low stage or canopied dais that's been set up against one wall of the loft, dominated by an elaborate golden throne. There are animal pelts draped across the arms and seat of the throne and great bunches of white flowers set out all around the stage.

"What the fuck?" I ask the fox boy. "Is that where the King of Birds gets his fucking crown?"

"No, it is not," he says and scowls at me, and I almost feel sorry for him, getting saddled with such a clueless git. "The King *has* no throne except the sky, and he has no crown at all."

"So, what's *that*?"

"The *show*," he says, his orange-red mouth making a perfect 0 of the word. "You'll see, *kitsune*. Be patient."

"Suck my cock," I reply, and he takes me literally and gets down on his knees in that absurd dress and takes me in his mouth, so that's taking me twice over. I shut my eyes, not wanting to be here, not wanting to see anymore—the dry old men and their frivolous playthings, the playthings who think this is fucking Paradise on Earth. I want to be home in my cruddy little apartment with my fox boy, only he wouldn't be a fox, and he wouldn't be attired for the court of *Louis le Dernier*, either. After the sex, we could watch an old movie and have microwave popcorn and maybe go out somewhere for coffee. Or we could just curl up and sleep. Either way would be fine with me.

His tongue flicks quickly, expertly, back and forth across the underside of my dick, and he holds me gently with his teeth.

And behind my closed eyes, we're lying in the fold-away bed. The window's open despite the cold and the snow, and the curtains flutter and flap in the icy wind. My fox boy is asleep beside me, and I'm trying to remember his name. I hear sirens and smell the smoke a moment or two later. Not my building, though, somewhere else in flames, somewhere else burning down to the ground and roasting a hundred people alive. And I'm about to go back to sleep, when I see something at the window, hungry eyes flashing iridescent in the dark, and then the mink slips silently over the windowsill, smooth as satin, and it's there in the room with us. I can hear its claws clicking on the hardwood, and there's a huge raven watching from the sill. The raven knows what's coming, just like it knows about the fire, just like it knows my fox boy's secret name.

And then I open my eyes, open them wide, because I don't need to see whatever the raven knows will happen next, and because my fox boy's tongue is magic and I'm coming so hard I think this might finally be the day and the second and the place that my heart stops beating, and the wasps and bees will be happy to know they have my head all to themselves. Now there's only the smoky room again and my hands tangled in his hair, only the animal masks and the sounds of men laughing and fucking and doing god knows what else to one another. He looks up at me, the fox boy who isn't me, and wipes his lips and smiles.

"Is that better, *kitsune*?"

"How about we both get the hell out of here?" I ask him, needing another drink so bad it hurts, not even sure where the last one went.

"Oh, no," he says, standing and dusting off the front of his gown. "We can't do that. That's not the way it works. No one leaves before the show. No one. Anyway, all the doors are locked from the outside. The windows, too. Didn't they tell you?"

"You're shitting me."

"No, *kitsune*. I'm not into that."

One of the bulldogs shows up then, this time with shot glasses of tequila and lime, and again I take two. Maybe, I think, there was more to the kitty flips than ecstasy and ket, maybe a dash of LSD, just to spice things up. Maybe more than a dash.

"Anyway," my fox boy says, turning towards the stage. "It's about to begin."

"What's about to begin?" and I toss back one of the tequilas before he can answer me.

"The changing of the guard," he says in a tone that is only slightly exasperated, only vaguely condescending, and he sits back down on the sofa and kisses me. He tastes like lipstick and semen and alcohol. And I realize that there's not so much noise as before, and almost everyone's turning towards the stage and the golden throne. There are black candles lit now, set out all around the edges of the dais, dozens of them, and on either side of the throne stands a nude man with a purple blindfold tied about his face. Each of the men swings a smoking censer suspended from chains. I want to ask why they're blindfolded, these men, why blindfolds instead of masks, but know my fox boy would roll his eyes at my ignorance, so I settle for the second tequila, instead.

"Like Mardi Gras," I mutter, speaking to no one but myself, perhaps believing I'd not actually *spoken* at all, and my fox boy sighs and shakes his head, but keeps his eyes on the stage.

"No, it's not like Mardi Gras," he says.

"I bet you it fucking is," I tell him, because both the shot glasses are empty and he's already disgusted with me again, so what the hell have I got to lose?

"It's not like that at all. You'll see."

"Ye Mistick Krewe of Comus," I say and lay my head on his shoulder, wanting to shut my eyes, wishing there would only be darkness if I did—not the wasps, not the staring raven on my windowsill, not the grinning mink boy creeping across my bedroom floor. "Endymion, Rex, Bacchus, Orpheus. The King of fucking Carnival. I've *been* to New Orleans."

"I'm sure you have, *kitsune*. Now shut up and watch."

"The goddamn Zulu Social Aid and Pleasure Club. I know *exactly* what's going on here, what all these queer old fucks are up to with their hokey-ass rituals and boy toys." But I'm not even fooling myself, and I have no idea what these dry old men with bird faces have set in motion. All of them rich and untouchable and stranded way out there in the cruel wastes of December, perched on the high-voltage wires strung across the end of the year, the end of life, and staring greedily, jealously back past crackling autumn leaves and Persian rugs and pretty fox boys to all those long-lost Junes and Julys.

"You give great head," I say, and my fox boy laughs.

Now the blindfolded men have been joined by a very tall ginger-skinned woman in a mask of peacock feathers. I'm about to tell my fox boy that I didn't think women were allowed. But then I see her dick, so never mind those perfect breasts and brown nipples and the yellow-brown curves of her hips and belly and legs. A she-male or some other transgendered creature, and maybe this will start to make sense in another minute or two, but I doubt it. There's a crimson jewel like a liquid drop of ruby poured into her navel and a belt of gold coins jingling about her waist, silver bracelets about her wrists and ankles, and around her throat a necklace of bleached white bones. She's too far away for me to guess what the bones might have come from. She bows to the crowd, and the crowd applauds.

"Okay," I say. "I will admit I didn't see that one coming."

"She is the Lady Salomé," my fox boy says; his green eyes sparkle, and I think I might have heard a scrap of something like reverence in his voice.

"Well, in case you haven't noticed, she's got an even bigger shlong than that mink son of a bitch."

"You're physically incapable of shutting up, aren't you?" my fox boy asks, and I don't bother to answer him. I look around for one of the bulldogs, but they all seem to have vanished.

"She's the daughter of King Herod," my fox boy says, and I'm straining to think through the fog of booze and drugs and wasps and crackling leaves, trying to figure out what the hell any of this has to do with the dry old men and their King of Birds, when the Lady Salomé is joined by Old Man Raven himself. He wears an elaborate golden crown, and I think the crown must be meant to be the sun, that somehow Old Man Raven has climbed into the heavens and managed to pull down the sun so that this night might go on forever, and we will always be locked in here with him, his private, pretend menagerie. He wears a long purple robe over his tuxedo, purple to hide his feathers the way purple hides the eyes of the men at either side of the throne. He bows to Salomé, and there's more drunken applause.

"Fucking Mardi Gras bullshit," I hear myself say, my words seeming to reach me from far, far away. I'm still resting my head on the shoulder of my fox boy, even though I'd have a better view if I sat up straight.

"No, but soon you'll see," my fox boy replies.

But I'm losing interest and thinking about my cock in his mouth, thinking maybe I should be a gentleman and return the favor, when everyone crowded into the loft—all the pets and the dry old men and even my fox boy—begins booing loudly. Some of them are cursing and shaking their fists at the ceiling, so I sit up to see for myself, tired of trading my questions for scowls. And I see that now a very muscular man in a leopard mask, dressed like a Roman centurion, is leading an emaciated, bearded man clothed only in rags roughly towards the stage. The bearded man's hands are bound behind his back, and his legs are cuffed, as well. He wears no mask at all.

"That is Jokanaan, the Prophet," my fox boy says, pointing towards the stage. "He is being brought before Lady Salomé and the King by Naaman, the executioner. This is the night of his judgment."

"You want me to blow you?" I ask him, already growing bored again and hoping maybe we can slip away together, find some unoccupied corner or closet or something of the sort, and leave the rest to their theatrics. But my fox boy only shakes his head and shushes me. He isn't going anywhere, not until it's over and done with, whatever *it* might be, and I wish once more that I wasn't so fucked up and it was safe to just shut my eyes and wait for all this pomp and fucking circumstance to pass me by.

"Do not *talk*," my fox boy whispers through clenched teeth. "It will not be much longer now."

The she-male or transsexual or whatever it might be—Salomé, the woman in the mask of peacock feathers—takes a sudden, eager step towards the bearded man. He keeps his eyes on the floor, or his feet, or both.

"Jokanaan!" cries out the Lady Salomé, and the booing and catcalls die away as suddenly as they began.

"Who speaketh?" asks the bearded man in rags.

"I am amorous of thy body, Jokanaan. Let me *touch* thy body!"

"Back, daughter of Sodom!" growls the ragged man, coming abruptly to life now, and I don't care, only want to taste my fox boy's lips again and find a bulldog with a sterling silver tray of martinis. But he's watching the show, my scarecrow bundled from autumn leaves and carpet scraps and stuffed into that fox-faced countenance and that immense, rustling gown.

"Touch me not!" howls the prophet. "Profane not the temple of the Lord God."

"Speak again, Jokanaan. Thy voice is wine to me!"

"Oscar Wilde," I sigh, and my fox boy looks away from the stage long enough to glare at me. I think his eyes are green berries not yet ripened, something that will turn red, then black, something for the beaks of the dry old men to pluck out and devour.

"*What?*" he asks, sounding genuinely angry now for the first time. "What are you talking about?"

"You know. It's Oscar Wilde. But it's all out of order. And where's Herodias and the young Syrian? They should both be in this scene, I think."

He's still glaring at me, those green berry eyes, those eyes I might like to taste myself—sour, but with some promise of sweetness yet to come.

"I'll find you later," he says coldly. "Maybe. Maybe I'll find you later." And then he's up off the sofa and disappearing into the smoke and the crowd before I can stop him, before I can say no, I'm sorry, don't leave me all alone in this place. And as he goes, I see there's a hole cut neatly into the back of his dress for two fox tails, luxurious tawny fur tipped with warning dabs of white and grown so long and bushy that they almost drag the floor behind him. And it's only the drugs that make them twitch and wag like living things. Only the drugs, the X and ketamine, the liquor and pot and whatever clandestine substances I might have unwittingly ingested, and nothing more. Nothing more at all. I let him go. I do not follow. I'll find him later, I tell myself, when this shit's over, and I'll make nice and apologize.

"Who is this woman who is looking at me?" asks the ragged man in chains. "I will not *have* her look at me. Wherefore doth she look at me, with her golden eyes, under her gilded eyelids? I know not who she is. I do not *desire* to know who she is. Bid her begone. It is not to her that I would speak."

"I am Salomé, daughter of Herodias, Princess of Judæa."

And now the Lady Salomé takes another step towards the cringing prophet. I glance from the stage to the crowd, hoping for some glimpse of my vanished fox boy. But there are only minks and tigers and lynxes, rabbits and toads and a hedgehog or two.

"Speak again, Jokanaan," purrs Salomé. "Thy voice is as music to mine ear."

"Daughter of Sodom," the prophet moans and tries to pull free of the executioner's grip. "Come *not* near me! But cover thy face with a veil, and scatter ashes upon thine head, and get thee to the desert, and seek out the Son of Man."

"Who is he, this Son of Man?" asks the Lady Salomé, standing so close now to the bearded man that her breasts brush against him. "Is he as beautiful as thou art, Jokanaan?"

"Get thee *behind* me! I hear in the palace the beating of the wings of the angel of death."

"Finish him!" someone shouts from the crowd, and the Lady Salomé grins a wide carnivorous grin for her audience. And I see that her teeth are not human teeth, but the sharp teeth of some night-stalking beast, the teeth of a shadow slipping over the windowsill.

"Put the sad old bastard out of his misery!" shouts someone else, a boy in a wolf mask snuggled up next to one of the owls.

"Fuck *that*! Put him out of *ours*!" shouts one of the rabbits.

"*Peace!*" bellows Old Man Raven with a voice like thunder heard from many miles away. "You are *always* crying out, you lot. You cry out like a *beast of prey*. Your voices weary me. *Peace*, I tell you!" And then he turns to the ginger-skinned creature. "Salomé, think on what thou art doing. It may be that this man comes from God. He is a *holy man*."

The crowd snickers, and there's a smattering of applause. "Indeed, he is!" shouts a rabbit. "He is *wholly* limp and flaccid!" An eruption of laughter then, and I want to go after my fox boy now. Not later. Later, he might have found someone else. Later, he might not even remember me.

"I will kiss thy mouth, Jokanaan," Lady Salomé tells the prophet, speaking past that mouthful of dagger teeth, her voice even more poisonous than the stingers in my head.

"I will not *look* at thee," the bearded man replies, his voice beginning to quaver. "Thou art accursed, Salomé, thou art accursed."

And now she seizes the bearded man by the jaw and forces his head up and back so he's staring directly into her predatory eyes. "But I *will* kiss thy mouth, Jokanaan," she tells him. "You will see. I will kiss thy mouth."

And then the crowd falls silent, and I can feel the simmering expectation lacing that silence like strychnine. The executioner draws his sword, and even through the smoke, the blade glints dully, and I know it's not a prop, not some toy for pantomimes and passion plays. The Lady Salomé releases her grip on the prophet's jaw, then turns and ascends the low stage and takes her place upon the golden throne. The silence has grown so heavy, it will soon crush me flat, I think, and I wish I were still lying unconscious and unknowing on the autumn carpet, or that my fox boy and I were still curled together in my fold-away bed, safe and warm beneath clean flannel sheets and goose-down comforters.

Look away, I hear my fox boy say, my rusty October scare-crow cooped up inside my aching skull with all the wasps and honey bees. But I'm not so far gone I don't know it's only *me* speaking to *me*, because he would *never* have me look away. He would have me see it *all*, would have me stare into the abyss until I am blind and can see no more, and still he would not have me look away.

The executioner—whose name I have already forgotten—raises his sword, and surely this is as far as it goes. Surely, this is where it *ends*, and in a moment there will be gales of laughter, fucking *hur-ricanes* of laughter, and I will feel so foolish at the way my heart has begun to race and the cold sweat beading on my palms.

The sword comes down, cleanly dividing the bearded man's head from his shoulders. He does not scream or cry out, does not make any sound at all that I can detect. Blood sprays from the stump of his neck, catching the executioner and Old Man Crow, though neither of them so much as flinch. His body sinks slowly to the floor; it seems to take a very long time for it to fall, and already Old Man Crow has retrieved the head and is placing it on a silver serving tray just like the ones the bulldogs have been using for martinis and cosmos and shots of tequila.

And I cannot look away. To save my life, I could not look away.

"Now, give me the head of Jokanaan!" says the Lady Salomé. And Old Man Crow, smug and bloodstained beneath purple robes and the sun fastened to his brow, offers up the severed head of the prophet to the temptress on her throne. She lifts the skull by its scraggly hair and holds it high so all may see her prize. Blood pools in her lap and streams down her long legs.

"Well," she says, "I know that thou *wouldst* have loved me, and the mystery of Love is greater than the mystery of Death."

And I feel hands upon my shoulders, smooth and soothing hands, hands that might yet deliver me from this nightmare, but I cannot look away.

"Ah," sighs Salomé. "Thou wouldst not suffer me to kiss thy mouth, Jokanaan. Well, I *will* kiss it now. I will *bite* it with my teeth as one bites ripe fruit. Yes, I will kiss *thy* mouth, Jokanaan," and then she does, pressing her lips to the lips of the dead man.

And where only a moment before, the room was filled with masked faces, it is occupied now with the snarling muzzles and snouts of things which have *never* been men and never shall be men, with lolling tongues and sharp white canines snapping viciously at the smoky air. And I feel my fox boy's paws resting there upon my shoulders, and he whispers the way a fox would whisper, "So you see, *kitsune*? Not like Mardi Gras at all. It is only like itself."

"Yes," I reply, wishing he would cover my eyes so I would no longer have to watch as the Lady Salomé finishes her kiss and begins to feed.

"I should not have left you here alone," my fox boy says. "That was not very kind of me."

"What happens next?" I ask him and realize that I am crying. "What do we do now?"

"Oh, that's the easy part," he replies. "Now we only have to take our places and join the dance." And a minute or two later, he steps around to the front of the cranberry-red sofa, my beautiful, beautiful fox boy in his Marie Antoinette gown, and I see that there is hardly any boy left of him now. Maybe there was never very much to begin with.

"You *can* dance, can't you?" he asks, and then he curtsies and winks and leads me down to the feast.

The Voyeur in the House of Glass

Somewhere out beyond this world which is only the rotating cages of steel and glass, the Barker's voice rises like a siren melody, luring in the hungry and unwary, singing a million wandering ships towards hidden reefs and jagged headlands. Two bits! he calls down from his high place in the spotlight glare. Just two measly bits, and we'll rip your hulls wide and drown you in the cold and briny deep, but never for a moment will you regret it, Sir or Madam. Never will you die unfulfilled. You'll thank us, yes you will, and ask for more. Just two bits and your immortal soul and whatever flesh you can or cannot spare—a small price to pay, a king's ransom, a steal, a bargain at thrice that amount.

And here I sit at the center of the wheel, the sparkling hub, the wheel within the wheel, sitting upright, never slumping on my stool, with his melodic naiad voice raining down upon me. But he did not sing me here; I would be here with or without his dulcet charms. I did not need the carnival's gaudy handbills, posters, and broadsheets to show me the way. I did not need enticements and main-street parades. My own bed of my own making, so leave me to it. Leave me here alone at the heart of the Barker's wheel. Do not even speak my name, for I will not look away. Not even for an instant. He has tried that trick so many times now, but I will not ever look away. This fantastic contraption built only for me— my desire's optic cradle—a hundred eyepieces positioned *just so* that I might simply lean forward and peer though, catching the precious light off roof and Porro prisms, images bounced with rare precision along the brass tubes of a dozen spy glasses. All these windows laced together with wooden struts and glue, steel rods and spot welds, thoughtful hand cranks placed *here* and *here* and *here* that I may easily reposition this or that portal to suit my momentary needs.

If there were ever a life lived outside this cell, a *before*, then it has passed far beyond the hinterlands of my memory. And I do not go looking for it. I have been always otherwise occupied. Always it seems, and so long has been my residency that I am become a standard, the old familiar beating heart of this sideshow. I have my own place on the painted canvas flaps, and men and women and children hand over their quarters and dollars and pennies for a glimpse of me, when all I ever do myself is glimpse.

Gaze upon him, Gentlemen and Ladies, this wretch so driven by appetite and lust that he might never linger very long at any delight, no matter how exquisite, for fear of what he might be missing elsewhere. Satisfaction, you ask? He's never heard the word. It isn't what he sees before him—though the beauty of it, the wonder and the horror and the glamour, might appease any one among you for all eternity—but what he *may yet see*, that nameless, unnamable sight which might await him. Do you begin to guess his affliction, he who stares so long and hard, but somehow never sees? Do not name it greed. That would be too gentle, love.

With this red switch *here*, I cause the wheel to advance, cell by cell, frame by frame, and with this green switch *here* I halt that advance until I am quite ready for it to begin anew. My bare feet rest upon an hourglass filled with sand from all the deserts of the world (or so the Barker says), and so I must surely appear like some absurd reject from a Tarot deck. The grains fall one by one, at the precise instant I flip the red switch, so ingenious is the contraption. Clever men build clever toys. The Barker tells the crowd the glass holds a million million grains. You do the math, he likes to say.

I flip the red switch.

And unseen machineries are set once more in motion—the spiral dance of spur gears and helical gears, cogs and shafts, rack and pinion clockworks, pulleys and ropes woven from the strongest hemp.

And the wheel turns.

Or I turn within the wheel. It hardly matters which.

The wheel or the hub, rolling ahead one space, and I squint through my favourite spyglass or set of antique opera glasses, waiting with sweaty palms and trembling hands as one scene is duly replaced by another. I have no doubt but that the delicious, bright anticipation *will* kill me, sooner or later, the anticipation like acid scalding my veins. And the whole wheel shudders, those great iron spokes groaning beneath the weight of their burden, and there is a distinct *click* somewhere in the mechanism as a new cell fills the space vacated by its predecessor. I flip the green switch, and somewhere above me in lofty sawdust balconies the crowd gasps, and the calliope falls silent, and the Barker waits for my reaction to this newest vision.

—The girl lies at the edge of the sea. She is not a mermaid, not yet, but this very morning she has come upon the oily carcass of a tiger shark, nine feet snout to tail, stranded in the seaweed and sand and shell litter. All she has ever wanted, this girl, a strong heterocercal tail, pectoral and anal and pelvic fins to carry her down into abyssal gloom that she might finally take her place in Neptune's lightless halls. She's hacked away the head and jaws a few inches above the gill slits and buries it in the dunes. Then she returns to the shark and slips herself inside, wriggling unwanted legs deep into the slimy, decaying gullet of the monster fish, burying herself to the hips. And with an upholstery needle and fine silk thread she begins to stitch herself to the dead shark, sewing her own pale, insufficient flesh to its sturdy predator's trunk. Later, she knows there will be some spark of magic, a marvelous alchemy of flesh and bone and cartilage to finish up the job, *if* she is strong and her will does not falter and she does not allow the pain to stay her hand. There will be a fusion, at the last, and answered prayers, and her pelagic longing alone will be enough to complete what she has begun. The sand all around her is spattered and splotched and stained with gore, and there's no telling which blood is her own and which belonged to the tiger shark. Hungry gulls and ravens wheel impatiently overhead, and the wind whispers secrets through green tangles of beach roses. She understands that she has to work fast, though the heat of the sun and the stink is making her ill, making her weak, slowing her down. She has to work fast, because the tide is coming in, lapping at that tail that is not yet hers...

Click.

And the wheel turns. For me, the wheel turns, again.

—Here now I see a dim and dingy room, unfurnished, three walls of bare concrete, and a young man kneels on the floor, or has fallen to his knees. I cannot tell which, and it does not necessarily matter. He wears nothing but a cloth blindfold, and his wrists are bound tightly behind his back. His head is bowed. Something immense squats over him, something glistening black as midnight, skin that may as well be leather or slick latex. It balances its bulk on long and jointed stilt legs. It purrs and sighs and sings the young man a breathless, toneless symphony of torture and transformation, of perdition and deliverance. I understand at once that he is not a prisoner. He is a willing supplicant, as this night-skinned thing would never come to a mere prisoner. It is a gourmand, this creature, and it does not come when called.

"Mother," he whispers. "Am I not pure? Have you not summoned me, and have I not answered the summoning?" The thing makes a comforting, keening sound, and now I see that the young man kneels within a wide ring of some white powder.

"I have waited so long," he says. "I have been faithful, and never has another touched me."

Hearing that, the black thing stops crooning and stands there above him, swaying almost imperceptibly on those long insectile legs. I quickly adjust the fine focus on a pair of Swarovski binoculars, pushing the insufficient opera glasses aside, and now I can plainly see the huge blisters on the creature's distended underbelly. The young man raises his head, looking up as though he can see through the blindfold and would now behold the sight of it, the sight of *her*. And then the blisters rupture, popping one after another, spraying him with foul corruption, the ichor of old and unimaginable infections. There is an expression of release and perfect elation on his upturned face, the face of a man standing at the gates of the only Heaven he has ever imagined.

Something the colour of a fresh burn slips from a slit set high on the creatures body, a proboscis or appendage of similar utility, perhaps, and it slithers and winds itself about the supplicant's torso, blindly feeling its way along the contours of his back, lingering at the base of his spine, and then sliding suddenly inside his ass. He moans and mutters obscene adjurations while the night-skinned thing fills him with its seed or eggs or something else that I cannot even begin to comprehend. I reach for the red switch.

Click.

And the cages roll, ferrying the scene away.

Above me, the Barker cackles through his megaphone.

Behold this Peeping Tom, this onlooker, starving though such a sumptuous banquet is laid out before him! Visions of such awful and exquisite ecstasy that even old Narcissus would be distracted from the reflection gazing back up at him from that still Thespian pool. But these spectacles we so thoughtfully provide are *not* enough, dear hearts. And why is this, might you inquire, being as you are of inquisitorial and meddlesome dispositions? Well, alas, I can only conjecture. But one must begin to suspect a certain peculiar emptiness in him, a hole or cavity, some spiritual cavern of such profound dimensions that it may never be filled up. He can not see *enough*. In all the wide universe, there are not sights sufficient to his unending need. Pity him, friends. And *see*...

The wheels turn, and I work the nearest hand crank, trading in one set of binoculars for a different pair. Below my feet, a single grain of sand falls, a single grain plucked from the Sahara or the Kalahari, the Karakum or Australia's Western Desert.

I do not feel their eyes on me.

I do not hear his booming voice.

—The stockade, a muddy pen enclosed by rough wooden posts and rails and a rusty metal gate held loosely shut with a twisted length of barbed wire. Mud the colour of shit, and the swineherd stands there in his tall rubber boots, a leather whip clenched in one fist. There are two or three others sitting on the rails, watching and shod with muddy rubbers of their own. In the pen, there are seven...animals...down on hands and knees, rooting about in the mud and filth. They might have been men and women once, long ago. There are still vestiges of that former humanity in evidence, of the lives lived and lost. They still have *faces*. Otherwise, there would be no reason to watch. This is the uttermost debasement of humanity, perhaps. I hold that thought a moment, and then push it aside. No, this must be only the *beginning*, and disgrace and humiliation beyond my stunted ability to apprehend still awaits.

The swineherd curses and strikes one of the animals—which I know was once a very beautiful woman—lashing it across the buttocks with his whip. It squeals in pain and anger, and there might almost be the ruin of words in there somewhere, as well. It rises up on hind legs amputated neatly below the knees, kicking out at the man with forelegs amputated just as neatly below the elbows. It snarls at the swineherd, bearing incisors and the short tusks protruding from is malformed lips. It has six flaccid breasts, and I wonder how many litters of piglets and not-quite-piglets have pawed and suckled at those teats.

"Yeah, that's her," one of the men sitting on the fence calls out to the swineherd. "That's the sow bitch bit me, right there."

The swineherd grins and hits the beast again, harder than before. "Is that it, piggy? You like to bite? You gone and got a taste for blood?"

She grunts and falls clumsily back into the mud, but only a moment later, two of the men from the fence have jumped down and seized hold of her short rear legs, and together they drag her towards the rusty gate. The swineherd is opening it, unknotting the barbed wire, and the gate creaks loud on corroded hinges. I know what's coming next, and I could linger here. I could see it through. The jute cords cinched quick around her stubby back legs before they strain and hoist her to hang head down above a galvanized aluminum washtub. Metal stained and scabbed from all the butcheries that have come before, and I could watch while she dangles there and squeals and screams like the woman she used to be, until the swineherd draws his blade across her throat—

I flip the red switch again.

The contraption bears the scene away, and I turn to the eye-piece of a spyglass I've been told was found amongst the effects of a certain Caribbean pirate. But that's one of the Barker's tales, so this instrument might have come from anywhere, anywhere at all.

Another grain of sand.

With thumb and index finger, I flip the green switch.

—And now there is a garden before me, a pretend rainforest dripping beneath wrought iron and greenhouse glass, stolen and patched back together from bits of Amazonia and the Congo and the jungles of Indonesia. There are long tables and workbenches, spades and empty terra-cotta pots and bulging bags of topsoil and fertilizer. Steam rises from thick clumps of philodendrons and scouring rushes and a hundred varieties of plants I do not know names for. The fleshy, drooping blossoms of the most exotic orchids, the sticky lures of bizarre carnivorous dicots, and here and there are primordial cycads and the trunks of tree ferns imported from New Zealand. For all I know, time may have begun here, in this garden, and I would not be surprised to see gigantic lizards watching from magnolia limbs or to hear the heavy air shattered by the shrieks of pterodactyls. There are two women—one older, the other somewhat younger, but both uncommonly handsome. The older woman's hair has begun to fade from black to grey, and her companion's hair is a shade that reminds me of crushed pecan shells.

They're sitting together on one of the benches. Neither is dressed, and their skin seems almost to glow in the warm sunlight sifting down through the arboretum glass. A fountain gurgles somewhere nearby, splashing droplets of fresh, clean water on the dark slate flagstones that pave the garden path. Between the two women there is a small parcel resting on the bench, wrapped in brown paper and tied up with twine. Something they have waited many years to receive, no doubt, some botanical rarity to at last complete their nursery, and the older woman snips the twine with a pair of shears.

"You are sure?" she asks her companion.

"Yes," the younger woman replies—too eagerly, too truthfully—and smiles, and then they kiss, there beneath those antediluvian fronds and epiphytic canopies. It is a long and hard and somehow desperate kiss, drawing from deep passion that might well be as ancient as all the forests of the world. There is tenderness here, and devotion, and love I cannot fathom, and I reach for the red switch.

But I have not yet seen the contents of the parcel.

And so my hand hovers, indecisive, above the control panel. Far above, the Barker chuckles and his audience holds its collective breath.

"You *have* to be sure," the older woman says, and this time her lover merely nods for a reply and opens the parcel. Just a simple cardboard box beneath the paper, but she reaches inside and produces a glass vial, corked and filled with an emerald liquid that sparkles in the sun. And there is a small manila envelope, as well, and she opens it and shakes out a number of pea-sized seeds into the older woman's outstretched palm. The very last thing from the box is something wrapped in cellophane, which she unwraps, and I see it's a small wad of clayey black earth.

I touch the switch, quickly losing interest, and I can feel the Barker, urging me on, taunting me with no words at all, only the steely glint of those eyes I have never seen and never shall see.

The younger woman is lying naked on the damp flagstones now, her legs spread wide to reveal the hidden cleft of her sex, and the older woman bends down over her. In her right hand, she holds the seeds, and in her left, the glass vial, which she has unstoppered. She whispers a few lines of poetry which I can clearly hear, passages in dactylic hexameter that might be Ovid's *Metamorphoses* and might be something else altogether. And now her lover closes her eyes and lies very still while the older woman empties the contents of the green vial into her companion's vagina. Next, most of the seeds are carefully placed within warm labial and cervical folds; the last two are tucked in snugly beneath the clitoral hood.

From my seat at the hub and through my lenses I can see it all, the finest details of that secret anatomy, the busy planting fingers, the expression on the older woman's face that might almost be sorrow and regret and whatever comes before the fact of a loss. I can see it all. For the moment, I have forgotten the red switch and what it signifies. I have forgotten, too, the Barker and his crowd and the dazzling spotlight halo.

The older woman kneads black clay between her callused fingers, then uses it to seal her lover shut.

"How long?" the younger woman asks, opening her eyes and staring up into tropical boughs and sunlight and the intricate framework of glass and steel.

"Soon now," the older woman replies, sitting down on the stones beside her. But I can see that it has already started, *this* metamorphosis; the younger woman's pubic hair has become a mossy thatch, and the yellow-green shoot that was so recently only her clit is pushing its way up through the clay plug.

I flip the red switch.

The Barker roars like a typhoon of fire and freezing wind, and another grain of sand falls beneath my feet.

Click.

Too much sentiment? the Barker howls, a question tumbling from the storm overhead, and then another on its heels. Too much inconvenient *feeling* getting in the way, when all he wants is raw, insensate exhibition? Look ye upon this poor, poor fellow. How he rushes ahead, pell-mell. How he grinds his teeth and anticipates and grows dizzy from his endless, irresolvable erection. Will he burst ere much longer, or are his balls, so long denied, gone dry and shriveled as the mummified testicles of an Egyptian pharaoh?

I flip the green switch.

—A boy stands before a tall looking glass, but for a moment I am too distracted by my *own* reflection there to notice anything else, just my face staring back at me through the pirates' telescope. So I reach for one of the cranks and quickly switch again to binoculars and a different angle, a different perspective. And yes, a boy standing before a looking glass—he cannot yet be twenty, maybe nineteen. His dick is hard, and he holds it firmly in his right hand. He has shaved his legs and wears black stiletto pumps and black silk stockings held up with a matching lace garter belt. His belly is flat and hard, but not so muscular that it spoils the illusion. He's spent almost a whole hour on his face and imagines his own scarlet lips closing tightly around the shaft of his swollen penis. He has never once seen any girl even half so lovely as himself, and never has he desired any man, either. He has made love to both, of course, but always those couplings have left him disappointed and confused. He is often haunted by phone calls and letters from discarded paramours, the ones who want more and cannot understand his disinterest.

If only I had a twin, he has frequently thought. *If only I had an identical twin, we would never have need of another.* Indeed, there have been times when he entertained fantasies of twins born and lost, born and hidden, born and then taken from him at birth. And one day they might meet by some unlikely happenstance. Someday, he might glance across a bustling street or the dining room of a crowded restaurant and see his own green eyes gazing back at him.

The irony is not lost on me. It never is.

I can *hear* the Barker's grin, and then the air around me and my contraption and my stool and the sand-filled hourglass beneath my bare feet trembles at his words.

If what he sees here displeases him, the Barker explains, if the wheel bears forth some perversity too distasteful or not at all to his liking, why, he's always free to move along. If he cannot bear the sight of a thing—if, perchance, it strikes too close to home or rings too true—he knows the drill. I would have it no other way, as so refined a palate must never be forced to tolerate that which has been poorly prepared or presented.

The boy in the mirror admires his hairless chest, his polished nails, his high cheekbones. If he only had a twin—

And I flip the switch.

The machine does as I've asked, and the wheel spins, or it's only me that spins, and the pretty, preening boy and his looking glass are immediately swept from view.

And I would turn away, would finally shut my eyes and find merciful darkness there to ease this relentless pounding in my chest. My mouth is drier than the hourglass sands, and it's been that dry as long as I can remember, not the meanest drop of spit left between my chapped lips and parched tongue. Oh, there is water, if I want it. There is a tall glass of crystal water always within easy reach. But there is no *time* to drink, and there is no time to turn away. There is only the carnival's contraption radiating all around me as it does, and these endless windows which are its hollow promises. There is only the ache between my legs and the constant craving...

One grain of sand falls, a descent that seems to go on for hours while the Barker roars and rages and the calliope wails. I hear autumn wind ruffling at the gaff banners and smell candy apples and popcorn and spilled beer. I smell the horses and the elephants. In this instant, I would gladly trade places with some simpler carny freak—Tom Thumb or the bearded lady, the Siamese Twins or the pinhead or that albino knot of stillborn flesh floating blind in its jar of spirits. I might be only something which is *seen*, only another sideshow geek or fakir, a tattooed fire eater or sword swallower selling Bibles and signed photos to the marks and mooches and lot lice.

Click.

I dutifully press the green switch with my thumb, and all thoughts of escape or compromise are immediately lost to me. For here is something *else* that I have never seen or even imagined, something I *must* see, for one day or night there will finally be that scene that will pacify and satiate my gluttonous hunger. They call it *faith*, to believe such things.

The Barker is pleased. I still hear his grin, but it no longer *hurts* to hear. It no longer grates like braking locomotive wheels grinding rails. His grin no longer throws molten sparks.

—A woman sits nude at the center of an empty room that has been painted the colour of a ripe pomegranate—walls, ceiling, doors, window casings, and the floor. The paint is still wet, and she sits on the last remaining unpainted patch of hardwood floor, her legs pulled up close to her chest, her arms tight around her knees. There is a terrible scar on her face, a keloid slash that might be the legacy of a burn or a knife or a razor or the jaws of a wild beast. I could not tell you which. Before the scar, she might have been pleasing to the eye, but somehow I sense that the real mutilation here is not so superficial. Something's torn apart *inside* her, something ripped asunder, some private, lonely wound.

Nothing she does not deserve, she would say, if I could ask. Nothing I didn't have coming to me after what I did. Her thoughts are the same shade of red as the drying paint.

There are two open buckets beside her, one empty and the other half full. There's a pool of paint inside a metal tray, and a brush, and a roller. She touches a fingertip to the damp pomegranate floor and stares a while at the stain this contact leaves on her flesh. And then she takes the roller from its tray and begins on her legs and thighs...

Red switch. Sand grain. *Click.* Green switch.

I wind another crank, and the binoculars are soon replaced by an 1861 Holmes stereoscope. Not just *any* 1861 Holmes stereoscope, not the way the Barker tells it, but one that once belonged to Madam Helena Blavatsky herself, one infused with special mystical properties by Hindu swamis and Tibetan monks. I grasp the walnut handle and place the leather hood against my face, staring out through those two panes of glass at what the wheel has delivered. Some impossible gift fallen here from anywhere and anytime. Some extraordinary demonstration that might even impress a sideshow voyeur...

—Flickering sodium-arc light, and heat haze, and the ceaseless clang of metal, an industrial cathedral of rust and verdigris and the innumerable corrosions all machines must in time endure. A cellar or furnace room, perhaps, hidden far below that soaring vault of girders and crumbling cement, pitched trusses and ancient bars of blister steel. Simply the Pit, as it is known to the damned and cast-off who have found their way down from the slag-littered hallways and parlors of ferrous superalloys far overhead.

And here, these two slowly untangle themselves from the rubble. These two, who must once have served some specific, special purpose, who must certainly have fulfilled the designs of a fickle Machine-Age god. But even they no longer know what that function might have been. Too much time and the dust that filters down to clog intake valves and gearboxes, the inevitable toll of oxidation, the casualties of out-gassing and simple wear and tear. A century ago, a millennium, an aeon, they might have walked together on rolling streets of chrome beneath a sky the startling blue of sapphires. Naive and programmed beings, they might hardly have guessed then at the existence of this underworld, the realm of the obsolete, maybe only a fairy tale from long ages before when the frailty of bone and sinew had not yet given way to the forge and the die, to exoskeletons of celestrium and cold algorithmic minds.

But for all that has been forgotten, these two still recollect the ghost of pleasure, the phantoms of automaton yearnings and needs. They have made dark deals with lesser simulacra, with nanite and nubot demons, and have spent time beyond reckoning on their own restorations. Parts that may as well be spare—as they will never work again—cut loose and traded for a few drops of hydraulic fluid, a milliliter of fluorocarbon lubricant, one perfect ball bearing. That long struggle only to reach *this point*, when one of them might raise a creaking tridactyl hand to caress the other's dented and scorched silicon shell. Something flutters, whirs, and is still again...

I hit the red switch and pull back from the stereoscope and these horrors, and the wheel does what all good wheels do.

It turns.

The Barker sighs, clears his throat, and begins to wind up his spiel. By now, there must be a fresh line of gillies waiting outside, and this bunch has surely gotten its dollar's worth by now. He didn't take them to raise, after all, and there are other freaks, other pitches, other shows waiting for easy marks. In the end, he says (so everyone will know it's almost time to leave), this is a sad and tragic tale—an *object lesson*, if you will—and we can only learn from this poor devil's predicament. A bird in the hand, Ladies and Gentlemen, is far better than a whole flock still waiting in the bush. Count your blessings. Know your place. And if any among you ever do go looking for your heart's desire, dare not look any further than your own backyard. Settle for less, because the only thing waiting at the end of the rainbow is more of the same. In a word, my good people, *moderation*. Thank you for your time, he says. Be sure to catch Spidora the Human Arachnid and Mr. Bones the Walking Skeleton. Please exit to the rear. No shoving…

And I sit here on my stool, a breathless scrap of meat snared forever in the bowels of the contraption.

And one grain of sand falls a thousand feet and lands upon the crest of the King of Dunes.

Click.

And I set my right eye to the Carib pirate's telescope, or set both eyes to a pair of Galilean binoculars manufactured late in the 17th Century, or lean into the heavy-duty, pedestal-mounted LittonEOS 20x120 rig the carnival picked up cheap somewhere from military surplus. All my indispensable, useless surrogate eyes. All my ocular augmentations, so I'll not ever miss a thing. I gaze into the eyepiece.

No one holds me here. Not the Barker and not the carnival bosses. You would find no locks, no chains, no manacles to keep me captive. Only this spinning carousel and the incessant visions it bestows, and only the infinity of depravities and pain and longing that I've yet to behold.

I sit up a little straighter and flip the green switch.

And I see…

Metamorphosis B

M^y mother, she collected shells," you say, hiding your left nipple beneath the shield of a cup-and-saucer limpet. "She had shells from at least a thousand different beaches, from all over the world." And the limpet stays where you put it, a dab of spirit gum on the underside of the shell to hold it in place. "But my father, he was never content to merely *collect* anything. My father, that old conjure eel..." but you trail off, and now I can only hear the wind and the wet crash of the sea against the rocky shore and a few hungry gulls wheeling high and far away. You sit naked on sand as white as sugar, and your shells are spread out in a bright scatter all around. You and I sitting together and always apart, inside the wide pentacle you drew in the sand with a piece of driftwood. The two of us, and your shells, and the bottle of spirit gum, a wicker basket of fresh seaweed, an antique looking glass and a camel's hair paint brush and the terrible old book bound in leather the colour of a scab. Prick at that cover, and you'll reopen some awful Noachian wound in the world. Pick that scab, and the brittle pages would turn, and time itself might bleed.

You sigh and select another shell, pausing to tell me it's a deep-sea scallop, *Placopecten magellanicus*, and then you glue it to your right breast just above the limpet. "He was a fisherman of sorts, my father, a trawler, and one day he took her in his nets. She almost died, because she couldn't breathe the air, of course. But then he kissed her."

I suspect that I would do well to follow the example of Odysseus' men and plug my ears with wax. And I almost say so. Almost. But the sight of you sitting there cross-legged on the sand

155

is enough to make me never want to speak aloud again. Once, when I asked your name, you said Parthenope. But only an hour later you said, no, it isn't Parthenope, it's only Ligeia, that your mother, *she* was called Parthenope by her father below the sea, before she was snared in a trawler's net and forced to live as a human woman on dry land.

"She begged him to give her back her gills and release her, but he was a wicked, greedy man, my father, and so he locked her up inside the forecastle and sailed for home." And then you search among an assortment of snails until you find exactly what you're looking for. You hold it out for me to see, and your skin seems unnaturally iridescent in the sun. "That's a dogwinkle," you tell me. "My mother found it at Folly Cove on Cape Ann when I was five years old." The tiny snail is the same shade of orangish red as a poppy. "This one ate nothing but mussels. You can tell from its colour. The dogwinkles that eat only barnacles are as pale as cream."

"He never set your mother free?" I ask, glancing anxiously at the evil leather-bound book with its scabby cover, wishing you'd left it beneath your bed today. Many nights, I've thought about taking it when you were asleep and burning it, or burying it in the dunes, or wrapping it in chains and sinking it in the bay. But cowards may entertain a million bold thoughts and never act upon a single one of them. I wait for you to answer me and watch while you use the dogwinkle to fill in a gap between the deep-sea scallop and the limpet hiding your nipple.

"He knew a spell," you reply, admiring your reflection in the mirror. "He knew a lot of spells. He could curdle milk and draw down lightning bolts from a clear sky. He could even make the sea's daughter forget how to swim. He put a glamour on her so no one might ever suspect what she really was. No, he never set her free. That's why she killed him."

Satisfied with the fit of the dogwinkle, you turn to the book, opening it, and I look quickly away. I've seen its pages enough times now. I do not need to see them ever again. I close my eyes and listen to the screeching gulls. And I remember a dream where the sky was *filled* with gulls, so many squawking, feathered bodies that they might have been the clouds of an approaching summer storm. I was in your ramshackle house beside the sea, but

I couldn't find you anywhere. I called your names—all the names you've ever told me might be yours—but there was no answer except the noise of the raucous gulls, their wings battering the sky above the roof. I passed your bed, and there was your father's grimoire, lying open on your pillow. The blankets and sheets were drenched with brine and dripping onto the floor. And what I saw in the book—what I *dreamed* I saw—these are not memories I want to keep, but they persist. I saw the words that bound a siren, the incantations that held your mother. I saw endless plains of black silt and marine snow and the bioluminescent ruins of sunken Atlantean towers. I saw jellyfish swarms and the slick ebony flesh and needle jaws of creatures that can survive the crushing water pressure a hundred fathoms down. Gulper eels and monstrous squid and the sinuous bodies of giant frill sharks and Greenland sharks, leviathan nightmares slipping silently along the walls of lightless abyssal canyons, all the demons and phantoms that haunt the perpetual gloom of the oceans' aphotic zones.

And turning away from that hateful book, I saw more water pooled on the floor, water that was also your footprints, and I followed them away from the bed and the open book. In the hallway, I paused before your tall curio cabinet, because the glass was cracked and smudged with mud. There was something watching me from one of the cluttered shelves, something peering balefully out at me from behind a large fossil ammonite, and its stalked eyes were not quite the same color as your own, that blue green of water that is just getting deep. It frightened me almost as much as the book on your bed, and so I didn't open the case to shoo it away, though I worried it might break something precious.

I hear you close the book and am relieved that I no longer need to avert my coward's eyes.

"One day, I asked her if she loved me," you say, chewing thoughtfully at your lower lip and trying to decide between the carapace of a speckled crab and the larger shell of a blue crab. "I was almost nine years old, I think. We were down at Scarborough Beach that day, because she wanted me to see the ruins of a nightclub that had burned sometime back in the forties. I asked, 'Do you love me, Mother?', because I never had asked, and she'd never said, one way or the other."

Dreaming, I followed your tracks back through the little house, and after a while they weren't water anymore. Instead, they were something sticky that glistened like the trails slugs leave on pumpkins and front-porch steps. They were no longer even footprints, really, just a long smear of slime leading at last to the bathroom door. It was closed, and when I tried the knob, I found it locked against me.

"What did she say?" I ask, even though I already know the answer, because you've told me this story before. Still, it would be rude of me not to ask.

You choose the blue crab and begin coating the edges of the carapace's underside with spirit gum. "She looked out at the sound, and I could tell the question had made her very sad. I wished I hadn't asked it, that I could stop everything and take it back. She said, 'I always have *tried* to love you. But part of you is him, daughter, and you only came to me because he stole me from the sea and raped me. Do you understand?' I said I did."

"That was a cruel thing to tell to a little girl."

"It was only the truth," you say, returning the camel's hair brush to the bottle of spirit gum. "I'll take cruel truth over kindly lies any day of the week."

"Did *you* love *her*?"

"Yes, I think so," you reply, then carefully center the crab's shell on your chest, between and above your breasts, a bare patch at the top of your sternum where the fine ridges of your clavicles almost meet. Then you press it firmly against your skin and hold it there, waiting for the glue to set. "She was my mother, after all. And it certainly was not her fault that my father had captured her in his nets and brought her back to land and forced her to be his wife."

And I would think this all a lie, or the fancies of a schizophrenic mind, were it not for the things the book has shown me, and the things you've shown me, and all those other things, which I've seen for myself. I am denied the easy mercy of dismissing out of hand that which would strike almost anyone else as insane or as lies made up by a lonely woman who will never believe that she does not need fairy tales to be interesting.

"She slit his throat with a common razor clam," you say and smile. I was there the day a dental student in Cambridge gave you those teeth, perfect ivory triangles of feldspathic porcelain, saw-tooth carinae so you'll never have to go looking for a common razor clam should someone's throat need cutting. "Then she fed him, piece by piece, to the sea. He had always been morbidly afraid of drowning, of his body being lost at sea. He feared—if he were not buried in consecrated ground—that his soul would be trapped *out there*, always," and you point eastward, towards the blue Atlantic horizon.

"But no one ever found her out?" I ask, and you laugh and select the tall, threaded spire of a wood-screw shell and paint one side with spirit gum. The shell is the colour of Baltic amber.

"She'd learned from the book, and it showed her how to cover her tracks. No one ever suspected a thing. Everyone thought the old bastard washed overboard in a gale. So what if the body never turned up. You don't need a corpse to plant a headstone somewhere. My grandfather had prepared a special place for him in the mansions of Poseidon, a vessel to contain his soul until the end of time. Occasionally, in my dreams, I'm down there, too, in the place where that vessel is kept. It's guarded by…well, I cannot *tell* you what guards it…but there *is* a guard, so no one and nothing can ever set him free. And sometimes, in my dreams—"

—I tried the knob, I found it locked against me.

And I turned and looked back down the hallway, past the invaded curio cabinet and your bedroom where the black book lay carelessly open on your pillow, spilling itself out into the house. I could still hear the sea gulls circling outside, and then, then I thought maybe I heard something else, and I turned back to the locked bathroom door.

"It's only me," I said, not whispering, no, but speaking very softly, my lips almost brushing against varnished splinters. "You can open the door for *me*, can't you?"

And you did.

The knob turned in my hand, and I wondered if it was ever really locked.

Using the looking glass, you center the wood-screw shell between your eyebrows, the place where your eyebrows would be if you didn't always keep that skin waxed smooth and hairless. I tell you it's perfect, and you nod and set the mirror aside. Gazing

ıozen dried starfish, you ask which I personally
rginated sea star or the *slender* sea star? I reply that
ıth, and you scowl, disappointed at my apparent lack
ion, that I answered so readily and have no preference
ıect.

ve to be absolutely *sure*," you say. "They don't even belong
to the same genera. There are almost 1,800 species of Asteroidea
alive today, and I only have a few to choose from. The pentaradial
symmetry has to be *just so*," and for a moment I'm afraid you're
going to open the book again to prove your point. Instead, you
choose the marginated sea star and hold it up above your head, as
though asking for the sky's approval.

In my dream, the tarnished brass knob turned in my hand
without my having turned it, metal gone suddenly cold as meth-
ane ice, and the door swung slowly open. Thick Arctic air flowed
out into the hallway, and my breath fogged. And all around me
there was that muddy, low-tide stink I've always hated, the stench
of low tide in the ponds and salt marshes back behind the dunes
and brambles and beach roses, the summer sun baking estuarine
slime and bloated fish and everything else that could not burrow
deeply enough or find sanctuary in shrinking brackish pools. I
covered my nose and mouth with grey frostbitten fingers and tried
not to gag.

"Do you really need to see that again?" you ask me, though
I've never told you any of my dreams. You're still holding the starfish above your head, and it casts a five-pronged shadow inside
your pentagram. "Wasn't once enough?"

"It was a dream," I say. "It was only a dream."

And you shrug and say, speaking of the starfish again, "See
how there are upper *and* lower marginal plates? See how only the
lower plates have any conspicuous spines? That's very important,
I think. I have to pay attention to all the details, the geometry."

"Is that what the book says?" I ask you. "Or is that what your
father would say?"

You only shrug again, not taking the bait, and begin apply-
ing a heavy coat of spirit gum to the ventral side of the starfish. I
have never once made you angry. I have never even seen you angry.
"I have to hurry," you say, glancing up at the afternoon sun. "It's

getting late. What did you see in the bathroom? You never have told me."

"I never told you any of it."

"Still, I'd like to know. Humor me," and I wonder if I have ever once done anything else.

"I saw you," I say, and then I almost add, *What that book made of you, what your* father *made of you.* But instead I only ask, "Were you there, when your mother killed herself?" Inside, I flinch at the measured cruelty of my own words, that you are so beautiful, there on the sand, and you have loved me for so long, and still I can be so contemptible, so petty.

"Is there some point in asking me questions you already know the answers to?" you reply, and find a place for the starfish directly below the blue crab's carapace. "Does it comfort you somehow?"

"Nothing comforts me anymore," I answer, and that's the truth, and you know it.

You shrug.

"Of course, I was there when my mother killed herself. She needed my help. She couldn't have ever done it alone. She'd tried." And now you turn your head and look me directly in the eyes. Your shimmering saltwater eyes that are neither green nor blue, and these are the stunted eyes of the child who helped her mother drown. The eyes of the girl who climbed into the bathtub and sat there on her mother's chest until it was over.

The freezing air pouring out through the opened door smelled worse than any low-tide miasma. It smelled like an entire continent submerged a hundred million years and by the force of some submarine convulsion thrust once again to the surface, all the wriggling, gasping, dying, dead things scattered across a thousand miles of drying muck and ooze turning hard to concrete. It reeked of burst swim bladders and blind eyes bulging from ruptured skulls. Exactly like the pages of your black leather book.

"She was my mother," you say. "She gave me life and kept me safe and taught me about the ocean. What else would I have ever done?"

And you watched me from the cast-iron, claw-footed tub with lidless eyes bruised dark as volcanic glass. You smiled your starving shark-toothed smile, crouched there inside a pearly shell you might well have stolen from some gigantic paper nautilus. But I knew this was no *borrowed* shell, but one that you'd been taught to secrete all on your own. Your skin become the glossy epidermis of nudibranchs or squids, competing shades of violet and yellow and red, and then something slithered over the side of the tub, coiling and uncoiling—

"It's getting late," you say again, still holding the starfish in place, waiting for the fixative to set. "One day, there will be enough time. One day, I'll get it right."

And I do not agree nor disagree. I shut my eyes and listen to the age-old interweave of waves and wind and gull voices. And try hard not to think about what might be waiting out beyond the steep and sloping edges of a continent's shelf, on those vast and sunless plains. Or about the fate of men who capture mermaids. Or their daughters.

Skin Game

By the moonlight, your skin seems like a saucer of frost and milk, your smooth, hairless chest as though you might still be only a boy, as if. Your nipples like dimes, and I press my lips to the taut muscles of your belly and try not to hear whatever it is you're saying. The words never make things any better, and I want only to taste you and hold you and be held by you. Your hand around my cock, encircling me, that would suffice, but you only have eyes for her, that bloated alabaster bitch sailing high above bare winter branches, scraping herself raw on sycamore fingers and the last shriveled leaves clinging doggedly to maple twigs. Your time of the month again, and you think I should laugh at a joke like that. I look up at your face, and she's washed your green eyes empty of anything but hunger and that need to run, to run and always run and never have to be held again within walls and locked windows and beneath roofs. Your eyes flash yellow gold, usually the gentlest greens of moss and verdigris but now flashing back some mean fraction of the fire she's poured into you. You laugh, since I have not, and that is still *your* laugh. And then you begin to sing in one of those ineluctable, inscrutable coincidences that attend these long nights.

Are the stars out tonight?
I don't know if it's cloudy or bright,
'Cause I only have eyes for you, dear...

"Hold me," I say aloud, realizing that I have said nothing aloud for so long, and the room has grown so very cold I can see your breath and my breath like smoke curling from our bodies which might begin to blaze at any moment. You let go of my cock, but you don't hold me, and you won't stop singing. Mocking me, as she is a jealous mistress and this is no secret, nothing you have ever tried to keep from me, the way she loathes my affections. The way she bares her teeth when we kiss.

The moon may be high,
But I can't see a thing in the sky,
'Cause I only have eyes for you dear.
I don't know if we're in the garden…

It's a sick, cruel joke, whether sprung from your own mind or her borrowed words slipping from your lips, either way a sick, cruel joke, and I rest my head flat against your chest, listening to your heart, instead of listening to that wicked, hateful tune. Your heart beats like a small, wild creature trapped in a cage of bone and blood and muscle, wanting out, wanting to be free again and free forever. She spills through the portals of your eyes and down your throat. You breathe her in, and she pools in the secret recesses of your heart so there will be no more room there for even the memory of me.

"The handcuffs," I whisper. "It isn't too late."

"Not this time," you reply. "Next month, the handcuffs. But no, not tonight."

"Hold me," I say again, and with your strong arms you feign some loose and disinterested half embrace. And when I tell you I love you and I wish you'd let me use the handcuffs, you say nothing at all. She has taken you to that place where I may never follow. Those airless, cratered halls and the endless grey plains of dust that were old even before the seas of this world swarmed with trilobites. I close my eyes, wanting to shut it all away, but I only succeed in opening *other* eyes, inner eyes to gaze out on scenes of retrospection and anamnesis. The tattered mess you brought back that had once been a young woman, and how many months ago was that? The last time you wouldn't let me use the cuffs, or the time before? There have been so many, and if you will excuse the pun, they bleed together. But you are crouched there on the bedroom floor, smeared with her, smeared with mud and shit and stinking of the woods and your own indiscretions, pine straw and all manner of detritus tangled in your long black hair. Her body like a broken toy, a torn and eviscerated rag doll, and maybe it would not hurt so much if you only hunted men. She lies sprawled there to call up all my doubts and insecurities, and how fucked up is that? You have done murder, again, more times now than I can name (and I do not keep any accounting), and I am worried that maybe you'd rather have a pretty *girl* than me, that here is the expression of some repressed, clandestine desire stripped down to spine and hollow ribcage for my benefit. Her throat is a sticky black hole, her face a mask that has gone missing, and you squat there above her corpse and sing your crimson love songs to the round white moon.

And then I am recalling some other corpse, some other butchery, and I am also remembering you in a bathtub of steaming hot water and me scrubbing the dirt and gore from your skin that is only skin. The water is stained the color of carnations, and the air smells like soap and scalding water and blood and the spicy, sweet sachet of forest loam lying underneath it all, a perfume of fungi and earthworms, soil and millipedes and at least a thousand species of decaying vegetable matter.

I scrub the incriminating stain of entrails and bile from your long-fingered hands, and you lick lazily at your thin lips and talk about werewolves in Russia. You say you know some spell or incantation, going alone into the forest, a copper knife driven into the bark of a fallen tree, and there are words, you tell me. I ask you not to speak them, and you smirk and call me superstitious.

"But the wolf enters not the forest," you say, and though I do not know whether or not this is some part of the incantation, I do not like the way the words press one into the other. "But the wolf dives not into the shadowed vale—moon, moon, gold-horned moon..."

Or it is some other bath, some other morning. And instead of Russian witchcraft, you're telling me the story of Lykaon of Arkadia, how he and his fifty blasphemous sons invited Zeus to dinner, then offered him a silver platter heaped with human flesh. Disgusted, the angry god cursed Lykaon and all his sons, that they would ever more be only wolves. And did you know, you ask, did you know that in 1827 a British naturalist named the African Cape Hunting Dog—*Lycaon pictus*—in honor of poor old King Lykaon? I shake my head, because no, I didn't know that, and squeeze fragrant shampoo into your hair. It lathers pink, and pink suds float in the carnation water.

You have stopped singing, and I open my eyes again.

"Soon," you whisper.

"Soon," I reply.

And now there is the softest growl or rumble from your throat, and in one fluid movement you rise and roll me over onto hands and knees, and with your right hand you force my legs apart—but there is nothing rough or brutish in these actions, and I do not struggle. You will take me, before she takes you completely, and I know this is almost an apology, that you are not stronger and that you are cursed and that I must share your affections with the jealous moon. You nuzzle and sniff at my most private anatomies, and I bite my lower lip and shudder, feeling first your tongue, pushing its way inside me as you indulge taboo and wolfish tastes. And then you mount me, and I want to scream, want to open my mouth wide from the pleasure and the pain and the knowledge of her watching us with that one pale eye through the windows. Not even this one moment can be ours *alone*, for she is ever and always in you and all around us. Your only goddess, waning or waxing, new or full, and I can only be grateful that you have not yet driven me away, that she has not yet decided there's no place for me in the ruin of your life.

Your teeth sharp on the back on my neck, forcing me down until I am lying flat on my stomach, your able jaws holding me still. And I think of that woman's corpse again, the gaping, sticky wound where her windpipe and larynx and throat had once been. My time will come, some night or another, because I will not leave you alone with her. Because I will not leave you. She will whisper in your ear, and you will forget yourself, and maybe you will even be sorry the next morning. I *pretend* that you will be sorry.

You have rarely ever broken skin, and I tell you that I love you, that I would not be here if I did not love you so very much. And you answer with a snarl and a breathless grunt and the grinding thrust of your hips, driving yourself still deeper inside me.

Break the shepherds' cudgels,
Cast wild fear upon all cattle,
On men, all creeping things...

There is so very little pain. The pain is unremarkable. And when you are done with me, I lie only a few feet away, silent and curled on my side, watching and wishing I were enough. She flows over you, radiant and insubstantial, dragging at your soul in a tide no different than the way she tugs the oceans to and fro. The water is rising now all about us, and you are drowning because you want not so much as to drown in her glow.

"Who will you hunt tonight?" I ask, my voice hardly more than a hoarse whisper. You do not reply, only smiling now, your lips curling back to show your teeth. "Do you know?" I ask, maybe only asking myself, maybe not asking you at all. "Have you looked into her eyes already?" It is not always a her, not *always*. Only more often than not.

You're at the window, on your knees and your face upturned to receive her monthly baptism, her precious sacraments of light and gravity. I would follow if I could, if I knew how. If the murmured incantations of Russian witches were enough, then I *would* follow. But I know better, because you have told me, time and time again. Lying together in our bed, you fevered and sweating, hurting, waiting for her to take the suffering away, you have told me how the moon came to your mother when you were only a very small child. The moon came, bearing gifts, and your mother was a lonely woman, starving for the attentions of any lover. A disregarded woman, your mother, and when the moon sang to her and froze her to the bone and laid a wolf pelt at her feet, your mother was smitten.

The moon wears many faces, and for your mother the moon wore the face of a beautiful young man. "Honor me," he whispered. "Wear this skin and think on me, and always will I love you and watch over you."

"I was seven," you've said. "I was only seven, and my brother and my sister, they were both much younger. She did not know I watched from the shadows while she stitched the wolf's pelt to her own skin."

I cannot say if this is true—if it is *literally* true, if it is a *fact*— or only a metaphor concocted to protect a child, and the man a child became, from the recollection of some more horrible event. Your father was a suicide, you've said. The month before the moon came to woo your mother, your father put the barrel of a shotgun in his mouth. So your mother was all alone and starving for comfort and for affection, starving for the love the moon came peddling like heroin and poisoned sweets, and you say that you have never once blamed her, but I think that's a lie. In her wolf-skin, your mother knew appetites she had never known before, and these were another gift of the moon. She gave you a key and begged and wailed until you locked her in her bedroom, and for days she hide herself away, and you sat listening to the terrible way she moaned, and to her mad laughter, and all the things she said to the moon.

Take it back, she said. Please, please, take it back. Take this hunger away from me.

And you cared for your siblings, as best you could, until the night she broke her bedroom window and slipped over the sill to run on all fours, baying beneath a full harvest moon. Before dawn, she came loping back, and you opened the door when she asked you to, because you were seven and so frightened, and even in the wolfskin, she was still your mother. She murdered your sister first, and then your brother, and you watched. She cut them up with a carving knife and ate until she was sick. And though you were very hungry, when she offered you some choice bit or another, you refused those delicacies.

I lie here on my side and watch you watching the moon. You are your mother's son, through and through, and it was always only a matter of time, you've said, before the moon came for you, too. When I have asked how the story ended, what became of your mother, there is always a different answer, perhaps because that part of the story does not matter, perhaps because it has passed beyond your recall, or it may be, I know, that all these tales are but some fancy of your weary, ravenous mind. She loved us, you say. She loved us and tried to keep us safe. She gave me the key.

And, truth to tell,
She lights up well,
So I, for one, don't blame her!

On your knees before the altar of the moon, which on this night is all the world. And I have your key on a chain about my neck. Even if you would not let me close those black steel cuffs tight about your wrists tonight, I carry the key always. I lie still, breathing as quietly as I may, and you turn your head and stare down at me with the eyes she has given you, your mother or the moon or the both of them conspiring. Those iridescent, night-seeing eyes, and for a moment I think this will finally be the night you do not love me *enough*. And for a moment, I wish that were the truth.

But then you turn away, and I hear, or only imagine that I hear, the staccato click of sharp claws against the wooden floors, and I'm alone again. I'm waiting again, and I do not care if the moon sees the malice and the anger on my face. I will not hide my resentment for her, and I will not hide my loathing of that grim celestial whore. I will lie here, still and listening closely to the night beyond these thin walls, listening for *you*, my love. And I will track her progress across the wide indigo sky, and when it is time and there is some hint of dawn, I will get up and dress and draw a hot bath so that you will not have to wait when you've come home to me again.

Ah, pray make no mistake,
We are not shy;
We're very wide awake,
The moon and I...

The Hole with a
Girl in Its Heart

Here," she said and pointed to a spot just below her sternum, below the cartilaginous tab of her xiphoid process. "It is here. When I swallowed it, this is where it settled. This is where it is."

There is never any sense that I am falling.

I open my eyes and watch that tortured patch of space, the blue star feeding the blazing accretion disk and the long pale axis of the relativistic jet geysering its stream of electrons and protons and more exotic particles away from the black hole, that stream traveling very near the speed of light.

I have come so far to fall, and now there is no sense at all that I am falling.

In her trailer, she sat alone, for never had she been anything but alone. Not since the night she'd wandered out among the dunes and found whatever it was lying in the sand and had taken it into herself. I now say *whatever it was*, for she would not ever name it herself. But she had placed it upon her tongue, that supermassive lozenge, and allowed it to move down her throat and the corridor of her esophagus, until it found that place where it had seemed most suited.

That is her story. The story she told me.

That is what I recall of her story.

"I was walking in the dunes, and then down onto the shore. At first, I thought it was only some glowing creature left stranded by the tide. I could not say how far it had journeyed to reach me."

She makes these assumptions—*it had journeyed to reach me*— and I let her, for she is the one who holds it in her chest, not I. She is the vessel, and never was I anything more than a supplicant. Five years, and I finally tracked her down a few miles outside Lincoln, Nebraska, living in an old Airstream travel trailer parked out behind a carnival sideshow tent. She'd been with the outfit—part thrill-ride sidestall midway, part Pentecostal revival—for almost six months. I never did learn where she'd been before that. I think they thought that I had come to take her away with me, away from them—the freaks and the swagmen, the roustabouts and the wild-eyed young woman who spent her nights speaking in tongues and leading lost lambs back to the loving arms of Jesus. I had not. It would not have mattered if I had, for there is no will in all the world that can overcome the gravity of her.

"They are all very sweet," she said, meaning the carnival people. "They are all lost."

"Even the preacher lady?" I asked.

"Oh, yes. Her most especially. She is the most lost of them all, poor thing. Sometimes, she comes to talk with me late at night when she thinks no one will know. She sees angels watching her from telephone poles and has terrible dreams about the end of the world."

I sat on the orange sofa crammed into one end of the Airstream trailer and sipped from the plastic tumbler of warm, flat root beer she'd given me. She talks, and I listen. There is a low shelf crammed with books, and I read the spines while she tells me about the day the show found her, starving and broke and hitchhiking her way across Nevada. Most of the books are hardbacks, almost all of them over my head—*The Large-Scale Structure of Space-Time*; *Principles of Physical Cosmology*; *Quantum Mechanics and Experience*; *The Meaning of Quantum Theory*; *The Conscious Universe*; *Mathematical Theory of Black Holes*. And there among all those weighty, intimidating volumes was one familiar face, a battered paperback copy of Madeleine L'Engle's *A Wrinkle in Time*.

"Now they think they could not survive without me. They could, of course, just as they survived before I came." The warm root beer was beginning to taste like Pepto-Bismol, and I sat the tumbler on a folding metal table.

"Put your hand right *here*," she said, smiling, only that was later, days or hours later. "Can you feel it?"

There is no sense at all that I am falling.

It is not at all what I expected. She promised me that it wouldn't be. I want to shut my eyes again, but it would not matter. I have seen it now, and shutting my eyes will not ever drive away the memory. I do not *want* to drive the memory away, but it is so much to have seen. It is so much to know.

I pressed my fingers to her chest.

"They come, like you," she said. "They hear that the show's rolled into town, and they come just to see, some of them. Or a man might come because all his life he's felt so empty, all his life he's felt there's this terrible knot of emptiness trapped in his belly or behind his eyes. Women have come because they've had a baby and felt empty ever since, or because they've never been able to conceive. Sometimes, they've come because even though they've never desired a child, there's still this vacant place deep inside. But they all come because, one way or another, they feel a terrible emptiness."

The late afternoon sun through the tiny windows of the Airstream was very hot and very bright, and her skin was clammy and slick with sweat.

"Can you feel it?" she asked me, and I could hear excitement in her voice, excitement and a gentle, unselfish sort of pride. "It knows you. It has known you all along."

But, for all my desire, for all my need, for all my emptiness, all I could feel was her sweat and the tiny, invisible hairs growing there below her small breasts.

"They come," she said again. "They come from all over. And they all have their different stories to tell. No two ever just exactly alike, same as with snowflakes and fingerprints. But they all have that one thing in common, because, you know, all snowflakes *are* snowflakes and all fingerprints *are* fingerprints."

I didn't tell her why I'd come. My own sob story. The reason for the knot of emptiness chewing me up inside. I never could have told her that, and, mercifully, she didn't ask, and I thought perhaps she was relieved that I'd kept it to myself.

"It's a myth," she said, "that black holes just sit out there gobbling up everything that comes too close. The gravitational field in the proximity of a black hole is no different than the gravitational field produced by any symmetric sphere of the same mass. Objects in space may orbit out beyond the edges of the event horizon indefinitely."

"You have to *cross* the event horizon," I said, and that made her smile again.

"You've done your homework."

"I've read a little bit, but nothing like you," and I nodded towards the bookshelf by the orange sofa, all those intimidating hardbacks and *A Wrinkle in Time.* "Just some of the popular stuff. Stephen Hawking, Clifford Pickover, you know. Books for the lay readers."

"Have you ever read Kitty Ferguson?" she asked, and I said no, that I hadn't, that I'd not even heard of her before. And there we sat together, in the hot sunlight, talking about books, my hand still pressed to that spot below her xiphoid process.

"Ah, well," she said. "No matter. It sounds like you read enough. Much more than most."

And then I felt it move.

I know the name of this star. I even saw a painting once, an artist's impression of the Cygnus X-1 system as a blue supergiant orbiting a black hole. It was a very pretty painting, but it cannot ever compare to what I see, squinting through the forward port-hole—the writhing flood of superheated matter flowing out from the young star across however many millions of miles of space to form the black hole's fiery accretion disk. Eight thousand light-years from Earth, and yet only an hour ago, and hour and a half at most, I was sitting with her in the sweltering aluminum trailer behind the freak tents, sitting there in the stark yellow-white light of a different star.

"For most all of them," she said, "it is enough just to touch."

If there had been any sort of a scar, I would have thought it no more than a hoax, that maybe it was nothing but a marble or a ball bearing or possibly some sort of body-piercing implant hidden there beneath her flesh. My fingers began to tingle very faintly, and she took a deep breath and shut her eyes.

"It is not really a *hole* at all," she said.

And I have no sense that I am falling.

"It's not enough for *me*," I told her. "I wish to god it were, but it's not. I think I must have been looking for you my whole goddamned life."

And I think that's when I saw her clearly for the first time. When I saw *her*, instead of merely seeing some object of my desperation, the fruition of my search, the bizarre and garish images painted ten-feet high on the flapping canvas front of the freak show. She was sitting there on a wooden stool, her T-shirt hiked up so I could touch her bare chest, no bra, her nipples brown, each surrounded by a small constellation of freckles. Her hair was the color of hay, her face thin but not severe, her eyes almost the same shade of blue as the star looming outside the porthole. Plain, no one I ever would have thought to call her pretty, and yet I had never seen any woman even half so beautiful. There were freckles below her eyes, speckling her cheekbones. Her lips were thin and chapped.

"It's not enough for me," I said again, because she hadn't replied, and I was beginning to think she hadn't heard me. The smile faded, and she glanced towards the trailer door.

"It's strictly a one-way trip," she said. "The mechanism, it doesn't swing both ways."

"There's nothing at all holding me here," I told her, wondering briefly if that *were* true, if I could fairly claim to be that entirely alone, if I had managed somehow to live almost forty goddamn years without picking up so much as a single string tying me to anything or any place or anyone else.

"I can't bring you back," she said, as though trying to make herself more clearly understood.

"But I wouldn't be the first?"

"No," she said. "You wouldn't. But I wish—"

"—it was enough for me to see it, to place my hands upon it?"

She looked at me again and nodded her head. Beneath my fingertips, something small and hard rolled inside her.

"Will it *hurt* you?" I asked her.

"No. It has never yet hurt me. It has filled me up with the debris of a thousand worlds, the secrets of galaxies, but it has never hurt me."

"Where did it come from?"

"Someplace else," she answered and smiled again, but this time I could tell it was forced. I think I was glad that's the only answer she had for me, because I'd half expected mad ramblings about gifts from God Almighty and benevolent aliens and the lost continent of Atlantis.

"I can't guarantee it's what you're after," she said, looking down at my fingertips pressed to her chest.

"I would never ask you to. No one ever gets a guarantee. Leastways, that's always been my experience."

"There are days," she said, then paused and swallowed. "There are nights I wish I'd never found it. It's a burden. I'd never want to *lose* it, not really, but I'd be lying if I said it isn't a burden."

I pulled my hand away then, because there was an unexpected rush of self-doubt and second thoughts, and the tingling in my fingers was becoming almost painful, spreading across my palm and encircling my wrist. I turned my head, looking directly into the brilliant glare of the setting sun shining in through parted drapes, and though I could not *see* them, I could *sense* them—the carny folk, waiting anxiously out there in the oatmeal patch of grass and weeds between the freak tent and the silver aluminum Airstream.

"They're so frightened that your coming here means I'm leaving them," she said.

I turned back to her, blinking at a dazzling swarm of yellow afterimages.

"I'm ready," I told her.

"I'm ready," I whisper, staring out through the starship's porthole, wishing she were here to see. But that was one of the stipulations, she said. One of the rules. She could serve as a conduit for countless others, but she could never travel this road herself.

Only an hour and a half ago, or maybe its been eight thousand years—and at this point I cannot see the difference—she took my tingling left hand and placed firmly against her chest. I could feel the hard, rotating object inside her, and I could feel her heartbeat.

"Close your eyes," she said. "Close your eyes now and then count to ten very slowly. Don't you dare open your eyes until you *get* to ten. Promise me that you won't."

"Like Orpheus," I suggested. "Don't dare look back."

"I'm not joking. *Promise* me that."

"I promise," I told her.

"Don't be scared," she said.

The blue light falls across the black metallic substance that forms the deck beneath me and washes warmly across my face. It fills my eyes, and I lean forward, craning my neck for a better view of Cygnus X-1, dark twin slowly consuming light twin in that great cosmic waltz.

She opened herself, and I'd already started counting.

The air smelled of burning leaves and dust. There was, as now, no sense whatsoever of falling.

And the terrible yawning emptiness inside me is gone, banished in the simple count from one to ten. This blue light fills me full, and I cannot now even imagine having once felt so hollow. I do finally shut my eyes, and I only imagine that I can hear heavy canvas flapping in a hot Nebraska summer wind, and that I can also hear her opening the door to the Airstream travel trailer and stepping down to stand among them. I only imagine their relief, and I only pretend she knows how grateful I am.

Outside the Gates of Eden

So easily do we lose track of time here, as easily as drawing my next breath, and sometimes with far less effort. Time is not quite absent, no, but neither does it press in at me with the old, persistent urgency. I lie here only half awake, but also only half asleep, dreaming but free of the subconscious' weight and nagging symbolism. The bed sheets smell like old roses, sweat, nectar, cardamom, rye whiskey, semen—all those bittersweet tinctures of you and me and the strangling moments that have passed between us. This will not ever be as simple as fucking, and I still haven't quite gotten used to that. Like when you say to me that it's not lycanthropy and not vampirism or schizophrenia or merely some glamour you've called up from the terrible old books you keep locked away behind glass. What it is, I will not say. It is not *for* me to say, to put my finger on, and I'd likely get it wrong, anyway. I roll over, and you're here on hands and knees, watching me, and your eyes flash red-green iridescence in the candlelight. "Come here, boy," you smile, and always I have to remind myself it's not a mask, for there can be no masks here. No deceptions, but only the merciless, perpetual peeling away of deceit and all manner of disguisement. "Come here, boy," and you slip your fingers between my legs, encircling my cock, winning from me a small gasp and a scrap of laughter. At first, I was surprised to hear laughter in this place, but now it seems as natural as the ubiquitous undercurrents of freshly turned earth and carrion and hothouse flowers that scent the air.

"Maybe I was busy," I say, feigning annoyance. "Maybe I was otherwise occupied."

"And maybe I've finally grown tired of the taste of your prick," you say, still smiling, still flashing those hyena teeth, nutcracker teeth to split open living bone, and your purplish tongue lolls from your black lips.

"Puppy," I playfully whisper, trying very hard not to laugh, and you growl and pull faces and show me much worse things than hyena incisors and canines and grinding carnassials. Your grip on my penis tightens, and I wonder how much it's going to hurt this time. But it's a distant sort of wondering, because I have not been afraid of pain for what must be years or months, at least. If it has only been weeks, I would be appalled. I have not been appalled in so long I cannot now quite recollect the sensation.

In your hand, captured in the circlet of your clawed thumb and index finger, my cock writhes, become now the roughest imitation of a serpent.

"You haven't been practicing," you frown, though of course I have. I have been practicing quite a lot, actually, but the trick does not come so readily to me. My flesh is too set in its ways, uncooperative hidebound me, and I am grateful you can see all this in my eyes without my having to speak the words aloud. You see my shame, as well, and you see how badly I want to impress.

"Well, it's better than last time," you lie, and let those reticulated coils of bronze and sepia and ginger wrap firmly around your wrist. I think about biting—no venom, just teeth as sharp and fine as sewing needles—and then decide that you might not be in the mood.

"It is not either," I reply. "It is not the least bit better. It wouldn't fool anyone."

"Be patient, boy," you tell me. "There's a lot still to forget, and forgetting isn't ever half so simple as most people seem to think." But already I'm taking it back, the malformed constrictor gone limp and withering, slipping from your hand and vanishing into the damp vaginal folds that have formed between my thighs. That's one I mastered almost right away, and the transformation pleased you then, but now you snarl and seal me shut with only a thought or a careless glimmer of those scavenger eyes.

"Fuck you," I say, staring down at the smooth nothing there between my legs, and I even wish for a moment that I had never met you, and you had never shown me the secret roads that lead down and down into this land where it is always neither day nor night, neither dusk nor dawn. A swarm of small white spiders washes across your cheeks and high forehead and is gone, and you watch me with a face that is almost human. And then I say it again, "Fuck you."

"Not like that, love," you laugh. "But don't worry. It's nothing you can't undo, not if you truly set your mind to it."

Far away, beyond the waxy black walls of our den, there are sounds I might once have mistaken merely for wind and thunder and rain falling on hot summer streets. And I close my eyes and try to concentrate on nothing but growing my penis back without your assistance.

"I brought a gift," you say, "something from the surface," and the *way* you say it, I can see it's meant as an apology. And I know, also, that you're probably not lying, because you still leave this place and scramble up the world's throat and then come back again, traveling from this tenebrous hollow and out into the light I used to know, but which now seems hardly even as substantial as time.

"I don't need your goddamn gifts," I reply and don't open my eyes. There's a faint tingle at my crotch, but nothing comes of it.

"I think you will like her."

I try to ignore you, because maybe this is only meant as a distraction, because I know how it must amuse you, your hapless, ephebic pupil, straining just to get back to square one. I open my eyes again, thinking that liquor might help; it sometimes does. I reach for the half-empty bottle of pear brandy on the walnut stand beside our bed. That was another gift from above, the brandy. You shower me with trinkets and baubles, sweets and intoxicants, a generosity that I know well enough I must never mistake for anything so crude as mere love or affection. We are beyond such base animal sentiments, you have assured me. But you will not have me wanting for anything I might need or desire—like brandy. I drink directly from the bottle, a few drops escaping my lips and running down my chin.

"I said that I have brought you a present, boy."

"You're trying to distract me," I say.

"That would be too easy," you reply and smile, revealing gums that have sprouted clusters of green-briar thorns and a few worn shards of cobalt beach glass in place of teeth. I hear wings, and the candles flicker, gutter, but are not blown out. We are never entirely alone down here, for there are many other beings like us, and they go and come with no concern for our privacy. Long ago—unless I have only been here a short while—you told me a wonderful story of how this place came to be known, how an Hungarian sorceress found the entrance in some ancient, evil Arabian book bound, of course, in human skin. A thousand years ago, two thousand, three, and maybe the sorceress wasn't Hungarian, but Egyptian or Persian or Syrian. Regardless, it was a good story, whichever way you told it to me. She had to bargain her way in, naturally, because there was a certain unsavory native element to contend with. But, in the end, it was nothing that could not be brokered with the proper incantations and sacrificial largesse. Eventually, others followed her, whether through independent discovery or the few abstruse hints she'd left behind. You say that we are pioneers, or you say that we are fugitives, or you say that we are unassimilated aliens, come here from our birth world. We are exotic transplants, you have said. You have also said that she is still here, somewhere, because no one makes the trip down and then returns for good. This place leeches its way into you, more addictive than heroin or religion, and we who have passed through the gates and wandered these labyrinthine passages of slate and charcoal, we who have slept beneath these vacant, starless skies, we shall not ever be free, excepting the freedom those above can't begin to comprehend. On occasion, I have thought about searching for her, but always you dissuade me.

I concentrate on the sweet burn of the brandy, and, straining, manage to sprout something from my groin that looks like nothing so much as the barrel of a revolver fashioned not from steel but pink-grey flesh.

"Nice try," you smirk. "At least you could take a piss with that."

"So what is my gift?" I ask, changing the subject because I'm too tired to try again right now.

"Something I found just beyond the portal. I think she might have been trying to discover the entrance. She had that stench about her."

"Her," I sigh, as I have never been shy about showing disappointment. "What will I do with a *her*."

"Don't be ungrateful, boy."

"I am certainly not being ungrateful," I reply, pouting now, as I know how much you love to see me pout, my petulance so much better than all the gratitude I could possibly muster. "But I don't know what I'm supposed to do with a *she*."

"Whatever you might wish. Don't be so thick."

Your face has become porcelain, a doll's glazed features cracked by age and the hands of children, and your mouth is a perfect Cupid's bow of reproach. Your eyes have filled with clockwork. I take another swallow from the brandy bottle and shrug my shoulders, dappled now with ebony down feathers and porcupine quills and the poisonous, variegated spines of a species of tropical lionfish.

"Show me," I say, and the porcelain abruptly shatters to reveal a skull carved from jade and sporting teeth carved from the ivory of a narwhal's horn. I *know* that face. The first one you ever showed me, and it always puts me at ease. Now there is a soft popping commotion from your chest and belly, and a moment later your torso opens wide for me, gaping like the maw of some Paleozoic monstrosity. Your whole body shudders, and then the girl you swallowed is disgorged, vomited up in a great slimy heap upon the sheets. She slides free from the tangle of organs and gears, blood and oil and stranger lubricants, and lies shivering at my feet. There is a pale umbilical cord leading from her throat, leading back to you, but it is quickly severed with a flick of your claws, and an alloy of Wharton's jelly and claret ichor spurts from the wound. The improvised, evacuated womb of your abdomen snaps shut, and now you hug yourself tightly and mutter, waiting for the contractions to end.

Somewhat more intrigued than I'd expected to be, I return the bottle to its place on the walnut stand, and for a long while (or so it seems) I sit staring at this *gift*. I think you've used the word in its loosest sense. She seems so close to death now that I might kill her with only a half-hearted contemplation of her undoing. She is naked, her body slicked with placental secretions and offal and glistening drops of pine resin. Her eyes are squeezed shut and her blue lips tremble with cold or pain or both. She is pretty enough, I suppose, if perchance you're into pussy. Her breasts are small and well-formed, but she's so thin that I think it must have been a very long time since she's bothered with getting enough to eat. And yes, even through the afterbirth I catch a whiff of that fragile, acrid perfume that led you to suspect she might be a pilgrim. Crush a handful of anise and dried foxglove, *Artemisia absinthium*, myrrh, a bit of fish oil, a pinch of mausoleum dust and antimony, and you'd get something not so very far afield from that singular fragrance. Her lips part and she gags, expelling a gout of some viscous, milky fluid, and then she's coughing and rising weakly onto her knees.

"She's certainly ruined the linens," I say, and now you have dissolved into an angry swarm of red wasps, darting to and fro, and I hear your buzzing, honeycomb voice crawling about inside my head. *Play nice*, you say, and *Try not to break her all at once*. And then all those thrumming, flitting bodies you've divided yourself into are swallowed up by the not-quite-solid walls, and I am left alone with this bestowal, this ragged distaff handout, when all I really wanted was the humdrum pleasure of your cock inside my ass.

She's watching me now, her watery eyes the color of ice at the core of a glacier, that exact opaline shade of blue. I can see that she begins to understand what has come of you, and though those eyes are filled with hurt and spite and hate, there is also an unmistakable glint of something like triumph.

She tries to speak, but only a hoarse wheeze makes it past her teeth and cyanotic lips.

"Take your time," I tell her, and I think about offering the girl some of the liquor, but I'm not yet certain it wouldn't be a waste, and it might be ages before you show up with another bottle of pear brandy. "You were looking for the way down?" I ask, and she nods her head.

"You're lucky," I say. "Last time he brought someone down, they made the journey lodged somewhere between his stomach and small intestine. And what with all that hydrochloric acid and pepsin and what have you, there wasn't a whole lot left by the time he spat the poor son of a bitch up again. I guess he's getting better at those delicate uterine forgeries."

She coughs, gags again, and grits her teeth, which I notice have turned to chrome. I could wait, were I that sort, and when she's able to speak clearly again and answer questions I might satisfy my curiosity—what path led her so near the portal; what was it she hoped to find here; what betrayal or loss or warping of her soul caused her to seek these deep-seated lands; has she come searching for someone who arrived before her? I like that last question best of all, for it opens up such exquisite realms of possibility. But I am not possessed of the sort of diligence or passivity, and besides, I've been bitten by pets before. Sometimes it's most prudent to let curiosity go unsatiated. And even in these grey quarters, there is a sort of Darwinian imperative at work, survival of the most imaginative, the least scrupulous, and least fastidious. And I think there's ambition in her eyes.

She reaches out and cradles my misconceived cock in her left hand. A rash of barnacles and the corpulent tendrils of sea anemones have begun to spread across her forearms.

"I know this game," she croaks, and a little more of the milky amniotic liquid dribbles from the corners of her mouth. And in her grasp, my sex at once blooms into something very like the calyx of an epiphytic orchid, unfolding to reveal a sunburst of sepals and petals and a swollen, throbbing labellum. I do not scream, though some part of me—surprised by such unexpected pain and unexpected skill—wants very badly to scream. She reaches inside the bloom she has created, finding and stroking the four erect stamens, and when she takes her hand away again, the tips of her fingers are stained saffron with pollen.

"I think perhaps he's ready now," she says, her voice still raw and rasping, but there's a smug humor there, regardless. She begins to lick the sticky granules of pollen from her fingertips as the air around our bed swells with the eager, anxious hum of a hundred or five hundred or a thousand red wasps. All those restless wings scissoring apart the darkness, a hovering cloud of piercing stingers and candy-striped bodies, and I take another swallow of brandy and lie back on the mattress and shut my eyes and wait for whatever it is you have in mind.

In the Dreamtime of
Lady Resurrection

*How I, then a young girl, came to think of, and to
dilate upon, so very hideous an idea?*
Mary Wollstonecraft Godwin Shelley
(October 15ᵗʰ, 1831)

"Wake up," she whispers, as ever she is always whispering with those demanding, ashen lips, but I do not open my eyes. I do not wake up, as she has bidden me to do, but, instead, lie drifting in this amniotic moment, unwilling to move one instant forward and incapable of retreating by even the scant breadth of a single second. For now, there is *only* now; yet, even so, an infinity stretches all around, haunted by dim shapes and half-glimpsed phantasmagoria, and if I named this time and place, I might name it Pluto or Orcus or Dis Pater. But never would I name it purgatorial, for here there are no purging flames, nor trials of final purification from venial transgressions. I have not arrived here by any shade of damnation and await no deliverance, but scud gently through Pre-Adamite seas, and so might I name this wide pacific realm *Womb*, the uterus common to all that which has ever risen squirming from mere insensate earth. I might name it *Mother.* I might best call it nothing at all, for a name may only lessen and constrain this inconceivable vastness.

"Wake up now," she whispers, but I shall rather seek these deeper currents.

No longer can I distinguish that which is *without* from that which is *within*. In ocher and loden green and malachite dusks do I dissolve and somehow still retain this flesh and this unbeating heart and this blood grown cold and stagnant in my veins. Even as I slip free, I am constrained, and in the eel-grass shadows do I descry her desperate, damned form bending low above this warm and salty sea where she has laid me down. She is Heaven, her milky skin is star-pierced through a thousand, thousand times to spill forth droplets of the dazzling light which is but one half of her unspeakable art. She would have me think it the totality, as though a dead woman is blind merely because her eyes remain shut. Long did I suspect the whole of her. When I breathed and had occasion to walk beneath the sun and moon, even then did I harbour my suspicions and guess at the blackness fastidiously concealed within that blinding glare. And here, at this moment, she is to me as naked as in the hour of her birth, and no guise nor glamour would ever hide from me that perpetual evening of her soul. At this moment, all and everything is laid bare. I am gutted like a gasping fish, and she is flayed by revelation.

She whispers to me, and I float across endless plains of primordial silt and gaping hadopelagic chasms where sometimes I sense the awful minds of other sleepers, ancient before the coming of time, waiting alone in sunken temples and drowned sepulchers. Below me lies the grey and glairy mass of Professor Huxley's *Bathybius haeckelii*, the boundless, wriggling sheet of *Urschleim* that encircles all the globe. Here and there do I catch sight of the bleached skeletons of mighty whales and ichthyosauria, their bones gnawed raw by centuries and millennia and aeons, by the busy proboscides of nameless invertebra. The struts of a Leviathan's ribcage rise from the gloom like a cathedral's vaulted roof, and a startled retinue of spiny crabs wave threatful pincers that I might not forget I am the intruder. For this I *would* forget, and forswear that tattered life she stole and now so labours to restore, were that choice only mine to make.

I know this is no ocean, and I know there is no firmament set out over me. But I am sinking, all the same, spiraling down with infinite slowness towards some unimaginable beginning or conclusion (as though there is a difference between the two). And you watch on worriedly, and yet always that devouring curiosity to defuse any fear or regret. Your hands wander impatiently across copper coils and spark tungsten filaments, tap upon sluggish dials and tug so slightly at the rubber tubes that enter and exit me as though I have sprouted a bouquet of umbilici. You mind the gate and the road back, and so I turn away and would not see your pale, exhausted face.

With a glass dropper, you taint my pool with poisonous tinctures of quicksilver and iodine, meaning to shock me back into a discarded shell.

And I misstep, then, some fraction of a footfall this way or that, and now somehow I have not yet felt the snip that divided *me* from *me*. I sit naked on a wooden stool near *Der Ocean auf dem Tische*, the great vivarium tank you have fashioned from iron and plate glass and marble.

You will be my goldfish, you laugh. *You will be my newt. What better part could you ever play, my dear?*

You kiss my bare shoulders and my lips, and I taste brandy on your tongue. You hold my breasts cupped in your hands, and tease my nipples with your teeth. And I know none of this is misdirection to put my mind at ease, but rather your delight in changes to come. The experiment is your bacchanal, and the mad glint in your eyes would shame any maenad or rutting satyr. I have no delusions regarding what is soon to come. I am the sacrifice, and it matters little or none at all whether the altar you have raised is to Science or Dionysus.

"Oh, if I could stand in your place," you sigh, and again your lips brush mine. "If I could *see* what you will see and *feel* what you will feel!"

"I will be your eyes," I say, echoing myself. "I will be your curious, probing hands." These might be wedding vows that we exchange. These might be the last words of the condemned on the morning of her execution.

"Yes, you shall, but I would make this journey myself, and have need of no surrogate." Then and now, I wonder in secret if you mean everything you say. It is easy to declare envy when there is no likelihood of exchanging places. "Where you go, my love, all go in due time, but you may be the first ever to return and report to the living what she has witnessed there."

You kneel before me, as if in awe or gratitude, and your head settles upon my lap. I touch your golden hair with fingers that have scarcely begun to feel the tingling and chill, the numbness that will consume me soon enough. You kindly offered to place the lethal preparation in a cup of something sweet that I would not taste its bitterness, but I told you how I preferred to know my executioner and would not have his grim face so pleasantly hooded. I took it in a single acrid spoonful, and now we wait, and I touch your golden hair.

"When I was a girl," I begin, then must pause to lick my dry lips.

"You have told me this story already."

"I would have you hear it once more. Am I not accorded some last indulgence before the stroll to the gallows?"

"It will not be a gallows," you reply, but there is a sharp edge around your words, a brittle frame and all the gilt flaking free. "Indeed, it will be little more than a quick glance stolen through a window before the drapes are drawn shut against you. So, dear, you do not stand to *earn* some final coddling, not this day, and so I would not hear that tale repeated, when I know it as well as I know the four syllables of my own beloved's name."

"You *will* hear me," I say, and my fingers twine and knot themselves tightly in your hair. A few flaxen strands pull free, and I hope I can carry them down into the dark with me. You tense, but do not pull away or make any further protest. "When I was a girl, my own brother died beneath the wheels of an ox cart. It was an accident, of course. But still his skull was broken and his chest all staved in. Though, in the end, no one was judged at fault."

I sit on my stool, and you kneel there on the stone floor, waiting for me to be done, restlessly awaiting my passage and the moment when I have been rendered incapable of repeating familiar tales you do not wish to hear retold.

"I held him, what remained of him. I felt the shudder when his child's soul pulled loose from its prison. His blue eyes were as bright in that instant as the glare of sunlight off freshly fallen snow. As for the man who drove the cart, he committed suicide some weeks later, though I did not learn this until I was almost grown."

"There is no ox cart here," you whisper. "There are no careless hooves, and no innocent drover."

"I did not say he was a drover. I have never said that. He was merely a farmer, I think, on his way to market with a load of potatoes and cabbages. My brother's entire unlived life traded for a only few bushels of potatoes and cabbages. That must be esteemed a bargain, by any measure."

"We should begin now," you say, and I don't disagree, for my legs are growing stiff and an indefinable weight has begun to press in upon me. I was warned of these symptoms, and so there is not surprise, only the fear that I have prayed I would be strong enough to bear. You stand and help me to my feet, then lead me the short distance to the vivarium tank. Suddenly, I cannot escape the fanciful and disagreeable impression that your mechanical apparatuses and contraptions are watching on. Maybe, I think, they have been watching all along. Perhaps, they were my jurors, an impassionate, unbiased tribunal of brass and steel and porcelain, and now they gaze out with automaton eyes and exhale steam and oily vapours to see their sentence served. You told me there would be madness, that the toxin would act upon my mind as well as my body, but in my madness I have forgotten the warning.

"Please, I would not have them see me, not like this," I tell you, but already we have reached the great tank that will only serve as my carriage for these brief and extraordinary travels—if your calculations and theories are proved correct—or that will become my deathbed, if, perchance, you have made some critical error. There is a step ladder, and you guide me, and so I endeavor not to feel their enthusiastic, damp-palmed scrutiny. I sit down on the platform at the top of the ladder and let my feet dangle into the warm liquid, both my feet and then my legs up to the knees. It is not an objectionable sensation, and promises that I will not be cold for much longer. Streams of bubbles rise slowly from vents set into the rear wall of the tank, stirring and oxygenating this translucent primal soup of viscous humours, your painstaking brew of protéine and hæmatoglobin, carbamide resin and cellulose, water and phlegm and bile. All those substances believed fundamental to life, a recipe gleaned from out dusty volumes of Medieval alchemy and metaphysics, but also from your own researches and the work of more modern scientific practitioners and professors of chemistry and anatomy. Previously, I have found the odor all but unbearable, though now there seems to be no detectable scent at all.

"Believe me," you say, "I will have you back with me in less than an hour." And I try hard then to remember how long an hour is, but the poison leeches away even the memory of time. With hands as gentle as a midwife's, you help me from the platform and into my strange bath, and you keep my head above the surface until the last convulsions have come and gone and I am made no more than any cadaver.

"Wake up," she says—*you* say—but the shock of the mercury and iodine you administered to the vivarium have rapidly faded, and once more there is but the absolute and inviolable present moment, so impervious and sacrosanct that I can not even imagine conscious action, which would require the concept of an apprehension of some future, that time is somehow more than this static aqueous matrix surrounding and defining me.

"Do you hear me? Can you not even *hear* me?"

All at once, and with a certitude almost agonizing in its omneity, I am aware that I am being watched. No, that is not right. That is not precisely the way of it. All at once, I know that I am being watched by eyes which have not heretofore beheld me; all along there have been *her* eyes, as well as the stalked eyes of the scuttling crabs I mentioned and other such creeping, slithering inhabitants of my mind's ocean as have glommed the dim pageant of my voyage. But *these* eyes, and this spectator—my love, nothing has ever seen me with such complete and merciless understanding. And now the act of *seeing* has ceased to be a passive action, as the act of being *seen* has stopped being an activity that neither diminishes nor alters the observed. I would scream, but dead women do not seem to be permitted that luxury, and the scream of my soul is as silent as the moon. And in another place and in another time where *past* and *future* still hold meaning, you plunge your arms into the tank, hauling me up from the shallow deep and moving me not one whit. I am fixed by these eyes, like a butterfly pinned after the killing jar.

It does not speak to me, for there can be no need of speech when vision is so thorough and so incapable of misreckoning. Plagues need not speak, nor floods, nor the voracious winds of tropical hurricanes. A thing with eyes for teeth, eyes for its tongue and gullet. A thing which has been waiting for me in this moment that has no antecedents and which can spawn no successors. Maybe it waits here for every dying man and woman, for every insect and beast and falling leaf, or maybe some specific quality of my obliteration has brought me to its attention. Possibly, it only catches sight of suicides, and surely I have become that, though *your* Circean hands poured the poison draught and then held the spoon. There is such terrible force in this gaze that it seems not implausible that I am the first it has ever beheld, and now it will know all, and it shall have more than knowledge for this opportunity might never come again.

"Only tell me what happened," you will say, in some time that cannot ever be, not from *when* I lie here in the vivarium you have built for me, not from this occasion when I lie exposed to a Cosmos hardly half considered by the mortal minds contained therein. "Only put down what seems most significant, in retrospect. Do not dwell upon everything you might recall, every perception. You may make a full accounting later."

"Later, I might forget something," I will reply. "It's not so unlike a dream." And you will frown and slide the ink well a little ways across the writing desk towards me. On your face I will see the stain of an anxiety that has been mounting down all the days since my return.

That will be a lie, of course, for nothing of this will I ever forget. Never shall it fade. I will be taunting you, or through me *it* will be taunting your heedless curiousity, which even then will remain undaunted. This hour, though, is far, far away. From when I lie, it is a fancy that can never come to pass—a unicorn, the roaring cataract at the edge of a flat world, a Hell which punishes only those who deserve eternal torment. Around me flows the sea of all beginnings and of all conclusion, and through the weeds and murk, from the peaks of submarine mountains to the lowest vales of Neptune's sovereignty, benighted in perpetuum—horizon to horizon—does its vision stretch unbroken. And as I have written already, observing me it takes away, and observing me it adds to my acumen and marrow. I am increased as much or more than I am consumed, so it must be a *fair* encounter, when all is said and done.

Somewhen immeasurably inconceivable to my present-bound mind, a hollow needle pierces my flesh, there in some unforeseeable aftertime, and the hypodermic's plunger forces into me your concoction of caffeine citrate, cocaine, belladonna, epinephrine, foxglove, etcetera & etcetera. And I think you will be screaming for me to come back, then, to open my eyes, to *wake up* as if you had only given me over to an afternoon catnap. I would not answer, even now, even with its smothering eyes upon me, *in* me, performing their metamorphosis. But you are calling (*wake up, wake up, wake up*), and your chemicals are working upon my traitorous physiology, and, worst of all, *it* wishes me to return whence and from when I have come. It has infected me, or placed within me some fraction of itself, or made from my sentience something suited to its own explorations. Did this never occur to you, my dear? That in those liminal spaces, across the thresholds that separate life from death, might lurk an inhabitant supremely adapted to those climes, and yet also possessed of its own questions, driven by its own peculiar acquisitiveness, seeking always some means to penetrate the veil. I cross one way for you, and I return as another's experiment, the vessel of another's inquisition.

"Breathe, goddamn you!" you will scream, screaming that seems no more or less disingenuous or melodramatic than any actor upon any stage. With your fingers you will clear, have cleared, are evermore clearing my mouth and nostrils of the thickening elixir filling the vivarium tank. "You won't leave me. I will not let you go. There are no ox carts here, no wagon wheels."

But, also, you have, or you will, or at this very second you are placing that fatal spoon upon my tongue.

And when it is done—if I may arbitrarily use that word here, *when*—and its modifications are complete, it shuts its eyes, like the sun tumbling down from the sky, and I am tossed helpless back into the rushing flow of time's river. In the vivarium, I try to draw a breath and vomit milky gouts. At the writing desk, I take the quill you have provided me, and I write—*"Wake up," she whispers.* There are long days when I do not have the strength to speak or even sit. The fears of pneumonia and fever, of dementia and some heretofore unseen necrosis triggered by my time *away.* The relief that begins to show itself as weeks pass and your fears fade slowly, replaced again by that old and indomitable inquisitiveness. The evening that you drained the tank and found something lying at the bottom which you have refused to ever let me see, but keep under lock and key. And this night, which might be *now*, in our bed in the dingy room above your laboratory, and you hold me in your arms, and I lie with my ear against your breast, listening to the tireless rhythm of your heart winding down, and *it* listens through me. You think me still but your love, and I let my hand wander across your belly and on, lower, to the damp cleft of your sex. And there also is the day I hold my dying brother. And there are my long walks beside the sea, too, with the winter waves hammering against the Cobb. That brine is only the faintest echo of the tenebrous kingdom I might have named *Womb*. Overhead, the wheeling gulls mock me, and the freezing wind drives me home again. But always it watches, and it waits, and it studies the intricacies of the winding avenue I have become.

> *She rolls through an ether of sighs—*
> *She revels in a region of sighs...*
> Edgar Alan Poe (December 1847)

Anamnesis, or the Sleepless Nights of Léon Spilliaert

1.

"Not the dreams," the girl with straw-colored hair and lips the same pale pink as fresh salmon replies. "It isn't the dreams. It's the always waking up. That's the worst of it," and the psychiatrist watches her the way that psychiatrists watch their prey, which is to say, the same way that cats watch their dying patients. The psychiatrist nods his head, meaning that the girl with straw-colored hair should continue, please, because mice are no fun anymore once they've stopped moving about. The girl sits on the sofa in the office three floors above the busy sidewalk, the office which is always much too bright, lit as it is by twin fluorescent suns that wink on and off at the merest flip of the psychiatrist's thin fingers. Four glass tubes filled with mercury atoms electrified and shocked so violently that they bleed ultraviolet, and the girl shades her eyes and watches the psychiatrist. When she does not speak, he grows impatient and prompts her. "The stairs are steep," he says, this man who has earned the right to pry inside her skull and pick apart memories and fears and slash equatorial divides between the hemispheres of any brain that should pass too near. There are framed bits of paper hung in the bright office that declare this to be so, calligraphy script and gold seals behind glass, so that the girl and anyone else may not forget his authority in these matters of the cerebrum. "The stairs are very steep," says the girl, whose name happens to be Acacia, though she has never thought herself to be particularly sharp, in any sense of the word. "They are so steep that were I to lean only a little ways forward I would fall. Anyone would fall. That's how steep they are." The psychiatrist nods his head again, as if to say *Yes, I've heard all this before.* Acacia squints and glances towards the clock, but it's only been fifteen minutes since she stepped into the office, and so there are still many more minutes in front of her than there are behind. "I sit down, and try not to lean forward. You can't ever see the bottom, but you can see the darkness that eventually swallows the stairs, down there where the sun can't ever reach, or the moon, either." The psychiatrist taps his pencil against a yellow legal pad, the ledger where he tallies all her sins and delusions, her weaknesses and nightmares. He taps his pencil and watches Acacia, and she knows that he only licks his lips because the air in the office is so cold and dry, not because he's a hungry cat (though he may well be). "You've never tried to find the bottom?" he asks, and she tells him no, which is a lie. "I sit down, and I listen to the birds and try not to think about how far it's going to be, making the climb back up to the top." The psychiatrist frowns and knits his brow and taps his pencil a little harder. "You've seen the top?" he asks her. "No," she replies. "I have never seen the top, or at least I can't recall ever having seen the top. It always seems that I'm already following the stairs down when the dream begins." He writes something, and the sound of his pencil—the deliberate scritch, scritch, scritch of graphite across paper—makes her skin crawl. "Why do you bother to put down the things I've said already?" she wants to know, and when he hears the question, the psychiatrist stops writing and licks his lips again. "Why do you feel compelled to repeat yourself?" he asks, and Acacia is never sure of the correct answer and would not risk the wrong one, so she shrugs her shoulders. "The stairs are so white," she says, thinking of the walls of the psychiatrist's office, which are white, as well. "I think that they are marble, but I've never seen such perfectly white marble. My skin is black against the stairs. Anything is black by comparison. That's how white the stairs are. Looking down, I cannot tell where my shadow ends and I begin, because the sun is so brilliant and the steps are so awfully white." He stops writing and starts tapping his pencil against the pad again. "It's nothing I haven't told you before," she says. "It's nothing I haven't said a dozen times." And then she apologizes, and he tells her there's nothing to be sorry for. The psychiatrist has the sort of face with no sharp edges, like a cat, and she can almost believe, sometimes, that it is a kindly face. "They are not symmetrical," she goes on, embarrassed by the unnecessary apology, or only at his identifying it as such. "The horizontal face of each step is much narrower, front to back, than the vertical faces are deep, top to bottom." And she is quite completely certain that she's being tedious, but in their way, the dreams are tedious, even though they terrify her. "So, they're very steep," she adds, and he scratches at his pad again. Acacia grits her teeth and watches the clock, which has made it almost all the way to twenty minutes past the hour. The weight reduced by five full minutes, but the dry, cold air seems no less heavier than it did before. "In the dream," says the psychiatrist, "you are always naked," and she says yes, in the dream I am always naked, and she can well imagine all the meanings and significances he might attach to that without having to hear them aloud. "The stairs seem to continue forever," she tells him. "On my left and on my right, they are so wide I cannot even begin to see the edges. But they curve, too, so I imagine perhaps the staircase is round. That if I followed one of them, in one direction or the other, someday I might return to the place where I began." *How would you know?* he does not quite demand. *How would you know, when you'd returned to the point where you'd started?* She squints at him a moment before responding, trying again to understand how his face can seem so kind. "Possibly," she says, "I have a piece of charcoal or a crayon. Then I might make a mark on the marble that I would recognize when I got back to it." He stares at her and says nothing at all. "Or I might break off a bit on my shadow and use that to draw the mark." And at this he smiles, and she catches the dull, wet glint of his nicotine-stained incisors. "That's something new," says the psychiatrist, as though she doesn't know, as if she hasn't just made it up sitting there on the sofa, shading her eyes from the fluorescent lights. "If you broke off a piece of your shadow," he mutters, scratching the words onto the yellow paper. When he's done writing, he looks up and nods so she knows it's time to say something else.

2.

She jerks awake from a dream that is not the endless staircase, and not the agate sea with her balanced precariously there above it, and not the whiplash trees, and not *The Curve of the Esplanade*. Acacia looks at the old wind-up clock on the table beside her bed and sees that she's only been asleep for seven minutes. It only seemed like a week or seven days, that mean time-stretching trick of dreams. She blinks, wipes a bit of spittle from her lips, then notes the hour and minute on a dated index card lying next to the clock. She does not note the particular dream.

She sits up and stares across the room at the dark window. She will not have draperies, as they have always seemed like an attempt to hide something or an attempt to hide *from* something, and she will do neither. From her bed, Acacia watches the night, first the broad star-dappled sky and then the brick building across the way. It seems, often, she is being asked to make a choice between them, and so each must represent something quite distinct from the other. The calculated order of one aging brick and mortar wall, versus the chaos of all the universe; unless, instead, it's the choice between a comforting barricade that she may only see just so far, and no farther, or a view that extends all the way back to the very beginning of time. She has by now considered a wide assortment of possible representations and the many choices that would follow from them. She has discussed it, on several occasions, with the psychiatrist—the problem of the night sky and the brick wall—but as always his conclusions strike her as hardly more than recited estimates meant to confine and comfort and dismiss.

Acacia switches on the lamp beside the bed, and the window across the room is rendered almost opaque in the incandescent flood. It's better that way. She knows that there are problems that do not present themselves in order to be solved, but, rather, to be appreciated, to disclose perspective or humility or awe. The wooden headboard is cool against her back, and she thinks how good it would be to get dressed and go out to the almost-empty midnight streets. But it's a bad neighborhood, as she has been reminded repeatedly, and no fit place for the long walks that might begin to ease her insomnia. The wee hours in the city are for wolves and worse things than wolves, just as the psychiatrist's office is for the teasing paws of cats that slowly grow bored. So, she has the window, the brick wall, and the sky. So, she has her dreams, which she would never have again if she might discover the secret of their exile. And she has the prescription bottle of pills she will not take, because if seven minutes seems but a week, how long might seven hours be?

Acacia pushes back the sweaty sheets and sees the blister on her left thigh, grown almost a big as a dime. At first, she thinks that something must have bitten her while she slept—a poisonous spider, maybe, or some species of fly. The blister, or boil, or pustule, is as black as the night waiting outside her bedroom window. She touches it, and there is no pain. It doesn't itch. The skin around it seems mildly inflamed, but there's no numbness nor any other sort of discomfort. In the lamplight, it glistens like a gemstone, a carbuncle of polished onyx or hematite, or an enormous pearl. It doesn't scare her, though she is aware that it probably should. She is also aware that she should get up and go to the bathroom to put something on it. A dab of antibacterial ointment, perhaps, or the spray she keeps on hand for mosquito bites. Instead, she sits in bed and stares at it while the wind-up clock ticks loudly on the table. Now and then, she presses the pad of a thumb or index finger against the ebony swelling; it feels almost as solid as stone. After a while, Acacia switches the lamp off again and watches the sky and the brick wall until sleep catches up with her once more.

3.

This is not a dream she's ever dreamed. Or if it is, it's one she has entirely forgotten. She stands alone at the edge of the sea, and the full moon has just begun to rise above the horizon, a jaundiced eye opening with exquisite slowness to gaze across the waves to the place where she stands on the night-swaddled sand. Behind her, there is the whisper of sea oats rustling in the salty breeze, and the waves murmur and hiss at her feet. They rush forward and then withdraw, as they have done since the first sea washed against the volcanic shores of the first continents. She watches the moon, and the moon watches her. A falling star streaks across the sky, and she thinks that never before has she seen one even half that bright. It leaves an afterimage when she blinks. Acacia sits down on the damp sand, because she must have walked a long way to reach the sea, which is nowhere near the city where she lives. She is not tired, but it's probably best if she behaves as though she were, lest the moon grow more suspicious than it already appears to be. There is a woman sitting beside her on the beach, and the woman is talking, so Acacia listens and realizes that the woman is speaking to her.

"You must be wearying of this," the woman says. "Surely, you must be sick to death of it all."

"I had not noticed," Acacia replies, then wonders if she's telling the truth, or if maybe the necessary games she plays with the psychiatrist and those other few people she ever has cause to speak with have led her to forget precisely how that's done.

"It smells like thunder," the woman tells her. "This sort of exhaustion. Have you never noticed, how they smell the same?"

"No, I never have noticed."

Then neither of them says anything else for a long moment or two while the sea comes and goes, while the moon watches warily on, while the stalks of sea oats rub dryly, one against the other. Acacia pushes her fingers into the sand and pulls them back out, embedding quartz granules and flecks of mica deep beneath her short nails.

"You cannot now remember why or how or when this started," the woman says. "You have waited too long, I think. Sometimes it happens that way."

Her words seem like a puzzle to Acacia, or a choice not so different from that between the sky outside her bedroom window and the brick wall. Not a puzzle to be solved, but only to be regarded.

The moon has risen above the restless plain of the sea and bleeds reflected light.

"It has been so very long," the woman says, "that you don't want to believe you ever knew. It's easier to think you never understood even the least part of it."

"Are you calling me a coward?"

"I am not calling you a coward. I am telling you something you won't hear otherwise, not unless I say the words."

And when Acacia wakes again, almost half an hour has passed, and the blister has grown as large as a ripe plum.

4.

She is standing at the bathroom sink, staring back at her reflection in the mirrored door of the medicine cabinet. Her hair is the color of straw and her lips are the pink of fresh salmon. Her eyes are the same cornflower blue they've always been, her naked body almost as pale as milk but for the spray of freckles on her cheeks and shoulders, the straw thatch of pubic hair, her nipples. The swelling on her thigh is the deepest black she has ever imagined, awaking or asleep. She is not frightened, and neither is she in pain. But her hands are shaking, and there are beads of sweat standing out on her forehead and upper lip. There is adrenaline and a taste at the back of her mouth like rust.

"What is it I've forgotten?" she asks herself, and in the mirror, her lips move in perfect pantomime. She covers the swelling with her right palm, so that the girl in the glass is only herself again. Only Acacia running from sleep and refusing to choose. The blister is not feverish, though it seems to her it ought to be. It also isn't hard, the way it was before she slept another thirty minutes and dreamt of the woman on the beach. Now it has gone quite soft, and yields to her touch.

"Would you force me to remember?" she asks the mirror, and uncovers the swelling again. "Is that what this is? Because I won't decide, the decision is going to be made *for* me?" And Acacia leans on the edge of the sink, not wanting to see her face, and not wanting to see the black thing sprouting from her flesh. And it occurs to her that she might not be frightened, but she is angry, more angry than she can ever recall having been before, and she opens the medicine cabinet and rummages about on the crowded metal shelves until she finds something suitable, a pair of stainless-steel tweezers hiding beneath a box of Band-Aids and a tube of neomycin. She closes the medicine-cabinet door and glares back at the girl with blue eyes and straw-colored hair.

"If I can't remember, there must be a good reason why," she says, herself or her reflection of the both of them speaking in unison. "And whatever it might be, I have a right to have forgotten. I have a right to not look back, to not recollect."

...if I followed one of them, in one direction or the other, someday I might return to the place where I began.

How would you know? How would you know, when you'd returned to the point where you started?

I might break off a bit on my shadow...

Acacia forces the tips of the tweezers together, then she and the girl on the other side of the medicine-cabinet door press the steel into the swelling on her thigh. And what spills out, it's warm, and it takes away the anger. And it smells more like thunder than anything else ever has. What was trapped inside, unremembered, now flows eagerly down her leg and also up across the very slight bulge of her belly. It does not spurt or drip or spatter to the ceramic tiles. When it slides between her legs and slips inside her, Acacia gasps, and the tweezers slip from her fingers and take a very long time to clatter to the floor.

...and use that to draw the mark.

She grips the edges of the sink with both hands so she won't fall, and she does not cry out, and she does not look away. It moves so quickly, possessed of a certainty of purpose that she has never known, or simply cannot remember ever having known. It spreads itself across her like a second epidermis, the thinnest coat of blackest paint, and it shimmers wetly in the light above the medicine cabinet. The stain only pauses when it has risen as high as her chin line, where it lingers, as if enough of that hideous urgency has been spent that it may now require permission or consent before proceeding any farther.

Acacia parts her lips, her thin salmon lips, and a drop of sweat rolls down her face to burst upon her tongue. In the mirror, her eyes have grown so wide, seeing so much all at once, so much she had imperfectly forgotten and meant never to remember. She turns loose of the sink and takes a single step backwards, and her legs feel strong and sure of themselves. The hole in her thigh has already begun to close, and when her black fingers brush the oily pool of her navel, ripples spread out across her body.

"What are you waiting for?" she asks the girl in the mirror, the gleaming black pearl, only asking herself and no one else. And in a fraction of another second, it is finished, and she stands on the impossibly steep white marble stairs leading down and leading up and away on either side. And it is the easiest thing she has ever had to do, taking that first, next step.

Scene in the Museum (1896)

In the long gallery decorated with pastoral depictions of carnage wrought by Cretaceous saurians preying one upon the other, the blind geologist sits with the girl named Mary. It is quite a small museum, built near the sea; indeed, its easternmost wall borders on the Old Mooring Road and so runs down almost to the quayside. By now, the sun has drifted below the western horizon, and the hoarse, wheeling gulls have fallen silent; the museum is locked up tight until the morning. At this hour, it might well be a tomb, laid aside for the world's most primeval burials, a mausoleum for vanished creations and bygone leviathans. The two women sit together on a granite bench amid the hulking shapes of tall glass cases and petrified skeletons patched together with plaster of Paris and held upright with welded iron armatures, and the murals and their faces are illumined in gently flickering gaslight. Though blind, the geologist wears pince-nez spectacles tinted an iridescent blue, an oily sort of blue that, in a certain light, appears almost green, shifting across the visible spectrum like the shell of a beetle or the buzzing wings of a dragonfly. She would have no one look upon the milky cataracts that scar her ruined eyes, and there is some minute comfort in having the finger-piece lenses perched there upon the bridge of her nose, set between herself and the gaping, curious scrutiny of men.

The girl sighs and shifts about on the bench—restless, impatient—and the silk taffeta of her skirts rustles softly.

"Is something the matter?" the geologist asks her.

"It's like they're watching us," the girl replies. "Those awful eyes up there, always waiting to pounce. It's a horrible thing to put upon on a wall, if you ask me."

"I didn't ask you," says the geologist. "At least, I don't presently recollect ever having done so."

"Well, it's horrible all the same."

"Are God and Nature then at strife, That Nature lends such evil dreams?" the geologist recites, then licks her chapped, dry lips.

"What's that? Is that scripture?"

"No, Mary. That's Tennyson. 'In Memorium A.H.H.'"

"A poem?" the girl asks skeptically, and the geologist slowly nods her head. "Well, I never heard it before, and it doesn't make me dislike those horrid things any less."

When the murals were painted, almost fifteen years before, the geologist was a young woman and still had the use of her eyes. They were still blue then, like the maritime skies, and she sat beneath the scaffolding and watched as the artist resurrected the *Lælaps* and *Hadrosaurus*, the toothsome pair of sea-faring mosasaurs, the *Iguanodon* of Bernissart and the *Megalosaurus* of Stonesfield Village. Ancient scenes from both the Old World and New England, recreated by the handsome landscape painter from Manhattan, following her careful notes and sketches and spoken directions. All his countless pigments hand-ground with mortar and pestle, and she looked on as he mixed the bright powders with egg yolks and casein and amber drops of honey. For her, he had brought the halls of silent fossils and muttering stones to life again, and for that she had always loved him, in her distant, secret way.

"That's no sort of poem I ever heard," the girl in the rustling taffeta says, and the geologist wants to inquire exactly what sorts of poems she *has* heard, if her experience has ever strayed beyond doggerel and burlesque, and whether all waterfront whores are such keen cognoscenti of verse. Instead, she recites a few more lines of Tennyson:

'So careful of the type?' but no.
From scarped cliff and quarried stone
She cries 'A thousand types are gone:
I care for nothing, all shall go.'

"I have a new dress," the girl named Mary says, driving the talk in another direction.

"Yes, I think I can hear it," the geologist replies.

"Ah, but you should *feel* it. Here, give me your hands."

At first the geologist keeps her hands folded in her lap; only rarely has she allowed herself to touch the girl. It is almost always enough to sit here in the gallery and talk. Usually, it is sufficient to smell the cheap toilet water that she wears, her sweat, a wilted flower in her hair, all the odors that the geologist knows her by.

"It was a gift," says the girl, those words not at all careless or trivial, but placed artfully, just so. And the thought of someone else spending money on this girl makes the geologist's heart flutter and begin to race, and clouds her thoughts with bright flecks of jealousy. Hesitantly, the geologist raises her left hand and, hesitantly, she lets her fingertips brush against the cool, stiff folds of taffeta. And then she quickly pulls her hand away again, as though the silk has scalded her, and Mary laughs softly to herself.

"What is the color?" the geologist asks.

"Let me see," says the girl, and there are a few seconds of silence marred only by the sound of the evening wind sighing off the harbor. "It is the red of the shadow on a rose. A *red* rose."

"Of course," the geologist says, though she'd actually imagined it might be a garish sort of aniline yellow.

"It's almost unnatural, this shade of red, so it took me a moment to think of it."

"I wish I could see it for myself. But I do recall that color."

"He said that he loved me," the girl says.

"Who said that?"

"He did."

"You mean the man who bought you this unnatural red dress?" asks the geologist, and her voice remains calm, steady, as deceptively indifferent as ever, for she is a woman who keeps her emotions to herself, except when she is talking about the murals or her fossil bones or Lord Tennyson. It hardly matters if this only makes her seem stranger to the pious, muttering people of the town, who have no end of rumors and speculations about the peculiar blind spinster who passes her days talking to rocks, and who lives alone in a garret above a sepulcher for ancient monstrosities.

"Yes," the girl answers. "He was the one. The man who bought me the dress."

"How do you feel about that?"

"Oh, I am quite cautious," says the girl. "You might not believe I am, but it's the truth, all the same."

"As well you should be," the geologist tells her, and now it seems as if her fingers are tingling, as if the fabric of the dress, tainted by some burning, caustic substance, some corrosive dye-stuff, has stained her skin. She wipes her hand against her own skirt and tries hard to pay attention to what the girl is saying.

"Perhaps *you* can make sense of it," says the whore.

"Possibly. Tell me what he said."

"Well, he would assume the role of my *protector*—his word, mind you."

The geologist stops rubbing her hand on her skirt and takes a deep breath. "Mary, do you feel like you need protecting?"

"I do not want to be alone—not like you—"

"Of course not."

"—but I certainly do not feel I need to be *protected*."

The geologist shuts her eyes, and never mind that it makes no difference, that there is no darkness greater, more absolute, to be found behind closed lids than the darkness that is with her every moment of every day. She shuts her eyes very tightly and hopes that the whore hasn't noticed.

"Do you love him?" she asks.

And the girl named Mary, Star of the Sea, laughs a cruel, quiet laugh, because it is a silly question.

"Would you please come nearer, Mary? I would have you sit nearer to me." And now there's a louder rustle as the girl scoots sideways on the granite bench, decreasing the distance between them by a scant few inches more.

"You should be grateful for the attentions of such a man," the geologist tells her. And this is only another part of the pantomime, forcing insincerities from her own throat, shaping deceit with her tongue. The words have no flavor whatsoever, no taste, no texture at all. "Indeed, you should be glad to have a willing protector."

"And why is that, Professor?"

"It's a hard world," the geologist replies. "I daresay harder on some few of us than on others."

"You mean harder on women like *me*," the whore says, and it would be impossible to mistake for anything else the cold, indurate note of pique that has crept into her voice. It is altogether too malapropos, too like finding a ruby lying amid the filthy cobblestones, befouled as they are with chamber-pot offal and horseshit and the refuse of fishmongers.

"Yes, Mary. I believe that I mean that precisely."

And the whore does not reply, and for a moment they sit, side by side, and listen to the Atlantic wind pressing cold and raw against the eaves of the museum.

"I need you to stand for me," the geologist says at last. "Just there, directly in front of me." And she points to a spot below the nearest mural, beneath the *Lælaps* and the dying *Hadrosaurus*.

"My feet ache something terrible," the girl complains. "I swear, sometimes I think I'd be better off without them."

"Please. Just for awhile. Stand for me, Mary. You may remove your boots, if it would help."

"Is that what you want tonight? You want me to take off my boots?"

"No, Mary. It does not matter to me one way or another. I only make the suggestion thinking that it might ease your discomfort."

"I'll keep my boots on, thank you all the same," says Mary. "These marble floors are cold, I bet. I bet they're almost as frigid as the goddamn bottom of the sea."

"Maybe," says the geologist. "I couldn't say for certain." And she listens closely as the girl gets up, the delicious rustle and swish of the new red dress, the friction of skirts against petticoats and stockings.

"You want me to stand here? Just stand?"

"Yes. That's what I need you to do."

"It's a queer sort of game you're playing at, you know that?"

The geologist swallows and licks her lips again, wishing that she were not so thirsty, that her parched mouth were not such a distraction.

"Do I pay you any less than the men who expect so much more?" she asks.

"No," the whore answers. "If you did, I wouldn't be here, Professor."

"In point of fact, do I not pay much, much *more*?"

The geologist can almost hear the whore smile.

"A girl has her reputation to consider," says Mary. "Risks weighed against the benefits and all. People talk, you know. There are already men on the docks who will not employ my services because, well, because…" but she trails off, and so the geologist finishes for her.

"Because you come to me, Mary."

"It makes them nervous, I suspect."

"But not your protector. It doesn't make him nervous."

"No. He understands that it's only because I'm so well compensated. He knows I'm not a tribade. That if I'm to be found tipping the velvet now and again, it's strictly business, and in no way pertaining to my habitual proclivities"

"Of course," the geologist whispers, so low that Mary almost doesn't catch the words.

"You just want me to stand here?" the whore asks again, and her heels sound almost like horseshoes clacking against the marble as she shifts from one foot to the other.

"Yes. That's enough for now," the geologist replies, slipping her right hand inside a pocket of her skirt. Her fingers close around the pearl-handled razor hidden there, and suddenly her mouth does not seem so very dry, and her heart is no longer racing in her chest. No rosary beads for her, no crucifix, but only the smooth curve of this solid shank for her fetish, her talisman. Nacre stolen from an oyster or mussel's inner shell to conceal the fine steel edge, which she keeps honed and ready with a leather strop. She squeezes it, imprinting its outline upon her palm, and opens her eyes again.

"Don't slump your shoulders," she says. "Stand up straight."

In dreams, the geologist kneels in the grey estuary muck of low tide, some tide so low that all the bay has drained away into the distance, and everywhere fish lie flopping and suffocating beneath a blazing summer sun. Cod and mackerel, haddock and flounder, starving gills and desperate, bulging eyes as the crabs move in to have their fill of this unexpected banquet. Here and there, the sea's retreat has exposed boulders which usually lie submerged, and the stones are clothed in fleshy, reeking mats of kelp and Irish moss and knotted wrack. She is naked, with not even a chemise to protect her from the blazing Cyclopean eye of this July or August afternoon, and already her skin has gone a delicate, pale pink; soon enough, it will turn the angry red of a boiled lobster and begin to blister. She has sunken so deeply into the mud that it reaches up above her knees, but at least, she thinks, her legs and feet are covered and safe from the devouring sun. Around her, the hulls and titled masts of stranded fishing boats jab at the blue-white sky, and the city is only a hazy silhouette of gambrel rooftops and church steeples looming above the quay.

"You will burn alive out here," the painter of landscapes and murals says, but when she raises her head to look at him, stinging sweat trickles down her brow into her eyes, and the geologist blinks painfully and stares down at the mud, instead.

"You'll bake, poor thing. In the end, this ooze will be your tomb, holding you secret as any trilobite. You will sleep away the ages while your shrouds lapidify about you."

"I will not dream of you," she whispers. She tries to stand, but the sucking, squelching mud holds her fast.

"I would have loved you," the painter sighs. "I would have carried you away from this stinking shore and given you the lights and wonders of the city. I would have given you all my love. I would even have given you a child."

"I never *wanted* you," she growls. "I never wanted you *or* your child." And now the geologist grits her teeth against the salt crystallizing in her eyes.

There's strange, piping music from the direction of the wharves, and the painter talks of sirens and Odysseus, of mermaids and Andromeda chained upon the Æthiopian shore by jealous Nereids and offered up as a sacrifice by her own father to the monster Cetus. The music is a fever, and his words are fever dreams. They fall from his lips and lie squirming all about her. At least, she thinks, Andromeda had the sea while she awaited death, cool Mediterranean waves lapping at her heels and toes, not this barren, uncovered littoral plain, this hellish expanse of dying fish and hungry crabs.

"It's that lie that holds you here," says the painter. "It's that lie that took your sight."

"It was an accident," she replies, trying not to remember the day and recalling it all too clearly, so many years past, but not the least bit forgotten or diminished, the day a small stoppered bottle of muriatic acid slipped from her fingers and shattered.

"That was what, a week after I returned home? Two weeks, perhaps? I missed my razor almost at once. You stole it from me, didn't you?"

"I'm not a sneak thief," she says, knowing it to be a lie in more ways than just the one.

He bends down, his hand cupped beneath her chin, the callused fingers that never touched her. He kisses her, but those are not the painter's lips. Those are the lips of Mary or some other whore, the first girl the geologist paid to come to the museum after sunset, or the second, or the third.

"You taste so sweet," the artist says, speaking with the borrowed voice of a dollymop.

"I am lost," she says. "I am lost forever."

"Not lost," the whore tells her. "You have merely been misplaced. You have lain yourself aside, that's all."

And then those callused, masculine fingers wander down to her nipples, the wide brown aureolae which have become encrusted round about with the sharp, scabby plates of barnacles. The painter and all the whores laugh to themselves, and then they are speaking all at once, though not quite in unison, not quite in perfect androgynous syncopation.

"You have need of no other lover than the sea and the stones that are forged within the night of its eternal crucible. You have not any exigency or desire for mere human hearts, nor touch, nor company."

"Take it back," she says, meaning the pearl-handled razor, not those indelible, damning words, for you cannot take back anything so tattooed upon one's soul. "I would not have it anymore. Take it, please, and then please leave me be." But she has left the razor in the bureau drawer where she keeps it when it is not tucked into a pocket, or when she is not sitting before her dressing mirror folding it open and closed, open and closed, admiring the polished gleam by lantern light. Marveling at the simplicity of so deadly an instrument just as she admires the teeth of venomous serpents or the sickle claws of Jefferson's *Megatherium americanum*.

So she cannot give it back, no matter how much she might wish to, and so the painter shrugs and shakes his head and turns away again, leaving her there in the muck. She has sunk in up to her thighs now, and the fleshy, stinging polyps of sea anemones sprout where once a brown thatch of hair concealed her sex. Across the mud, a regiment of crabs are coming for her on jointed, scuttling legs, their pincers held high, waving in time to the music from the docks.

In dreams, she is consumed by silt and sand, by every hungry thing that waits below the waves. She is a feast for all Poseidon's offspring, and as they enter her—that host of chitinous shells and slithering, eel-formed bodies—and as she screams, a fantastic, towering shadow rises in the east and a roar rides out before it, like the commingled voices of all the tempests since time's beginning, as the mighty wave bears down upon the town.

Below the murals, the whore named Mary stands up straight and the geologist sits stiff on her granite bench, pretending that she can see the girl. That she can see the *unnatural* red of the noisy new dress, and the insatiable eyes of the painted Dinosaurian gargoyles leering down from their place upon the wall, and that she can see, too, the girl's unremarkable face, which she has only ever felt with her hands. She inhales the musty smells of the museum; the faint and omnipresent scent of the sea; the whore's bouquet. She listens, straining now to hear something more than the wind, more than the faint hiss from the gaslight sconces and a buoy clanging disconsolately in the harbor.

"Mary," she says. "I would ask a favor of you."

"A *favor*? Does that mean I have a choice?"

"You always have a choice," the geologist replies. "It's not like I'm holding a gun to your head, is it?"

"No," the girl admits. "It's not like that. So, is this a *favor* I can do sitting down?"

"No," says the geologist as firmly as she dares, and she grips the razor tighter still. "You should remain standing."

The girl sighs almost as loudly as the wind.

"There is something I would ask you to do, my precious Star of the Sea."

"Don't you call me that," the whore says.

"Why not, Mary? It's only what your name means. *Mary*, from the Latin, *Maria*, or the Hebrew *Miryam*, and you *are* precious to me."

"I'm not some sort of goddamn Jewess," the girl sneers, and the geologist draws in a very deep breath and allows herself the indulgence of folding the blade partway open. When she speaks again, there is only the slightest tremor in her voice.

"No, Mary, you are surely not that. But you wear the name of the Blessed Virgin, the very Queen of Heaven. And you wear it like a crown, like a jeweled diadem, like a new red dress. You wear it well, and always you shine like the brightest star hung above the ocean's abyss. Even to my blind eyes, you shine."

"Fine. So what's the *favor*? I already told you my feet hurt, didn't I?"

"There is something I would ask you to do."

"Isn't that usually how it works, Professor?"

The geologist shuts her eyes again. "Please, Mary, do be quiet. Unless you would have us stop this now, and so seek your evening's wages in some other, less strenuous quarter."

The girl shifts fretfully from foot to foot, heel to heel, toe to toe, and again the clacking of her boots on the marble puts the geologist in mind of the stamping of some bizarre bipedal horse.

"I have appetites," the geologist says, opening her eyes and folding the razor shut. "And I freely confess, they are strange to me, Mary. I have *terrible* appetites."

The whore coughs nervously, and then, in a smaller, less strident voice, she says, "I think you would find my blood sour and fouled with spirits."

The geologist wants to laugh, but she doesn't. She only permits herself a smile, instead. "I don't want your blood, Mary, my Star of the Sea. Don't be so ghoulish. I only suffer from lesbianism. I am not a vampire."

"And I was only making a fucking joke," the girl says, unconvincingly. "My feet are killing me, Professor. I don't see why I can't do this favor *sitting*."

The geologist sighs and leans towards the whore, leaning forward but an inch or so, leaning into and through something far denser than the long night of blindness or the stagnant, antique atmosphere of the museum, leaning through her own desire. "*No,*" she says. "I need you to stand, and so you *will* stand. Or you will leave. The choice is yours, as always."

For a few seconds there's not even the sound of Mary's restless feet, just the wind, and the geologist begins to wonder if perhaps tonight she's pushed too hard. But then the girl's skirt rustles, and she scuffs at the floor with the toe of a boot.

"I *am* standing," she says.

"Thank you, Mary. That is very kind of you. Many in your line of work are not so tolerant of my whims. Now, would you come closer, please, and would you kiss me?"

"Will you remove your spectacles?" the whore asks. "I've never seen your eyes."

And you never shall, the geologist almost says, almost, but then there's a sudden and unfamiliar flutter in her belly, some unexpected and not wholly unpleasant twinge. None of them have ever seen her eyes, not even the ones she has undressed for and lain with. None of them have ever looked upon the sickly opalescent sheen eclipsing her pupils and retinas, corneas and sclerae. None of them has ever had the gall to ask that she remove her spectacles.

"I warn you, it is not a pretty sight," she says.

"I don't expect it to be. It's a hard world, and I daresay harder on some few of us than on others. I see a lot of ugly things, Professor. Only, sometimes they don't seem that way to me, if you know what I'm saying."

"You are an odd one, Mary. Possibly, I have not given you due credit."

"Possibly, you think all whores cut from the selfsame cloth," the girl replies. "But I have seen such sights, and never have I turned away. I have seen the ravages of typhus and cholera and the pox. I have seen the innumerable disfigurements life at sea works upon the body of a man. Once, I saw a sailor who'd been mauled by a shark. It took away everything below his waist, and yet, by God, he lived on an hour afterwards."

Again, the flutter deep in the geologist's gut, and she folds the razor open once more. She hears the girl take a step towards her, and then another. *If I reach out,* she thinks, *if I reach out, I could touch those silken folds again. I could cut—*

"I'll tell you something else," the whore says, speaking now with an air of confidentiality, and the geologist realizes that she is being seduced by this filthy, unschooled guttersnipe, this scheming bit of meat and gaudy raiment. But she sits still, and she listens. The razor's blade is cool against her palm.

"What, Mary? What will you tell me?" she asks.

And the whore takes another step nearer the granite bench.

"It was the damnedest thing," she says. "When I still lived in Gloucester, it came up in the nets of a whaling barque, though I don't recollect the ship's name or the name of its captain. But I saw it sprawled there on the dock, after it'd been run through and killed by one of the harpooners. I thought it might have been a mermaid, at the first, like you hear of in tales and chanteys and the like. But it weren't no mermaid, I'll swear to that. And if your eyes are even half as fucking unseemly as the eyes I saw that day, I'll give you the night's snatch for free."

"That's a bold proposition," the geologist replies, trying to imagine what the girl might have seen lying dead and speared upon the Gloucester docks, what she might have first mistaken for a mermaid.

"My feet hurt like the devil, Professor, and discomfort always makes me bold."

With her left hand, the geologist removes her pince-nez from the bridge of her nose and then sits and stares unseeing at the spot where she knows the girl is standing. The razor is still open, and the fingers of her right hand have begun the bleed, a fresh gash or an old one reinaugurated for the occasion.

"No, that's not so fucking terrible," Mary says, and she bends and cups the geologist's chin in her hands, and though a streetwalker's palms are not so soft as the supple hands of idle women, they are sometimes softer than anticipated.

"No?" asks the geologist, folding the razor closed.

"Nothing to make me turn away, but like I said, I seen some unlovely fucking exhibitions of the Almighty's handwork. So it might be I'm not the one to ask."

And then she kisses the geologist, exactly as she has been bidden and paid to do, as she has done many times before. Outside the museum, the wild, salty wind cries like a widow mourning at her husband's grave, and somewhere in this moldering and ramshackle town fetched up like so much foam and flotsam at the edge of the sea, a bell begins to toll the hour.

The Madam of the
Narrow Houses

She has never called herself a medium, this furtive, brown-eyed woman who lives alone where Hull Street crosses Snow Hill Street and runs down to the glassy, slow river. She does not seek to profit from the bereaved, nor to offer solace to grieving widows, widowers, or orphans. She does not hold séances in hushed and darkened parlors, and never has she practiced automatic writing, nor even once communicated with otherworldly spheres via planchettes and elaborate codes of table rapping and the cracking of knuckles. She does not call the dead, for always have they come to her unbidden, in their own time and in their own service. Rarely do they speak to her, and when they do, it is even more rarely that they share words she would dare repeat.

By day, she is a sempstress, an architect with needle and thread and thimble, clothing well-bred Boston women, and she minds her spools and stitches. She has a fondness for old hymns, and often hums them while she works, though she is not particularly religious. Religion has always seemed to her the domain of questions which will be answered in the fullness of time, one way or the other, by and by. Or they will not, in which case it hardly seems they matter very much. She lives in the high gabled house left behind by her mother and father when they passed—only one month apart, one from the other—and she imagines that she will live there until the end of her own days. She has an especial liking for yellow roses, and for mulled cider, as well, and late autumn, and the inscriptions she finds carved on slate headstones when she walks between the rows at Copp's Hill. Of the latter, she has two favorites, both of which she has copied down and pinned upon the wall near her chifforobe. They offer some comfort on those infrequent occasions when it occurs to her, in passing, that perhaps she is a lonely woman who has simply never paused to recognize her own particular sort of loneliness. One reads:

Sacred to the Memory of
MR. SAMUEL WELLS,
Who resigned this life Nov. 13th,
1804
in the 26 year of his age.
Stop my friends; in a mirror see
What you who ere so healthy be,
Tho' beauty with rosebuds paint each face.
Coming death will strip you of each grace.

and the other goes:

Here lyes ye body of
MRS AMNEY HUNT
Wife of Mr Benjamin Hunt who died
Nov 20th 1769 aged
40 years
A sister of Sarah Lucas lieth here,
Whom I did love most dear;
And now her soul hath too its flight
And bid her spiteful foes good night.

That both Mr. Wells and Mrs. Hunt died in November has always seemed significant, and sometimes this sempstress who is not a medium imagines it a portent of some sort, conceivably that she herself will perish on a chill November day, only after the crisper delights of October have finished, and that thought bestows a certain solace.

She sleeps always above the blankets, for no reason in particular and following from no superstition. This bed was once her grandfather's, as was once this house the property of that same man, who made his meager fortune importing tea and exporting tobacco. She keeps a sachet filled with dried lavender and thyme beneath her pillow, and on the beside table she keeps a small box made from cherry wood. The lid is finely carved with a scene from Greek mythology—Narcissus gazing longingly at his own reflection while Echo watches bitterly. Inside the box, wrapped in a white linen handkerchief, she keeps her baby teeth and two she has lost as an adult. There is also the cracked arm of a china doll she found lying in the street, years ago, and there is a silver coin, tarnished mostly black, which she thinks must have come from Portugal or Spain.

She does not call them to her. Always, they find her by their own secret wiles, the spirits who come when she is sleeping, or lying awake waiting for sleep. They find *her*, following whatever compass a ghost might hold, slipping in through the inevitable, stingy gaps afforded by all closed doors and windows. They rise up through floorboards, or sift down through sagging ceiling plaster. Or they appear somewhere in the room without having seemed to have entered by any obvious, material route. So, she knows there must be a multitude of invisible doorways that her living eyes cannot discern. They have also risen from the scorched glass chimney of the oil lamp that sits on the table along with the cherry-wood box, and from beneath the bed, too. On more than one instance, they have emerged suddenly from the brick maw of the chimney, sooty and fire lit and scattering ash and embers across the room.

The first one came when she was only fifteen years old, and it merely sat at the foot of her bed and watched her with its sunken coal-lump eyes. She was not afraid that night, and she has never yet been afraid of them since. They come with needs, with the unfathomable and insatiable hungers and desires of all dead things, but they do not come maliciously. And though she understands, instinctively, that they are all jealous of her flesh and of her ability to taste and smell and touch, envious of her every breath, she also understands that she is an unlikely banquet, and that the loss of her would be an almost incalculable loss to these uninvited visitors.

Sometimes, they bring her gifts, though she has never asked or expected anything from them. Once, a withered bouquet of violets, found afterwards on her pillow, and on another night, a page torn from a book of poetry by Longfellow, and after still another liaison, she found a blue China bowl of milk waiting in the hallway outside her bedroom door.

She was a sickly child, prone to unaccountable fits and agues, and her parents were convinced on more than one night that she would not live to see the dawn. Certainly, hearing the grim pronouncements of the physicians who attended her, they had not expected their daughter and only child to reach adulthood. But she did, and now she has outlived them both by almost fifteen years and grown to be a fit and sturdy woman, though still somewhat thin and of a paler complexion than she'd prefer.

One of the few times she has spoken with her spectral callers, she asked, "Why was I always so sick?"

And the ghost hesitated only for a moment, then replied in a voice like winter wind along shingled rooftops, "We have ever been near to you."

Emboldened by its response, she asked, "Why, then, am I always well now, hardly ever suffering even so much as a runny nose?"

"Because," the ghost told her, and she thought possibly the tone of its voice betrayed a hint of impatience, "we are ever near to you."

Because you need me, she thought, but would not have spoken those four words aloud. If they need her, she has come to need them at least as much, and she can no longer comprehend the tedium of an existence without their nightly company. She is proud of her skill as a dressmaker and of her position in the shop on Hanover Street, but she knows that the work and the demands of her craft are hardly sufficient to give meaning to her life. She has seen and felt too much to live as others live, to be no more than a spinster and a sempstress dwelling alone in the high, old house in the city's North End. And it is not necessary that she flaunt her certainty of her visitors' need for her; it is enough to know they do, to sense, from time to time, their anxiety that they will come some evening or another and find her gone.

She has overhead whispers and gossip, in the shop and on the street, when others think she is not listening or out of earshot. "Such a shame she never married," someone will sigh, feigning pity, pretending to sympathy. Or, "An odd one, that woman, and have you heard...?" and then there will be some hushed tale of strange lights from her windows or peculiar sounds heard in her presence. Perhaps the smell of dying flowers or brimstone whenever she passes by, and were it only two centuries earlier, she might be hauled before magistrates in powdered wigs to be interrogated, accused of congress with demons, found guilty of witchcraft, and then hung from the limb of a convenient tree. But, by chance or providence, she was born into an enlightened age of Science and Medicine and gas streetlights. So, usually, she ignores the whispers, because none of them even begin to suspect the truth, and none of them can steal the nights away from her.

She lies in bed, naked and unashamed of her nakedness, shivering but unmindful of the chill, and she watches the restless patterns the lamp throws upon the walls. Sometimes, they come to her as no more than shadows, and when she happens to consider the unperceived form that *casts* those shadows, there is a delicious twinge or prickling at the nape of her neck or deep in her belly. So often, it is not what she glimpses, but what she will never behold that seems to nourish the greatest revelations.

In her right hand, she cradles the page ripped from a volume of Longfellow and left upon her pillow, and she has underlined this passage:

> *Let us go forward, and no longer stay*
> *In this great picture-gallery of Death!*
> *I hate it! ay, the very thought of it!*

> *Elsie. Why is it hateful to you?*

> *Prince Henry. For the reason*
> *That life, and all that speaks of life, is lovely,*
> *And death, and all that speaks of death, is hateful.*

> *Elise. The grave is but a covered bridge, leading from light to light, through a brief darkness!*

Often, she has wondered which one of them left it for her, and precisely what those lines may have meant to them, but she has never found the courage to ask any of the visitors. Lying there with the page crumpled and brittle in her hand, worn smooth by her fingers and all the nights she has held it, she broods over the truest meaning of the stanzas and whether they might hold within them any truth beyond the pretty conceits of all poets, great and minor and those who have died completely unknown. It might be that Elise has spoken the truth to the Prince, or it might be that the darkness of the grave runs on forever, that it is not a covered bridge at all, but a well bored through solid granite, which never again emerges into the light of day. Or, she thinks, it might be a deep reflecting pool, where the weight of souls bears them down to the grey-green half-light, through murk and silt, to settle amongst the knotted roots of water lilies, disturbing only the fitful slumber of turtles and newts.

In a corner, near the bedroom door, something stirs and is still again. She watches, but only from the edges of her vision, because sometimes they are shy, especially if they have never visited before. For the moment, this one seems hardly more than a shredded slip of lightlessness, not even as solid as the fleeting wisp of smoke when a candle has been snuffed. She smiles and lets the page of Longfellow slip from her fingers to the floor, and then she rolls onto her back and raises her knees, spreading her legs in a wordless act of invitation. She turns her head until her right cheek is pressed against the blanket, until she can once again keep her indirect watch upon that corner of the room. She wants to whisper some further, slight encouragement, but keeps quiet for fear that even the softest voice might be too much. This one will come, or it will not, and she can make no more overture than the simple offering of herself that has been made already.

For an instant, a span measured in shallow breaths and the uncontrollable metronome of heartbeats, she watches as the angles of the corner become somehow more acute than their usual ninety degrees. The portal swinging open, stretching and straining that only apparently fixed intersection of the room's north and eastern walls, and she parts her knees the slightest bit more. What was only a slip or a smoky wisp has already taken on a more substantial form, flowing into this world from when- and wherever Nature or Super-Nature consigns that part of the human mind that survives death. Then the walls are merely plaster walls again, the corner no more or less than any corner in this house, but filled now with a roiling, slowly revolving material, the singularly gossamer filaments of a being sewing itself together with naught but longing and urgency and dim memories. It is not exactly translucent, nor quite genuinely opaque, and its shifting surface glints with a greasy sort of polychromasia.

And this is when she always looks away, prudently turning to face the ceiling, instead, averting her gaze, for there is something too horribly vulnerable about her visitors at this stage of their manifestation. Neither quite here nor there, half in and half out, raw and exposed to any prying, curious eyes that might fall on them and stare without understanding or mercy. The lamp on the bedside table flares suddenly, glowing almost painfully bright, and then it gutters as if an unfelt draft is about to extinguish it. But soon enough the flame grows steady again and retreats to its former, fainter brilliance, and she is grateful that the presence in the corner has not seen fit to douse the wick and leave her blinking at afterimages and waiting in the dark.

That is kind of you, Sir or Madam, she thinks, and at once there is a dry, fluttering noise, the rattle of fallen leaves or castoff feathers blown across parched earth or cobblestones, and it may or may not have been anything meant for her ears. She knows that the apparitions hear her thoughts, sometimes, but other times, it seems her mind is closed to them. Or that they simply choose not to listen. She lies as still as she may, at ease and unafraid and open to the approach of her coalescing guest, waiting for this night's ministrations to begin in earnest. She takes a deep breath, filling herself with the air in the bedroom which has become laden with all the familiar, astringent odors of ghosts, and exhales through her nostrils.

And were there anyone alive—a sister or mother, a friend or father confessor—to whom the sempstress might ever divulge these unions, she would readily admit that while the visitors do not frighten her, the reactions of her own body to them often do. Which is to say, the unconscious reflexes of her sympathetic flesh to the appetites and yearnings of non-corporeal intelligences, and no doubt it would leave the spiritualists in awe, and surely they would deem her possessed of some mighty gift or talent. It has been her experience that people are often eager to praise or envy that which they themselves have never had to endure. The cold begins in her belly and rises quickly into her chest, that ache, that unfolding bloom of frost, as though she is about to cough up the dirty slush of a January street.

She swallows, blinks, and sees that it is standing at her bedside now—no, not *it*, but *him*, for the features have solidified into the face of a young man. There is a keen sadness to his expression, which is unusual; rarely do they show her sorrow, regardless of what the living might expect of those bereft of blood and bone. More often than not, there is relief that they have found her, that she has welcomed their arrival, and so their eyes beam and glisten for her, all gratitude and release. They wear the echoes of smiles and the faint remembrances of joy, no moaning phantoms dragging the burden of clattering chains, no weeping haunts. So this gentleman's downcast countenance is unexpected, and she almost asks him aloud to tell her, to talk if he can, and if, perchance, talking might help, but then she catches herself and keeps the questions to herself. If he wishes her to know, he will explain, when and how it suits him. The ghost leans nearer, and she knows there would be tears if the dead did not, inevitably, forget how to cry.

And here is the same fact they all bring to her, and it might overwhelm or disappoint or insult another, but never yet has it lessened her enthusiasm for these encounters. The fact—they do not come to see *her*, but, rather, they come to see what she can *show* them. She is merely the instrument capable of sounding those old tones which they have dragged themselves up from pine boxes and moldering, worm-gnawed sod to hear, just as they are merely the musicians capable of playing her. In this improbable symphony, as in all orchestrations, neither one is anything without the ability of the other. He reaches out, and she can almost feel his fingertips brush gently across and through her erect nipples, and trapped there within the bower of her ribcage, the cold has redoubled and swelled into a blizzard. She can hold it inside just so long, and never a single second more.

He kisses her then, and his lips are flavored with dust and the clicking language of ebony beetles. She does not shut her eyes, and he does not close his, and so they share this one moment between them before she can no longer forestall what he has *truly* come here for. But it is enough, and she stops fighting what cannot be defeated, as the ice inside flows effortlessly along the trough of her throat, answering his unspoken pleas and rising up to meet her visitor.

"Death," her father says, and he smiles so that the word does not seem so ominous. "When all is said and done, it is hardly more than a covered bridge."

And here she is standing down on the street, staring up at the gauzy white drapes that cover her bedroom windows like cataracts obscuring blind and aged eyes. A carriage passes behind her, the horses' iron-shod hooves throwing sparks as they strike the pavement.

And here she is only seven years old, lost in the throes of a fever, and her mother is sitting next to her bed, holding her hand and wiping her face with a cool, damp cloth.

"Life, and all that speaks of life, is lovely," her mother says, and even though she sounds very afraid, the authority in her voice will brook no argument and accept no compromise. "Do you hear me, young lady? Death, and all that *speaks* of death, is hateful. Do you understand?"

"Yes, mother," the sempstress whispers, keeping her eyes on the inconstant shadows hunched all around, pressing in from the years she has not yet lived.

"So, you're staying *here*," her mother tells her, "with us. You're not going *anywhere*."

"No," the child replies, the child who knows what lies ahead because these are only recollections seen through the distorting glass of time. "I would never leave."

The frowning young man with sad grey eyes touches her face with intangible hands, and a glacier pours across her tongue and teeth and out her open mouth.

"A shame she never married," mutters the greengrocer's wife, who has five children and loves none of them. And the sempstress thinks, *But I am a married woman, and my husbands and my wives and all my children are scattered across the ages and always seeking me.*

"An odd one," sighs the dour, scowling wife of a butcher or a banker or a Presbyterian minister. "You wonder what she gets up to, left all alone in that abominable old house. Oh, I've heard stories, but it's nothing I'd care to repeat, being a Christian woman."

From the shingle of a rocky beach, she watches as the day draws to its sunset end and the advancing tide rises by slow degrees from the eternal, devouring sea; her father laughs and places an especially pretty shell or rounded pearl of blue beach glass in her palm.

"She is your mother," he says and sighs. "What did you expect she would say?"

She does not know, because she cannot even remember the question.

"Fear whatever you can avoid, and be mindful where you step, sure. But death, child, is only a bridge, leading you from light to light, through a brief darkness. Fear it all you wish, and sidestep all you like, it will change not a thing in that regard. Your mother knows that as well as I."

And now her soul hath too its flight
And bid her spiteful foes good night.

As saltwater and foam rush across sandy shores and weathered stone, so, too, this flood spills from her, rushing over her chin and across her bare chest and shoulders. Disregarding gravity, it flows back and upwards, as well, entirely shrouding her face, filling her nostrils, sealing her eyes. There is only a passing, reflexive fleck of panic, that initial shock when she can no longer breathe or see and before she remembers that this is not what will kill her one day, somewhere farther along, and that she has done this thing so many nights before *this* night and, always, she has lived to entertain the needs of other visitations.

"Don't waste your days afraid of ghosts," her father says and bends to lift another piece of flotsam from the beach. The buttermilk sky is filled with dappled wings and the cries of wheeling gulls.

The viscous, colorless matter expelled from some unknown recess of her anatomy or mind or spirit has already heard the ghost leaning low over her, that sorrowful man who has come here to find something lost and not yet restored to him. Someone who still breathes, perhaps, or someone dead who has yet to cross his path, and maybe there are so many roads on the other side of death's covered bridge that souls might wander all eternity and never find reunion. And, because she was born to be a violin or cello or a penny whistle, and because she is incomplete without a melody, she has disgorged this second, telepathic skin to read his thoughts, and that membrane expands and wraps itself tightly about her body until it has been pulled as thin as any human skin. Her face is no longer her own, but is the face *he* needs to see, the face that she was birthed to show him on this night when at last he has found his way to her bedroom. The caul hides away the indecent flush and warmth of her mortality, and now he can *touch* her as though the two of them were living or the both of them were not even as solid as a breeze.

He kisses her again, and the sempstress does not need to see to know that he is no longer frowning.

The preceding stories first appeared in *Sirenia Digest*, Issues No. 1-29, December 2005-October 2007. The author would like to thank all the people who have made, and continue to make, the digest possible, beginning with the subscribers, and including William K. Schafer, Vince Locke, Kathryn Pollnac, Gordon Duke, Sonya Taaffe, and Geoffrey H. Goodwin. You guys keep the wolves at bay.

"A Child's Guide to the Hollow Hills" and "The Hole With a Girl In Its Heart" originally appeared as "Untitled 23" and "Untitled 26," respectively.

About the Author

Trained as a vertebrate paleontologist, Caitlín R. Kiernan did not turn to fiction writing until 1992. Since then, she has published six novels—*The Five of Cups, Silk, Threshold, Low Red Moon, Murder of Angels, Daughter of Hounds*, and, most recently, *The Red Tree*. Her short fiction has been collected in *Tales of Pain and Wonder; Wrong Things* (with Poppy Z. Brite); *From Weird and Distant Shores*; the World Fantasy award-nominated *To Charles Fort, With Love; Alabaster;* and *A is for Alien*. She has also published a short sf novel, *The Dry Salvages*, and two volumes of erotica, *Frog Toes and Tentacles* and *Tales from the Woeful Platypus*. She has scripted graphic novels for DC Vertigo, including thirty-eight issues of *The Dreaming* and the mini-series *The Girl Who Would Be Death* and *Bast: Eternity Game*. Her many chapbooks have included *Trilobite: The Writing of Threshold, The Merewife*, and *The Black Alphabet*. She is currently working on her next novel.